What You Want to See

Also by Kristen Lepionka

The Last Place You Look

What You Want to See

A ROXANE WEARY MYSTERY

Kristen Lepionka

Minotaur Books
New York

WHAT YOU WANT TO SEE. Copyright © 2018 by Kristen Lepionka. All rights reserved. Printed in the United States of America. For information, address St. Martin's Press, 175 Fifth Avenue, New York, N.Y. 10010.

www.minotaurbooks.com

The Library of Congress Cataloging-in-Publication Data is available upon request.

ISBN 978-1-250-12053-3 (hardcover)
ISBN 978-1-250-12054-0 (ebook)

Our books may be purchased in bulk for promotional, educational, or business use. Please contact your local bookseller or the Macmillan Corporate and Premium Sales Department at 1-800-221-7945, extension 5442, or by email at MacmillanSpecialMarkets@macmillan.com.

First Edition: May 2018

10 9 8 7 6 5 4 3 2 1

For Columbus

What You Want to See

ONE

Urban renewal was in the air on Bryden Road. The dilapidated house across the street from my apartment had been condemned, foreclosed, and eventually purchased by a fighty grad-student couple who appeared to be using the renovation process as experimental marriage counseling. Then my upstairs neighbors moved out and were replaced by a twentyish hipster with a name I could never remember and dreams of starting a farming collective in the building's narrow backyard. I knew this because she had long, loud phone conversations about it all day long.

It was a Tuesday, the kind of perfect June day that made it easy enough to forget how undesirable the weather was in Ohio most of the time. I was on my porch, listening through her open windows to Bridie or Birdy—whatever her name was—talk about the Brahma chickens she was thinking about buying for her farm. As annoying as she was, there was something compelling about it, like a hipster radio drama playing out one floor above me.

It goes without saying that aside from being pathologically nosy, I was also currently unemployed.

I was finishing my second cup of tea when the car pulled up. Tan Impala with no hubcaps and LED light strips behind the grille, easy enough to spot as an unmarked police-issue vehicle.

A regular old cruiser was a more common sight in Olde Towne East, but an unmarked one wasn't out of the ordinary either.

Upstairs, Birdy said, "There are cops on the street. Again. Do you think it's, like, safe here?"

I thought about calling up to her, "Not for Brahma chickens."

But I decided against it when the passenger door of the cop car opened and Tom got out.

That meant they were here for me.

Tom didn't look happy about it. Neither did the other guy, who was short and dense with salt-and-pepper hair razored into a bristly buzz cut like a vacuum attachment. I didn't know him, but his expression said that he knew something about me.

I put my mug down on the ledge and stood up. "I didn't know I was getting company."

"Hey, Roxane," Tom said. His face was unreadable. "This is Detective Sanko. You got a few minutes?"

"To?"

"Chat."

"About?"

The vacuum attachment scowled at me. "You talk just like your dad did," he said. "And you look like him, too."

I sighed. "What's up, friends?"

Sanko said, "Do you want to do it out here, let everybody on the block know your business?"

Upstairs, Birdy was silent for the first time in what seemed like days. "Why don't you come in, then," I said.

I led my visitors into the front room of my apartment, which served as an office of sorts. I tried to catch Tom's eye but he still wasn't playing. "So what's this about?"

Sanko looked around my apartment, his eyes sweeping over an end table piled with laundry and a nearly empty bottle of Crown Royal. "Nice place you got here."

"Ed, don't be a dick," Tom said. He looked at me, finally. There was tension in his face.

"Marin Strasser," Sanko said once he finished his inspection. "You familiar with her?"

I stared at him.

Although I had no idea why they were here, I never would have guessed it'd be about her.

Until a few days ago, I'd been following Marin Strasser everywhere she went. Her fiancé had hired me to find out if she was cheating on him. She wasn't, not so far as I could tell. Which wasn't very far, because less than a week into the case, the man's retainer check bounced and that was the end of it.

Or so I thought. "Yes."

"How?"

"I recently did some work for her fiancé. Why?"

They exchanged glances. "Because she's dead," Sanko said.

A week earlier, I had met with Arthur Ungless at the print shop he owned on the north side. It was in one of those stucco office parks where rows of one-story buildings housed an oddball mix of businesses; the print shop was nestled between a bulk candy distributor and a karate studio. The office smelled like ink and paper and had a pleasant hum of activity murmuring from somewhere on the other side of Arthur's closed door. Business was apparently good: a slow but steady stream of cars coasted past the window behind his desk. "Norm said you were very discreet," he was saying. "And easy to talk to. I need that. Telling a complete stranger that I think the love of my life is having affair. This is all very uncomfortable, see. Embarrassing."

"I get that," I said. I did a job here and there for Norm Whitman's personal-injury law firm, surveillance stuff that fell on the dirtier end of the spectrum of the cases I took on. But money was money, and I valued Norm's business enough to take a referral from him seriously. "But you've got nothing to be embarrassed about. I'm on your side."

Arthur smiled faintly. "Well, you do seem very professional," he said. "I like that."

I straightened up in my seat. I wasn't sure how professional I seemed. I was wearing a black T-shirt, jeans, and an old olive-colored military jacket I'd had for fifteen years that had sort of come back in style recently. But I'd brushed my hair for the meeting, and I was sitting here instead of having this conversation amid the laundry in my home office. So compared to my past self, maybe this *was* professional. "Why don't you tell me about your fiancée?" I said.

Arthur nodded somberly. He was about sixty, short, barrel-chested, with reddish hair going silver, a wide mouth, and washed-out hooded eyes. The cuffs of his blue Oxford shirt were dotted with ink and rolled up to his elbows, revealing a faded Marine Corps tattoo on his left forearm. He struck me as a hardworking, friendly guy. By contrast, the woman in the photograph on the desk between us was coldly pretty, a well-dressed blonde at least fifteen years younger than him. "Marin," he said. "Marin Strasser. You're probably thinking what the hell does she see in me, good-looking woman like her."

"No, no," I said. But I could see what he meant. If *leagues* were a real thing, Marin would be out of his. I wrote her name down in my notebook and underlined it twice. "What makes you think she's cheating on you?"

Arthur sighed and leaned back in his executive chair, idly fiddling with the end of his tie. "Well, we got engaged last October. We were at dinner at M when I asked her. You been there?"

I nodded. "Romantic."

"She was so happy, just over the moon. We've had some real good times together, me and her. Trips and such. This year we've done Palm Beach and Vegas already, and we're talking about Mexico for Christmas. I like taking her places, taking care of her." He paused, his expression clouding over. "But honestly, something's different now. She's different. I can just tell. She's distracted, and jumpy. She'll get phone calls at all hours—that's not really new, her clients are very demanding—but she'll get up and leave the room sometimes too."

I glanced down at the photo again, wondering briefly if she was an escort. "Clients?"

"Marin's an interior decorator," Arthur said, and then I felt like an asshole. "That's how we met—she came in here to get new business cards." He shook his head briefly. "Anyway, when I ask her about it, ask her what's going on and all that, she says it's just the stress of wedding planning. I don't know. Feels like more than that. And I gotta be sure, about her. I can't get married feeling like this. Doubting her, doubting myself."

"Do you have any suspicions about who she's seeing?"

"None," Arthur said.

I waited.

"Marin doesn't have a lot of friends. Neither of us do. That's partly why we got close so fast."

I looked down at Marin's picture. I highly doubted a woman who looked like that had few friends. "Okay," I said, "if you don't know who, do you have any thoughts about when or where?"

He shook his head again. "We live together, so I'm with her every night. But during the day, I don't know exactly what she's up to. No idea. She doesn't keep an office or anything. I know she spends a lot of her time buying for her clients, so she's in and out of furniture stores a lot."

I tapped my pen on my notebook for a second, then wrote

furniture stores down under Marin's name. So far it was not shaping up to be the case of the century. "So you'd want me to keep an eye on her during the daytime hours."

"Yeah. I usually leave home around seven, and I get back home by eight. Weekends, I usually only work in the mornings."

I restrained an unprofessional sigh. "Arthur," I said, "cases like this can get expensive fast. Especially if you're hoping to have someone on her for thirteen hours a day. Say it takes a few days, or a few weeks, even. Are you prepared for that?"

"Trust me, money is not a problem."

I told him my hourly rate, and he didn't bat an eye. So maybe that was what Marin saw in him: either his unwavering dedication, or his bottomless pockets. I figured she was probably having an affair. Part of me wanted to tell him to save his money, because the very act of hiring me more or less meant he'd never be able to trust her again. But if he was determined to pay somebody for answers, it might as well be me.

Arthur wasn't kidding when he said Marin was in and out of stores a lot. She didn't buy much, mostly just wandered around sort of touching things at random. She spoke to very few people, and she didn't sleep with anyone either. For four days, I followed her from one end of the city to the other. We went to an estate sale, the architectural salvage by the fairgrounds, an antique shop in Powell, two overpriced clothing boutiques and a string of art galleries in the Short North, and a hot yoga class. The most interesting thing that went down during those four days was that I spotted Catherine Walsh in one of the galleries, and I did the mature thing and hid behind a sculpture made of chicken wire and fake fruit. But that had nothing to do with Marin Strasser, and everything to do with the universe's habit of putting the same lesson in front of you over and over until you learn it. I was trying, where Catherine was concerned. She'd gotten a cell phone recently and I had yet to respond to any of her texts because there wasn't anything left to say.

If she saw me, she did the mature thing too and walked on by.

Finally, on Friday morning, Marin and I hit up Grandview Heights, and while she spent a very long time looking at pens in a stationery store, I was reconsidering my assessment of the situation. She didn't seem like a woman in the throes of an affair at all. Nor did it seem like she was busy with her allegedly demanding clients. It just looked like she was killing time. But since I had a professional reputation to live up to, I had every intention of following Marin around until Arthur lost interest or ran out of money.

That happened a hell of a lot sooner than expected. The money, not the interest. Sitting at a two-top in Stauf's with a cup of mint tea and the crumbly remains of a blueberry muffin in front of me, I received an alert on my phone that Arthur's retainer check to me had bounced. I stared at the screen. No one had ever written me a bad check before, and I'd worked with plenty of clients who seemed far more likely to do it than Arthur Ungless did. Marin, meanwhile, was flipping blithely through an issue of *Dwell* magazine. She was wearing a black sleeveless dress that looked like it cost more than my entire wardrobe. I'd been able to tell she was attractive based on the photo Arthur gave me, but in person she was gorgeous, with long, artfully streaky blond hair hanging halfway down her back. Her bare arms were smooth and tanned, wrists adorned by an array of bracelets that made a hollow rattling sound when she turned pages in her magazine. She looked aloof and rich, which made the bounced check even more confusing. But it wasn't like I really knew anything about her. Surveillance work was nothing but an odd, shaded view into someone's life, like watching television with the sound off. I ate the rest of my muffin crumbs and thumbed through my inbox in case Arthur had emailed me an explanation of some kind. He hadn't. I didn't know what to do. But when Marin put her reading glasses away and stood up to leave, I didn't follow this time.

Instead, I went back up to Arthur's office. When I was there earlier in the week, he had proudly given me a tour of the facility, name-checking the highlights from his customer list and his cutting-edge techniques like intaglio and microprinting for document security. Today, though, he just slumped in his executive chair and spoke to his desk blotter instead of to me.

"I don't want you to think I don't have the money," he said, his tone disbelieving. "I mean, I have the money. Of course I have it. Look, I'm real sorry about this. I went to the bank and I got you, what is it, twelve hundred here." He picked up a white drive-up envelope, thick with cash. "I still very much want your services."

"Arthur," I said for the third time. "I think we should maybe hold on this for a bit."

"No, no, I have the money," Arthur said. "It is not a problem. There must have been some kind of mix-up, some accounting thing. I'll have to check into it. The shop had a bad couple years but things are turning around. So I have the money. This is embarrassing, okay, but it's just some mistake."

We looked at each other for a minute. "Please," he said, his eyes welling. "I have to know. I just have to."

I reached out and touched his wrist. "Let's give it a few days," I said. "You can get your books sorted out or whatever you need to do, and if you still want to me to pursue it after that, give me a call. Okay?" I thought I was doing him a favor. The twelve hundred bucks on the desk between us barely even covered the time I'd already put into following Marin Strasser around, so I was taking a risk that he might not call and I'd just be out three days' pay altogether. But I felt bad for the guy, and I didn't want to leave him both brokenhearted and penniless at the same time. I wasn't *that* much of a professional.

"Okay," Arthur Ungless said finally as he roughly wiped his eyes. "That's fair. I'll be in touch."

We shook hands, and I left his office distinctly wondering if I'd regret not taking the money and staying on the case.

And now I had my answer. I sat down heavily on the edge of my desk, picturing Arthur's big, sad eyes. "What happened?"

"Tell me about this *work* you were doing for Arthur Ungless first," Sanko said.

"That's confidential."

Sanko said, "Heitker, you told me she'd cooperate if you were here."

"Roxane, come on," Tom said. "You know it's not."

He was right. But I didn't want to spill Arthur's business without knowing the circumstances of Marin's death. I could guess, though, since homicide cops don't come around asking questions like this about car accidents or aneurysms. "Since when don't I cooperate?" I said.

A smile tugged at the corner of Tom's mouth. He was on the tall side, six-one, maybe twenty-five extra pounds on his muscular frame but he carried it well. He always looked like a too-serious cop, whether he was in jeans or dressed in a suit, like he was today. And he always looked good, a fact that I was doing my best not to notice these days. I always felt like anyone could look at us and see it, the kind of familiarity that only happens between people who've slept together before. It had been months since the last time. But that didn't make it any less weird around his colleague.

"Can you just tell me what happened? For Frank."

"Frank," Sanko muttered. But then he gave a small shrug. "She was shot. Friday night, around nine o'clock. Victorian Village, on Hunter Ave. Kind of an alley between Dennison and Neil."

A creeping dread worked its way up my spine. Eerie, how just hours before that I'd been sitting behind her in a coffee shop, watching her read a magazine. "What was she doing there?"

"You tell us. You were the one following her, right?"

"Not by Friday night," I said. I explained about the check. Tom and Sanko didn't look surprised, so I assumed they'd heard the same story from Arthur. "I wish I'd still been tailing her, though. I could have seen what happened, or intervened—"

"No, we might just have two victims in that case," Tom said.

I raised an eyebrow at him. "So what is this, a mugging?" The neighborhoods surrounding the Short North had their fair share of street crime, mostly of the car break-in variety. "When I was following her, she never went anywhere near Neil."

"She had her purse and all her jewelry," Sanko said, "so it's not looking like a mugging, no. According to your client, they had dinner at the Guild House. They met there, Mr. Ungless was working late. They had a bit of an argument, over the fact that Ungless had employed your services, and Marin left, upset. We figure she may have parked somewhere near the crime scene."

I didn't know what to make of this. If not for the technology that allowed my instantaneous access to banking information, I would have continued to tail Marin for another two or three days before I knew Arthur's check had bounced. It was like a glitch in the universe, a loophole. "She drove a black Jeep, with matte black rims," I said, and rattled off the license-plate number.

"I know," Sanko said. "We're looking for it. So about this work you were doing for Ungless. She was having an affair?"

I shook my head. "Not that I saw."

"What did she do? Who'd she do it with?"

"She shopped. By herself. And she went to hot yoga."

"Hot yoga?"

"It's like regular yoga, but the room is like eighty degrees."

"Why would anyone do that?"

Tom cut in, "Never mind hot yoga, Ed. Roxane, how did Arthur seem to you?"

"Embarrassed."

"And?"

"And, that's basically it. He was embarrassed about the check. Surprised, too, I guess. I got the feeling he's not accustomed to being short on cash."

"And how did he seem regarding his fiancée? Angry?"

"No. He wanted me to keep her under surveillance."

Sanko scowled harder. "It was me, I'd be angry. If my pretty, younger lady was stepping out?"

It seemed like my initial instinct to hedge had been correct. "He wasn't angry," I said. "He was sad and confused."

"People react in different ways. Maybe he was pretending to be sad, for your benefit."

"What, he hired me to follow her around but wrote me a bad check so I'd stop right before he murdered her? You've got to be kidding." I turned to Tom. "Did anyone see or hear anything?"

Tom said, "It's Ed's case, and his call. I'm just here to make introductions."

I tried to look as cooperative as I could. "Please?"

Finally, Sanko shrugged. "Neighbor reports hearing raised voices in the alley before the gunshot. A man and a woman, arguing. Then *pop*. A bullet to the chest. A thirty-eight. You know who owns a thirty-eight?"

I waited for the punch line.

"Arthur Ungless. And conveniently, he can't locate it."

I saw Arthur's face again, pleading for my help the other day. I was thinking that I needed to find a criminal lawyer for him, because he obviously didn't have one. A murder victim's significant other was usually the first stop, and for good reason. But I didn't buy that my client killed his fiancée, argument or no. "You said Marin left the restaurant first," I said. "So can anyone put Arthur still there at the time she was killed?"

Now Sanko shook his head. "We came here to get information out of you, not vice versa."

I folded my arms over my chest. "I don't know what I can tell you," I said. "Marin didn't meet up with anyone while I was following her. Other than a few salesclerks, she didn't even talk to anyone. She didn't go anywhere unusual or do anything unusual. And Arthur was not angry."

Sanko thrust a business card at me. "Right. Sure," he said. "Call if you remember anything."

I said, "About Marin, or about Arthur?"

"Yes. And don't go doing your girl detective routine in my case."

He turned to head for the door. Tom said, "I'll be out in a second." Then he paid a lot of attention to the dying plants on my fireplace while he waited for Sanko to be out of earshot.

I didn't care if Sanko heard me though. "Girl detective routine?"

Tom gave me half a smile. "Sorry. I would've called, but the first I heard about this case was ten minutes ago. He grabbed me on the way back in from court and said he needed my help. He hated Frank's guts, and apparently you by association."

I shrugged. "So not a compliment when he said I look and sound like him, then."

He didn't respond to that. He didn't have to.

"I should go. We'll talk later. And hey, be careful around this Ungless guy."

"He's harmless. Tom, there's no way he had anything to do with this."

His face told me he had his doubts. "Be careful anyway."

TWO

The sun was warm on my back as I stood on Arthur's front porch. He lived in a modern ranch overlooking Rush Run, a woodsy ravine that felt isolated even though North High Street was less than a half a mile to the west. I'd spent some time here last week, sitting in the car down the block as I waited for Marin to emerge. Today, though, I parked right in front. I was expecting to see a long line of cars in his driveway—my mother had received an endless stream of visitors in the days after my father was killed last year—but Arthur's driveway was empty except for his own vehicle, a dark grey Jeep similar to Marin's. His and hers. I knocked a second time and the curtains fluttered and then Arthur opened the door and squinted out at me, his face pale and stunned with pain. "It's you," he said softly.

"Arthur, I am so sorry about Marin," I said quickly.

He stared at me, slowly palming the front of his shirt. His eyes were rimmed with red.

"I spoke to the police this afternoon," I continued. "I apologize for showing up like this, but I wanted to talk to you about—"

"The police." He cleared his throat. "Oh. I guess I shoulda given you a heads-up. I wasn't thinking."

"No, no, don't worry about that."

He ran a hand over his face. "I just—look, ah, why don't you come in for a minute. You'll have to ignore the mess, though."

Behind him, I could see that the house was decorated in a nineties sort of outdated opulence—overstuffed furniture, a black and grey geometric area rug, and a glass-topped coffee table. It was a strange aesthetic for an interior decorator's house, but more notably, the house looked like a windstorm had blown through it. An entertainment stand on the far wall stood empty, its contents flung across what I could see of the living room, doors hanging open. A bookcase had been knocked on its side, paperbacks spilling off the shelves like a waterfall.

As I followed him inside, I said, "What happened in here?"

"My gun," Arthur said. He shoved a stack of magazines off the sofa and sat down. "I can't fuckin' find it anywhere." He turned around to face me. "The police, they got the wrong idea. I mean yeah, we were fighting. In the restaurant. I'm the first to admit, it was a pretty bad fight. But I would never hurt her, even after—after everything. I just need to find my gun. If I find it, they'll have to listen, right?"

I perched on the edge of the coffee table. What he said was a bit of an oversimplification. If my last big case had taught me anything, it was that the police could sell any story they wanted. "When did you see it last?"

"I got no idea. Haven't seen it in years. Years. I bought it when I lived over in Linden, there was a string of break-ins on the street. But that was, what, twenty years and two houses ago." He looked around a little helplessly. "But it's got to be here somewhere. Christ, what a thing to have to think about at a time like this."

I looked around at the mess. I was good at finding things—that was why I became a detective—but probably no one would be able to locate a handgun that hadn't been seen in two decades, and it was hard to say how much that would help anyway. Finding

Arthur's gun could only prove that this particular gun hadn't killed Marin. Thanks to Ohio's complete lack of gun laws, there was no registry or anything to prove that Arthur didn't own ten other thirty-eight-caliber weapons. I said, "Arthur, can I ask how the gun came up with the police?"

"They asked me if I owned one, so I said yeah." He ran a hand over his face. "I mean, was I supposed to say no?"

"Have you talked to a lawyer?"

He crossed his arms over his chest. "I got nothing to hide."

I bit my tongue for a second. The fact that he was looking for the gun told me that he was worried, even if he didn't want to admit it. "Do you have one?"

"Well, Norm."

"Norm is a tort lawyer," I said, with measured patience. "He's not going to be able to help in a criminal case—"

"But he's real good in the courtroom—"

"Criminal court is completely different—"

"You know he referred me to you in the first place," he said. "So have a little respect."

I held up my hands. I had no interest in arguing with him, not about the objective fact that a personal-injury lawyer wasn't ideal in a criminal case. Nor the part about how Norm's referral had gotten me exactly no money for my trouble. Arthur was grieving, so I figured I should give him the benefit of the doubt. For another few minutes, at least. The vague guilt that brought me here was giving way to vague irritation.

"Sorry," he said after a beat.

"It's fine."

"But what the hell am I supposed to do. Call that detective and say okay, I got a lawyer now, wanna question me again? No, thanks."

"No, but if they come back to talk to you a second time, you ask to have your lawyer present."

He leaned back and covered his eyes with a hand. "But they'll just think I'm lying, then. Hiding something."

I got up and went to the kitchen, looking for a scrap of paper to write down the name and phone number of a firm specializing in criminal law. They would do worlds better in a police interrogation than Norm Whitman would, his courtroom record of victories against uneven sidewalks aside. I could write down this number and be on my way. If I wanted to feel frustrated without getting paid for it, I didn't need Arthur Ungless. I could do that all on my own. But I stopped when I got to the kitchen counter. There was an open can of chicken noodle soup next to the sink, a spoon inside. I peered into it, hoping that Arthur had just been about to pour the soup into a pot when I interrupted him. But the can was two-thirds empty. Again I thought back to the days after my father died, about the casserole dishes brought over by well-meaning neighbors and distant relatives. I glanced back at him—still sitting on the couch with his hand over his eyes—and then I quietly opened the fridge. Not a casserole dish in sight. That didn't mean much, but between the empty driveway and the sad fact of his cold-soup meal, I got the feeling that something else was going on here.

"Arthur," I said as I returned to the living room. "Do you have family in town?"

He dropped his hand to his lap. "No," he said. "My daughter's in Erie. She's really all the family I got left, except some cousins."

"Have you talked to her?"

"No," he whispered.

"Have you told anybody what happened?"

He took longer to answer this time. "No."

I couldn't imagine what was going through his head. "Arthur, why?"

My client looked at me. "Because I'm embarrassed."

"Embarrassed of what?"

Arthur fell silent again. I thought back to what he said when I first arrived—*I would never hurt her, even after everything.* Then I said, "I want to help you if I can. Do I have the whole story here?"

He cleared his throat. "No."

I stepped back into the kitchen and found two rocks glasses and a bottle of Irish whiskey. I poured us each two fingers' worth and sat next to Arthur on his couch. He took the glass, eyes flicking to his watch for just a second.

"It's kinda early," he said. But he took a small sip.

I glanced at his watch too and saw that it was almost five.

Not that early.

I sipped my whiskey and motioned for him to tell me what the hell was going on.

"After you left on Friday, I got with Janet, she does my bills and whatnot. I thought maybe there was some kind of bank issue that caused it, the—you know, the check to bounce. Janet doesn't touch my personal accounts, so she didn't know anything about it. But we looked at the statements together and, well," he said, "there'd been all these checks. Big checks, payable to cash. With my signature."

I didn't like the sound of that.

"And I remembered, shit, the wedding stuff. I've been giving Marin blank checks to pay the deposit on the venue, the flowers, all that. I thought it would be a couple hundred here, a couple hundred there. But the money's gone. All of it. And what kind of venue wants a deposit in cash? She was lying to me."

"Ouch," I said. I pictured Marin's slightly snooty profile, the dress, the shoes. Aloof and rich. And dishonest as fuck. "How much are we talking here?"

"Seventy-five."

"Hundred?"

Arthur raised his eyebrows and shook his head. "Grand."

Okay, so *ouch* didn't quite cover it. "Christ," I said. "She stole seventy-five thousand dollars from you. When did this start?"

"January. That's when we set the date and she started planning the wedding. I tried going with her at first but it was too hard with my schedule, so I figured, it's easy enough to sign a check and let her take care of the amount, whatever. And I know, it's partly my own fault—for not paying attention to my account balance, for keeping that much in checking in the first place."

I shook my head. "No, it's not even a little bit your fault."

"I just didn't think about it. All my personal bills are auto-withdrawals, so I guess I never even look anymore. I hate dealing with that stuff, you know?"

"Sure," I said. "I do too. Mind clutter. What happened then?"

"So this was Friday, three, four o'clock. I didn't know what to do, I didn't know what to think. I mean, I wanted to give her the benefit of the doubt, but what explanation could there possibly be? And the worst part is, whatever she needed that money for? I would've given it to her no problem if she'd asked." He shook his head and tossed back his drink. "So we were supposed to go to dinner at the Guild House. We had reservations. I was getting ready to go home early, talk to her before dinner and all that, but we had an issue with a customer and I got stuck there till after seven. Marin called and left a message that she was going to head down to the restaurant so we didn't lose our table. And I had no choice but to meet her down there."

If I'd been in Arthur's position, I wouldn't have just calmly gone to dinner. Then again, I couldn't exactly pretend I had never put up with any nonsense from the men or women I'd dated. I had some more of my whiskey. "Go on."

"Well, I shoulda called her back and told her to forget it. I don't know what I was thinking, going there. I lost it. I completely lost it.

I told her I knew about the checks, and I even told her how I found out—that I'd hired you because I thought she was having an affair. And then she got just as mad as I was, and we were practically shouting at each other in the restaurant. Worst night of my life. Finally, she got up and stormed out."

"And you didn't go after her."

"No, I stayed, had another drink." He shook his head. "Then I came home. Middle of the night, I'm passed out right here on the couch, and the police come to the door. It's just unbelievable."

"Did you tell the cops?" I said. "About the money she stole."

Arthur nodded. "And I think it might've been a mistake, because the fat one just acted like that was practically proof that I'd been mad enough to kill her."

Interesting that the police had left this out of what they told me, although, as Sanko had said, they came to my apartment to get information out of me and not the other way around. "What was she doing with that money?" I said. "Do you have any idea?"

"She wouldn't say. She wouldn't even admit to it."

"Does she use drugs?"

"No."

"Gambling?"

"No."

"Anyone in her life with a problem? Friends or family?"

"She doesn't have any family."

"None?"

"None. Her parents died in a plane crash when she was nine, and she was an only child. Her aunt, her mother's sister, took her in for a while and was abusive. So Marin had to cut ties with everyone. She hasn't spoken to them in over thirty years. And friends, I mean, we've got our mutual friends. But she's shy, she's an introvert."

I thought his assertion about Marin having no friends the other day sounded a little shaky, but this story was clearly a load of crap. "Mutual friends," I said. "You mean your friends."

He looked at me for a second and nodded.

"Arthur, I have to say. This is very strange. She made seventy-five thousand dollars disappear. She didn't do that on her own. Introvert or not. Did the police look through her stuff, take anything?"

"No."

I sighed. It didn't sound like Sanko was trying all that hard. I thought about the places Marin had gone while I was following her. They were maddeningly ordinary, nothing to explain why she had been blatantly stealing money from the man she lived with. Unless her secret was that she had a pathological addiction to expensive pens. "Her cell phone," I said. The device itself was likely in her handbag at the time of her death, and therefore tied up in evidence. But her call records could be illuminating. "Do you pay her bill?"

"No," Arthur said.

So much for that.

"I told her we could get one of those, you know, sharing plans. But she didn't want to change her number, because of her business."

A bullshit excuse. She could have easily transferred her number to a new carrier. But speaking of her so-called business, now I wondered if that was any realer than the rest of her. Marin hadn't acted like someone conducting business of any kind while I was tailing her. Then again, if someone were tailing *me*, I might not either. Still, the outdated look of Arthur's home gave me pause. "Did she have a website for her company, a trade name, anything like that?"

"A website?" Arthur said. "You know, I'm not sure." Then his eyes lit up, relatively speaking. "But I still have one of her cards, the cards we printed for her over at the shop." He went into the kitchen and opened and closed some drawers. Then he returned and thrust a cream-colored card at me.

Marin K. Strasser. Sophisticated decor for your home.

Then her email address and phone number.

That was it.

Anyone could get business cards that identified them as anything. I knew this from experience, because I had a bit of a library of them myself. Depending on the context, I called myself a detective, a production coordinator, a claims adjuster. There was nothing official about a business card, but if your actual business was manipulating people, you'd know that they gave a story an air of authenticity.

I wasn't sure what kind of gambit involved posing as an interior decorator, though.

Who the hell was this woman?

"Maybe her business was in trouble," Arthur offered feebly. "And she didn't want to tell me. And now I'll never know."

I swirled around the last bit of whiskey in my glass. "Maybe, yeah," I said, not sure what else to say.

"Listen," he continued, "talking it all through with you right now, it makes me realize. I'm in a bad spot."

"Your circumstances could be better, yes."

He gave me a faint smile. "I know I already owe you money. But can I hire you again, to find out what the hell happened?"

"Arthur—"

"I know," he said. "I know you got to protect yourself and all that, and nobody wants a deadbeat client. But look, I have other accounts. Honest. Tomorrow, maybe Thursday, I could give you five, ten grand. Cash."

I sighed. I was intrigued, and I was also worried for him. The fight at the restaurant, the gun—it made for a good enough argument, if you weren't paying much attention. But it was clear that there was more to the story, and it wasn't a good sign that Sanko seemed less than interested in finding out what it was. I had zero confidence in Arthur's ability to procure five or ten thousand dollars in cash by tomorrow or Thursday, but I also didn't like how things shook out after the last time I told him to keep his money.

"All right," I said. "*If*, and only if, you contact a lawyer too. That will help you more than I can, okay?"

Relief flooded through his washed-out eyes. "Thank you, Miss Weary. Roxane."

I finished my drink. "Don't thank me yet."

I stopped at the Angry Baker on the way home. They were closed already, but Shelby was waiting for me outside with a grease-spotted bag full of what I hoped were chocolate-iced doughnuts for me. I knew she didn't make much money working there part time, but the free day-old doughnuts had to be worth something. She was talking to a girl, a cute girl with an intentionally lopsided haircut, maybe a couple years older than Shelby's brand-new age of eighteen. I rolled down my window and looked out blankly, prepared to ask for directions or something as a ruse in case she wanted to ditch our plans and hang out with her new friend. But when she saw me, she gave me a little wave and quickly ended the conversation before hopping into my car.

"Who was *that*?" I said once the window was closed again. "I was trying to give you an out, but you blew it."

Shelby laughed, her face turning pink. "That's Miriam. She comes in every afternoon for a coffee and a croissant."

"And to see you."

"*No*, jeez, we were just talking today because she liked my shirt."

I glanced over to take in Shelby's faded Tori Amos tee. "Good taste. So when's the wedding?"

"Stop it, OMG." But she was grinning as she thrust the paper bag at me. "Here. Payment for spending your Tuesday night looking at an apartment with your surrogate niece."

I tapped the brakes to pause at a stop sign and reached into the bag for a doughnut. "Surrogate niece?"

"Well, aren't you kind of like my cool aunt?"

I liked the sound of that. "Yeah, okay," I said, "surrogate niece. So where is this place?"

"It's at Rich and Eleventh. My dad said it's going to be crappy like the other ones, but the pictures seemed nice."

"Well, let's hope." I shoved the doughnut into my mouth.

I'd met Shelby and her father, Joshua, on a case the previous fall and since then found myself in a role I couldn't entirely explain, but *cool aunt* covered it pretty well. Shelby needed a cool aunt, or at least a friend. And I needed her a little bit too; Shelby and Joshua reminded me of the fact that, once upon a time, I'd done something right—a welcome reminder after what had happened with Marin Strasser.

"It has this great kitchen, like, twice the size of the one at my house," Shelby went on. "With a brand-new stove. Well, range. That's what the ad said. Range. Is that a stove?"

I nodded, chewing. "Gas or electric?"

"Gas. I've never used a gas one before. I probably wouldn't even know how to turn it on, actually."

"It's a lot easier than an electric," I said. I elbowed her. "Does this mean I know something about cooking that you don't?"

"Ha," she said. "Now, listen. Let me do the talking this time, even if I get all flustered, okay? I'm trying to get better about that."

"Got it." I turned onto Rich, squinting at the street signs. We were on the far edge of Olde Towne, almost to Franklin University.

Despite everything, Shelby was doing okay: in the last six months, she came out to her father, graduated from high school, found a job, registered for fall classes at Columbus State, and was at work on a plan to get the hell out of Belmont. Joshua was taking it all in stride—better than my own father had on the coming-out front—but he thought her goal of moving out already was a bit too soon. I saw his point. But at the same time I didn't understand why he wasn't in a hurry to get the hell out of Belmont too. "Okay, Rich and Eleventh," I said.

"Right there." Shelby pointed at a two-story grey brick building with little archways over the door. A young guy in a popped-collar polo stood on the sidewalk in front of it, scowling at his phone. He glanced up at us as I parked the car, then made a show of checking his watch.

As requested, I let Shelby do the talking, and while the popped collar gave her a halfhearted tour of the place, I hung by the window and scoped out the cars parked on either side of the street: regular old sedans, for the most part, not too new and not too old. It wasn't exactly scientific, but the state of the vehicles on any given block always seemed like a good indicator of its vibe. The apartment itself was tiny, a first-floor studio with badly patched walls and a sloping hardwood floor. It did have a lot of natural light going for it, plus a big kitchen, with the sort of new but cheap fixtures that screamed tax-benefit renovation. It wasn't a horrible place for a first apartment. But it was nothing to get excited about either. The popped collar scowled snobbily at Shelby as she looked around. He seemed cut from the same cloth as my new upstairs neighbor—a gentrifier, someone who wanted to make the neighborhood into something other than it was.

This became obvious when he started listing off the terms of the rental agreement: "Thirty-five-dollar application fee, and that's per *tenant,* not per unit. Security deposit is two months' rent—that's eight hundred a month." He rattled on, but Shelby's face fell.

"The Craigslist ad said six-fifty," she said, her voice small.

The guy stopped and sneered. "Sorry, that's a mistake. It's definitely going to go for eight hundred. Now, where was I. Okay, security deposit is sixteen hundred, there's a nonrefundable pet deposit of three hundred . . ."

Shelby looked like she was about to cry. The popped collar wandered into the kitchen as I went over to her, the uneven floors creaking under my feet.

"They can just put one thing in the ad to get you to come and then suddenly it's higher?" Shelby whispered. "That sucks."

"Yeah, it does, Shel," I said. "But you can do better than this place."

"Not really. You saw the other places. They were way worse. That grey carpet left over from an office building? Bars on the windows? I thought this was going to be a good one. Six-fifty, I could swing. But eight hundred?"

"No, eight hundred is a racket for this place. I don't even pay eight hundred and I have five times as much space."

"Yeah, but that's because you've lived there forever," she said.

"Rent would be way easier if you were splitting it. Maybe you could get a place with a friend?"

Her cheeks went pink. "Roxane, I literally don't have any friends."

I opened my mouth, momentarily speechless. The popped collar chose that moment to walk back over and interrupt with, "Eight hundred is a *very* good deal for the area."

"Um, great," I said. Now I was the one who was flustered. "We'll have to think about it. Do you have an application or something we could take?"

"Ma'am, that stuff's all online now."

"Never mind," Shelby said, making a beeline for the door. "I'm gonna go wait in the car."

She hurried out of the apartment, leaving me face-to-face with the popped collar. "Eight hundred is insane," I told him before I walked out too.

Shelby was in the car with the door propped open, fiddling with her phone. I got in behind the wheel and cleared my throat. "Shelby," I started.

"We don't have to talk about it," she said. Even though she didn't look up at me, I could see the tension and embarrassment on her face, hear it in her voice.

I sighed. "You know I want to help. That's why I've looked at, what is it, eight places with you? And I'll look at eight or twenty or a hundred more, okay? We'll find something. It might just take a while. And it's not like you're on a deadline."

"I *am* though," Shelby said, her head snapping toward me. "I have to get out of there. Every time I look at her house, I just—" She stopped and took a deep breath.

She was referring to Veronica Cruz, her next-door neighbor and best friend—and longtime crush. Veronica was doing well enough after her abduction ordeal in November but had moved to Oregon with her mother for a fresh start. No one, Shelby included, could blame her for wanting to start over. But that didn't make it any easier. I said, "I'm sorry, I wasn't thinking when I said that."

"It's really hard, okay? There's this sad For Sale sign in Veronica's yard and it's never going to sell, right? No one wants to live in Belmont now. There's like four houses down the street on the market already. That's why my dad says he can't move, because there's no way anyone would buy our house. And I get that, but it doesn't mean *I* have to stay there."

"No, of course not." I rubbed my forehead. I'd already let my client down, and I hated doing the same to Shelby. For whatever reason, I still felt responsible for looking out for her. I hoped it wasn't some kind of biological-clock situation kicking in randomly at the age of thirty-four. "I'm telling you, we're going to find you a place before school starts. I promise." I gave her a quick hug over the console. "And don't say you don't have any friends. You have me. I know I'm not Veronica, but I'm not so bad, right?"

Finally, she smiled. "No, you're pretty okay."

I stuck my hand into the paper bag for another doughnut. "Come on, have one so I don't feel like a total pig. We can toast to *pretty okay.*"

She groaned. "But I've already had like four of these today." Then she got a doughnut out of the bag and tapped it against mine. "Oh jeez, I didn't even ask you how you're doing," she said.

I shook my head as I chewed. "Don't."

THREE

I woke up to the *beep-beep* of a large vehicle backing up behind the building. My dream, in which the beeping was a submarine sonar, fizzled out and left me staring blankly at the ceiling. The previous tenant had put glow-in-the-dark stars up there, but in the ashy light of dawn they just looked like weird yellow blobs. I checked the clock: 6:25. Then I rolled over and tried to go back to sleep, but it was immediately clear that I wouldn't be able to with that racket outside. I got up and retrieved my jeans from the floor and pulled them on. I stepped out onto the back patio and glared ineffectively at the box truck. Bluebird or whatever her name was stood in the yard, motioning for the driver to continue onto the grass.

"What's going on?" I called to her.

She looked over her shoulder at me, oblivious to my glaring. "Raised garden beds. Glenn said it was okay."

I doubted that my cranky, ancient landlord had said anything of the sort, but I shrugged and went back inside while the beeping continued. I closed some windows to turn on the AC. The perfect weather from yesterday had spoiled overnight, giving way to the kind of lank humidity that comprised most of an Ohio summer.

After I made a cup of tea—cinnamon, with a splash of whiskey to take the edge off the early morning—I sat down at my desk, then opened my computer to the remains of last night's background search on Marin Strasser. I hadn't gotten very far. Or, rather, I'd gotten much farther than I usually did without getting many hits. Round one: social media—nothing. Round two: previous addresses—nothing other than Arthur's place, where she had lived for a grand total of ten months. Round three: the general trappings of bureaucracy, such as court records, property information, business filings, voter registration, or speeding tickets, all of which could be good sources for personal details. Except this time, I found nothing. Marin Strasser didn't own a car or a house or a business that was registered with the state; she'd never gotten a traffic citation or even so much as a parking ticket. She had a Social Security number, so she did exist—but she'd never held a job or opened a bank account either. For some reason, she was very careful about not leaving a trail. So basically, after three hours of checking every source I could think of, the only paper trail I could find on her was a *Dispatch* entry about her murder. I didn't even get any of the junk search results that offer to give you every piece of information about a person, if you just enter your credit card number and sign up for their useless monthly subscription.

It was weird. Not that she didn't have a Facebook profile or a car or an old nineteen-hundred-dollar debt that Citibank had sued her to collect, but that she didn't have any of it. On paper, Marin Strasser was basically a ghost. Under-the-table living was certainly possible, but it was hard in the modern world.

Now, I tapped my fingers lightly on the keyboard without typing anything for a few seconds. Marin had stolen a big chunk of change from my client, so obviously she wasn't on the straight and narrow. I could see how Arthur would be an easy mark: he was wealthy, lonely, and a little bit naive. But what kind of mark were we talking about, and why? I pictured the way she'd walked through clothing stores, idly trailing her fingers across the merchandise almost compulsively.

Maybe she was just crazy, or maybe there was way more to her than it seemed.

I called Arthur and asked if I could stop by to look through Marin's possessions. He said yes and gave me instructions on how to find his spare key, since he was currently out securing cash for me. I imagined that this meant pawning a coin collection or something. But I headed over to his house around ten, found the key hidden under one of those fake plastic rocks that fooled no one, and went inside.

The house had been put back together slightly, although yesterday's sad soup meal remained on the kitchen counter. I did a quick search of the junk drawer: matches, batteries, expired coupons. I moved on: three bedrooms, one of which was used as an office; two bathrooms; first-floor laundry; back balcony with great views of the ravine, which seemed to glow in the midmorning sunlight. The decor throughout the place was outdated like the living room: heavy lacquer dressers and headboard in the bedroom, white carpet, a desk chair in the office with that nineties pattern that looked like paint swatches.

It was hard to picture Marin, alleged purveyor of *sophisticated decor for your home,* living in this space. And not just because of the ugly upholstery in the office, which appeared to be Arthur's domain. There weren't many signs of her anywhere, honestly. Guest room: an empty Samsonite suitcase labeled with her name and Arthur's address. Bathroom: a pink electric toothbrush and a makeup bag full of Dior. Bedroom: a handful of chick-lit titles on her half of the headboard, a hundred bucks in twenties folded up on her nightstand, a stack of small slips of paper in the nightstand

drawer, plus a small bag of weed, a bottle of body lotion, and a vibrator. I opened the baggie and sniffed—cheap stuff, nothing to get
excited about. The paper slips were curious though: printed with
QR codes and random strings of letters and numbers. I shuffled
through them, unable to discern any meaning. They were printed on
thermal paper, like from a fax machine, and most of them had been
torn off of another slip or a roll. I pocketed one of them and
I moved on to the closet. It was split evenly between Marin's and
Arthur's clothes. She had a lot of dresses like the one she'd been
wearing when I saw her last: dark-colored, fitted, size four. Shoes,
size eight. Handbags, expensive and numerous. I felt through a
bunch of them but found nothing except loose change and forgotten sticks of gum.

I paused to check my phone for messages and saw there was
only a new text from Catherine. Just three dots.

. . .

Since she'd never had a cell phone before, I figured she was still
learning. But it wasn't my job to educate my ex-whatever on the nu-
ances of texting. She'd first messaged me from the new number
with the same message she probably sent to everyone she'd ever
met—*Hey! It's Cat. I joined the twenty-first century xx.* I didn't respond. A few weeks after that, she started with a full-on campaign
to get me to text her back. *I miss you. Why are you ignoring me?
Are you dead? If you're dead I'll REALLY miss you.*

I still didn't go for it. I tried to tell myself I'd learned that lesson
already, that Catherine never meant anything she said. Eventually,
she stopped using words, just went for the dots. Perhaps supposed
to intrigue me into breaking my resolution not to engage with her,
no matter how insistent she became. I knew I should just block the
number, but I also knew I'd never do that. Not in a million years.

I went back to my search. I was feeling like a perv, rooting through a dresser drawer full of sexy underthings when I finally found something: a cedar cigar box, wrapped in a web of nylons. I sat down cross-legged on the floor and considered its secrets. A passport, for STRASSER, MARIN KENNEDY, which contained no stamps, and an ugly silver locket wrapped in an Hermès scarf.

I opened the locket and squinted at the tiny picture inside. A little boy in a suit with a bow tie, standing stiffly in front of a tall Christmas tree, not smiling. A thin sheet of cracked, yellowing plastic lay over the image, making it impossible to tell how old it was. I used my thumbnail to dig the picture out, but I still couldn't tell. The back of the tiny oval offered a portion of the Kodak logo, which probably did not count as a clue.

Needing another break, I walked away from the box and sat on the edge of the bed. Tried to imagine what someone could find about me while searching my apartment. Probably not much, except the fact that I was bad at housekeeping.

But I didn't have anything hiding in my underwear drawer.

So was any of this stuff worth concealing from her fiancé, or was this just her version of a safe-deposit box?

After I left Arthur's house, I drove over to Victorian Village for a look at the crime scene before I dove wholeheartedly into researching locket-dating techniques or whatever I needed to do to make something out of the random collection of items I found among Marin's possessions. Hunter Avenue was a narrow cobblestone strip running through what was probably some of the priciest real estate in the city. On the east side of it, big old mansions facing Goodale Park and their carriage houses, separated from the alley by tall fences. On the west side, a string of apartment buildings and doubles, which, while more modest in their architecture, probably still pulled in four times as much rent as I paid in Olde Towne for more space. Victorian Village wasn't even necessarily safer, as evidenced by the high number of car break-ins and, obviously, the bloodstain in the middle of the street from Marin Strasser. I stood in the alley with my hands on my hips, wondering why she'd been walking through this area. It was a bit of a hike from the Guild House to this spot, and if she was looking for her car, it seemed a strange choice, since all of the metered spots were bordering the park and closer to the restaurant. Maybe, though, she was blowing off steam after her fight with Arthur. Planning to return to the restaurant after she cooled down, or maybe trying to sober up before driving home. In that case, she could have parked anywhere, and no one would ever find her car or figure out why she was here. I wondered if she kept personal stuff in her car, and if the police had found it or even started looking. I glanced around but spotted no public parking areas in any direction. I didn't know how hard the police had looked for her Jeep—probably not very, considering that they'd already found a suspect—but it seemed possible that they had looked exactly this hard and then gave up.

I walked south on Hunter from Buttles to where it dead-ended into the freeway, then looped back along the vaguely Gothic mansions facing the park. The sun was hot on my shoulders. I could keep this up all afternoon and get nothing for my trouble but a sunburn, I realized. But when I got back to the spot where Marin had died, something caught my eye: ruffling curtains from one of the apartments in a U-shaped block of town houses arranged around a small courtyard. All of the apartments had big front windows, and most of them would have had a good view of the street. I headed that way and told myself that I was only taking a break from the search for Marin's car, not giving up completely.

A big, anxious, mulleted man opened the door to the town house a few inches and stared out at me with one eye, the rest of his face hidden on the other side of the door. The smell of pipe smoke wafted out from inside the apartment. Eccentric heir to some kind of mundane fortune, like from plumbing parts, I assumed.

"Hi there," I said, pushing my aviators into my hair. "I'm a private investigator and I was hoping you might have a minute to talk about what happened here on the street the other night." I didn't say *murder*, not wanting to spook him.

"A private investigator?" He squinted at me. "You don't look like a private investigator."

"Do you know any?"

"What?"

"Never mind," I said. I showed him my license. "See there."

"Huh. Private investigator."

"Yes. Roxane Weary, pleased to meet you."

He gingerly shook my hand. "Edward Bennett Wilkington," he said.

Definitely an eccentric heir to a plumbing fortune. "Now, did you know there was a shooting out here on Friday night?"

He nodded and opened the door slightly. The smell got stronger.

"Were you at home?"

Another nod.

"Did you see or hear anything?"

"No, not until the police came. I was . . . busy. I didn't hear it," he finished. Eccentric heir to a plumbing fortune who missed a murder outside his window because he was playing *World of Warcraft*, maybe.

No judgment.

"Okay, thanks."

"Do you want to come in?"

I turned back. "For?"

Now he blushed a splotchy pink. "I have some lavender lemonade. It's good for anxiety. Not that you are, um, anxious or anything. I just thought. Ahem." He had the eyes of a drowning man.

"I can't right now, but thank you," I said, giving him one of my cards. I wondered if a woman had ever graced his front porch before. "If you happen to remember anything, okay?"

He took the card like I'd just given him a sacred artifact. "Is this your phone number?"

I wondered if I would regret giving Edward Bennett Wilkington my contact info. I had been wondering if I would regret a lot of things lately. But I nodded. It was hard to dispute that the number was mine.

"Okay, bye," he said, and slammed the door.

It takes all kinds, I reminded myself.

I went from door to door, trying all of the apartments that faced the courtyard. Most of my knocks were unanswered, and I got quite efficient at scribbling a note on the back of a business card and sending it through the mail slot. The people who *were* home were from the odder spectrum of humanity. I spoke to an old woman who'd heard the gunshots and then hid in her cellar for the next hour, as well as a teenage babysitter who didn't live in the neighborhood and a pair of stoners who weren't even aware that there'd been a murder just outside their front door. Finally, in one of the last apartments in the building, I found someone who could possibly help me.

"I called 911," the woman said. Her name was Meredith Burns and she was in her mid-forties with grey hair in a long braid that hung down her back. "As soon as I heard the shot. You always hear people saying, oh, *maybe that was just a car backfiring, in the city you never know*. Well, clearly they've never heard an actual gunshot right outside their window. I knew. It was horrifying."

"Yeah, it's kind of different up close and personal."

She shook her head. "That poor woman," she said. "I even heard them arguing before it happened, a woman and a man. And I was just annoyed at the racket. I was watching television and I even got up to close my window."

"Really," I said. "Did you see anything?"

She shook her head again. "It happens a lot around here, especially in the summer. Drunk people arguing in the street."

"They sounded drunk?"

"Well, not really. But at first I just assumed."

"Did you hear what either of them said?"

Meredith pressed her lips together, thinking. "The man said something like *what did you do*. That's what he said right before I closed the window. *What did you do?* And then I turned a fan on, because it gets so hot in here without the windows open. And just a few seconds after that, bang. I grabbed the phone right away and went into the bedroom and I didn't come out until the police came." There was something guilty in her face. "The 911 operator told me to stay inside so that's exactly what I did."

I showed her a picture of Marin, but she had no recollection of seeing her in the area before. Ditto for a black Jeep.

I guessed it was back to the locket.

FOUR

At home, I sat down and dumped my meager collection of clues onto my desk: a business card for a business that might not exist, an unused passport, a locket with some kid's picture, and a weird paper slip. I examined it closely, still not sure what I was looking at. I Googled *slip of paper with QR code* as a warm-up, not expecting much. I got a few pages of results concerning lottery game slips, cryptocurrency, contest entries, transit tickets.

Fascinating.

I looked at the locket next. Not much bigger than my thumbnail, the locket was a tarnished silver oval with the letter "M" engraved into the surface, a spray of flowers behind it. It hung on a rope chain, slightly tangled. I slid the picture out again and examined it under a loupe. The kid was blond, slightly chubby, maybe six years old. I scanned the photo into my computer before I lost it forever in the mess on my desk, then set the necklace aside.

The passport was useless. Its leather Kate Spade cover spoke to Marin's good taste, like her clothes, her shoes, her glossy blond hair. I thought again of the outdated furnishings in Arthur's house.

Sophisticated decor for your home.

I picked up the business card. Name, phone number, email. I ran a few searches on the three in various combinations, finally hitting on something when I typed in her phone number with *Columbus sophisticated interiors.*

A Craigslist ad posted to the antiques section twenty-nine days ago, titled "BEWARE!!!!! THIEF IS BACK."

I clicked to read the rest of the text.

> There is a lady listing a RARE Taylor neon thermometer for sale but she is a THIEF DO NOT BUY PLZ BEWARE I bought a 9 tube herschede from her in January 2007 and she said she was an interior designer selling antiques for her customers. SOPHISTICATED INTERIORS yeah right later I found out she STOLE the herschede and the police came to MY SHOP about it and I had LOTS OF LEGAL PROBLEMS FOR MONTHS!!!!!!! Well now she is BACK selling this taylor neon thermometer and unless you want to get ACCUSED OF BEING A FENCE and IN TROUBLE WITH POLICE then avoid this seller she is a LIAR AND A THIEF!!!!!!!!!!!!!!!!!!!! If anyone knows who this lady is PLZ CONTACT ME because someone needs to stop her!!!!!!

It went on to give Marin's phone number and a physical description of her—"rude trashy blonde"—plus a screenshot of the neon-thermometer listing in question.

I laughed out loud in bewilderment. There was a lot going on here. "Liar and a thief" definitely seemed to fit Marin's MO, but I stared at the date—January 2007—and figured it had to be a typo. Unless this person had been nursing a grudge for over ten years?

There was no way to identify whoever posted this, because Craigslist used an anonymous email relay system, but I could possibly convince the poster to reveal themselves. I clicked the reply button on the ad and copied the email address to send them a quick note to attempt just that.

For verisimilitude, I did a quick search to see what the hell a "9 tube herschede" was—an expensive antique grandfather clock—then wrote:

> Hi, saw your CL post about the clock lady and I think
> I know who she is! Can we talk in person? Would
> rather not discuss on email. Thanks!

I sprinkled in a few more exclamation points for good measure and sent the message.

I went to my mother's house for dinner every Wednesday—just the four of us now, my brothers, my mother, and me in the kitchen of my childhood. Beige tile floor, plaid wallpaper. Original to the house, so this was probably the kitchen of another family's childhood too. I always felt the tiniest bit out of place here, like it was still my father's house, like he still made the rules. Even with him gone now for over a year, the rules still stood—like how my mother still wouldn't smoke in the house, or how she still wouldn't go into his office upstairs—Frank's personality so strong that he could keep us all in check just through his memory. Not all the memories of my father were bad. But they weren't all good, or even okay, not in my mind, and not in my mother's, either. She'd never say it out loud, though, one of the many ways that I was more like him and not like her.

"Rita's daughter-in-law just had her baby, did I tell you that?" my mother, Genevieve, was saying while she poked at something in the oven. I stood at the counter with a cutting board and a jumbo

Vidalia in front of me, because she was an eternal optimist and still thought I'd learned how to chop an onion properly at some point in my life.

"A boy. Ten pounds! His name is August. Isn't that cute, Roxie? A June baby named August."

"I wonder how many times the kid will hear that joke in its life," my brother Matt piped up from the living room, where he was watching LeBron crush it in the NBA playoffs.

"*Its*?" my mother said. "Matthew, this is Pietro's son. You remember how he idolized you way back when, right?"

Matt, cranky as usual, grumbled something unintelligible.

I wiped away the beginning of an onion tear. I had not, to my knowledge, ever met Rita's daughter-in-law, although Rita had lived next door to my mother as long as I could remember. Then I got an idea. "Rita's youngest girl. She still commuting to OSU?"

My mother nodded, gingerly setting a pan of crescent rolls from the oven onto a cooling rack. "Why?"

"Just wondering if she has plans to move out, get her own place with another girl. I know someone who might need a roommate soon," I said. Shelby's living situation was still weighing heavily on my mind.

She looked at me with hesitation. "I don't know. Alexandra's real shy, such a sweet girl. Sheltered."

The way she said it made it sound like anyone I'd know would undoubtedly corrupt shy, sweet Alexandra. I wasn't sure if I should be offended or not. I knew she didn't really mean anything by it, but still. I opened my mouth to say something but then my other brother breezed into the house on a cloud of cigarette smoke and aftershave.

"Andrew!" my mother exclaimed, tipping her face up toward him for a kiss on the cheek.

Andrew was her favorite among the three of us. I didn't blame her for that, because he was also mine.

"Brought you something," he told her, holding out a bottle of white wine with a swank label. He deftly passed a whiskey bottle to me with his other hand and winked. We had it down to a science here, the delicate art of pretending my father's liquor cabinet wasn't empty. Neither Andrew nor I wanted to call attention to how quickly we'd cleared it out by making a show of restocking it. "This is called a traminette. It's sweet. You'll like it. Rox, you want me to help with that?"

I looked down at the mound of large, uneven onion chunks on the cutting board. "Sure," I said. I let him take over. I couldn't exactly deny that I was doing a shitty job with the onions. The kitchen was too small to have three adult people in it at the same time so I grabbed two rocks glasses from the cupboard and relocated the whiskey bottle to the dining room. The bottle of Powers was open already, probably nicked from the hotel where Andrew was a bartender.

He was also the first stop hotel guests made when they wanted to unwind with an ounce of weed along with a drink.

But he probably hadn't brought any of that.

My mother was saying, "Did you get that adorable invitation to Tom's party? Pam is just such a sweetheart. She's so good for him."

There was that word again: *sweet*. Every time my mother said it was like a reminder that she'd never use such a word to describe me. Probably no one would. Which was fine, because I wasn't. But it was something my mother valued in a person. Their sweetness. Their niceness. Yet another way in which I took after my dad. The very last thing he ever said to me was *Be nice but not too fucking nice.* So was it really any wonder that I turned out this way? I swallowed the inch of whiskey I'd poured into my glass and closed my eyes.

"Can I see the invitation?" I said. I knew about the party, all right. I'd somehow found myself agreeing to help Pam plan it. In fact, I was meeting up with her tomorrow to discuss the arrangements. Tom was going to hate every minute of a surprise party, possibly as much as I was going to hate party planning with his girlfriend. I wasn't aware Pam was sending out invitations though. I refilled and carried both glasses back into the kitchen.

"I'm sure yours is in the mail, hon," my mother said. "It's on the sideboard, by my purse."

Andrew said, "You can't miss the thing, it could be seen from space."

I looked at him. "*You* got an invitation?"

"Well, it's not like I'm going."

Neither of my brothers liked Tom much. I was never entirely clear on why—maybe something to do with the fact that my father was fonder of Tom than he ever was of either of them, or of me, really.

I didn't mind Tom.

But I had my own reasons.

"Andrew, we should all go," my mother said. "Tom's always been like a part of this family."

I went back into the dining room and located the invitation in a stack of mail on the sideboard, a shiny affair proclaiming *SECRET SUMMER SOIREE.* I wondered again why I hadn't just said hell no when Pam asked me to help her. Or, more importantly, why she even thought she needed my help in the first place. Clearly she had it all figured out. I set the little card back down on the stack, catching a glimpse of a thick, folded, legal-looking document. I nudged it, took in the somber text identifying it as the last will and testament of Francis J. Weary.

Over a year later, and the estate still wasn't settled. I already knew that. But something stabbed at my chest when I thought about my mother having to deal with the day-to-day of it. She put up a relentlessly cheerful front, but if there was anything the Weary family was good at, it was putting up fronts.

As quietly as I could, I refilled my glass again.

FIVE

The neighbor's car had been broken into during the night. At a quarter after eight, she started screaming bloody murder about it, so much raw emotion in her voice that I grabbed my gun from my desk drawer and dashed outside, only to see her sobbing in front of the busted front window of her Honda. Bluebird—or whatever her name was—looked at me and wailed, "Oh thank God. You have to help me! What do I *do*?"

I shoved my gun into my jeans at the small of my back. "About your window? Call Safelite or something—do you want their number?"

"No! It's my purse. My purse is gone."

"Oh," I said. That seemed to fall under problems of her own design. "Um, you have to be careful about what you leave in your car around here—"

"Like this is *my* fault?" She stomped her feet. "God! Everyone here is *so mean!*"

I shrugged and went back into the building. Alejandro, who lived in the apartment next to me, was just opening his door. He looked sleepy and fabulous in a white satin robe. "From the way she was screaming, I thought somebody *died* out there. Between this and those ugly things in the garden now? Worst neighbor."

"Don't forget the Brahma chickens," I said.

Alejandro giggled. He was Bluebird's age or maybe younger, but infinitely less terrible. We'd bonded immediately as the only non-straight people in the building when he moved in last year. He said, "I gotta go back to sleep though, it's way too early for this bullshit. But we need to have drinks soon, girl, mmkay?"

I told him to text me and went back inside. I had been sitting at my desk, hoping to get a response from the angry clock person. But now I wondered if going back to sleep was a better idea anyway. I went into my bedroom but then heard my phone start ringing from beside my computer.

"Everyone here is so mean," I muttered.

"Did I wake you up?" Tom said when I answered. "Sorry."

"Surprisingly, no. But I didn't sleep well. And I don't think you're sorry."

"Well," he said, a smile in his voice, "how about you buy me breakfast then?"

I sat on the edge of my desk. "Okay. Do you have news?"

"News? Not really. Just some questions. Can I bring a date?"

My jaw tightened. "What?"

"Sanko," Tom said quickly. "He wants to talk, ask you some more questions."

I covered my eyes with a hand. "Okay. But why am I buying you breakfast?"

"You're not. I was kidding. Fifteen minutes, at Jack and Benny's?"

The restaurant was over near High and Broad, only a few minutes away from my place in Olde Towne. But although I was nowhere ready to be seen in public yet, a perverse desire to appear low-maintenance made me agree to the time. "Sure." Then, assuming I'd be late, I added, "Order for me?"

"Waffle special and black tea?"

"You know it."

The plastic-and-Formica booths at Jack & Benny's Downtown Diner were small, and Tom and Sanko looked a little silly there, two not-small men seated across from each other, not speaking. "Hello," I said, squeezing in next to Tom.

He looked happy enough to see me, but Sanko didn't. "So how come you didn't mention the other day that you're working for Ungless again? On *my* case?" he said.

"Okay, wait a minute," I said. "Let's cool it with the third degree."

"Come on," Tom said at the same time.

Sanko frowned. He was wearing the same blue suit as Tuesday, but this time with a bright red and yellow tie that someone had obviously told him looked *peppy*. Tom was in a dark grey suit with a tie that Pam had probably picked out.

Focus.

I cleared my throat and said, "I wasn't working for Arthur the other day when we talked. I didn't even know what had happened to Marin until you told me. But I did talk to Arthur afterwards. I'm not trying to step out of my lane or anything here. I only want to make sure he stays out of jail, because he doesn't belong there."

"You don't get to decide that."

"Believe me, I know," I said, "but it's not like you told me everything either. The seventy-five grand? Obviously there's more to Marin than just a fight with her fiancé, right?"

"We're looking into it."

"How?"

"Is she always like this?" Sanko said to Tom.

I opened my mouth to respond, but then the waitress appeared with our food. I shut my mouth and looked down at the golden beauty of my waffle, by far the best thing about this day. Once we all had our plates in front of us, Tom said, "Look, Roxane solved a case last year that even *Frank* couldn't close. So hear her out. She knows her stuff."

"Aw," I said.

Tom shook his head, but he was smiling. "Yeah, she's always like this."

Sanko grabbed a saltshaker and liberally dusted his eggs with it, saying nothing.

"Maybe we can help each other out," I offered. "I'll tell you what I know, et cetera."

"And what do you know?"

"Not a whole lot," I said. "But I do know that Marin's got a pretty thin file, except for Arthur. How'd you connect her to him?"

I could tell Sanko didn't want anything to do with me, but he looked at Tom and shrugged. "Well, he was in her phone as the emergency contact. You know, ICE. And she had his address on her driver's license."

"Well, I think I may have a new angle for you."

I told them about the Herschede clock and the Craigslist vendetta, but Sanko just glared at me.

"Oh, sure, like a freaking Craigslist post is the secret to this case. We already have a suspect, thanks. When you see hoofprints, look for horses. You ever hear that, Miss Weary?"

"No, never," I said, "but it sounds very wise. What makes you so sure it's that simple?"

I felt Tom tense up beside me as he contained a laugh. Sanko scowled thoroughly. "What makes me *sure*," he snapped, "is what the staff at the Guild House had to say about them two, okay?"

We all chewed in silence for a minute or so. "Well, what did they have to say?" I asked finally.

He let out a put-upon sigh and looked at Tom again in a way that made me wonder what Sanko owed him. Then he said,

"The restaurant was this close to asking them to leave." He held his thumb and forefinger a hair apart. "One of the waitresses thought they might need to call the police, but then Marin got up and left on her own. Apparently they were screaming at each other. Eff this, eff that, eff you, and so on. Arthur threatened to kill her."

I felt my jaw drop. "No way."

"Way," Sanko said. He reached into his blazer and pulled out a small notebook and flipped backward through its pages. "He said, and I quote, 'You lying cunt, I could just put my hands around your pretty little neck and squeeze the life outta you right now.'"

Next to me, Tom shifted his weight. I cleared my throat. I didn't like the sound of this at all. "But Marin was shot, not strangled," I said a little feebly. "And she got up and left. Do you know how much time passed between when she left and when Arthur did?"

"No."

"What time was Arthur's check paid? There should be records."

"You think I didn't check that?" Sanko said.

That was exactly what I thought.

He continued, "He left without closing out his check. He dropped a pile of cash on the table. So no, we don't know how much time. Marin walked out of the restaurant just before eight-thirty. Ungless ordered another drink at eight-forty. It was after nine when his waitress completed his cash payment in the computer. He was already gone by then, and no one can say exactly when he left. I don't know why I'm even telling you this."

"Was it gone?"

"Was what gone?"

"The drink he ordered. Did he finish it?"

"He had plenty of time to catch up with her, if that's what you're asking."

We chewed in silence for a while longer.

"So," Sanko said eventually, "he's got no alibi. He's got a hell of

a motive, means, and opportunity, and in fact was seen by a restaurant full of people threatening to take Marin's life less than an
hour before she was killed. That's pretty solid, in my opinion.
Which brings me to my point—I don't need you involved here any
further. This case is winding to its inevitable conclusion. I gotta
piss and then we need to go, Heitker."

I had to admit that his theory seemed valid. If we were talking
about someone I wasn't working for, I might have even agreed with
him. But we weren't, so I didn't. I sighed and put down my fork.
My window was closing fast. "Any chance I could see her cell
phone?" I said.

"No, of course not."

"Are you checking out the numbers she called?"

Sanko gave me a tight little smile and squeezed out of the booth
without responding.

As he walked away, I tried, "Have you found her vehicle yet?"

But Sanko didn't answer that either.

Tom let out a heavy sigh. "He told me he was going to be nice to
you."

I got up and switched seats so I was facing him. "Honestly, I
think that was being nice, for him. And to think I even considered
buying you both breakfast." I reached across the table and picked
up my tea, which I had barely touched. "So what do you think?
Really."

Tom thought about that for a second. "I think I want the rest of
your waffle. Is that weird?"

"Probably."

He was holding his fork expectantly.

I added, "But go for it. What do you think about this case?"

He cut off a section of my waffle and moved it to his plate.
"I think this is a mess."

"Thanks."

"Seventy-five grand? Cash like that can buy a lot of trouble. It doesn't look great for your guy."

"*Lying cunt* doesn't make him terribly sympathetic, does it?"

"No, not exactly. But you're pretty sure about him?"

"I'm pretty fucking sure."

He nodded. "Those famous Weary instincts." He gave me a smile. "You want me to look into her vehicle at least, see if it's been recovered yet? I think that's worth checking out."

Our eyes met for a moment and I felt myself smile too, for the first time all morning. "Would you?"

"Sure," Tom said. Sanko stomped back to the table and stood there, tapping his foot. Tom stood up and pulled out his wallet and tossed a twenty on the table, shooting me a wink. "I'll let you know," he said, holding his hand up like he wasn't sure what to do with it. Then he dropped it to my shoulder and squeezed. "See you."

As soon as he was gone, the waitress brought the check over. "You two are always so adorable together," she said.

SIX

I was pretty sure I wanted to like Tom's girlfriend. But I was almost positive that I didn't. Before I met her, I irrationally decided Pam was one of those women who buys her friends the same bejeweled "Will work for wine or shoes" tote bags every year for Christmas and orders a *triple Venti extra-hot half-caf half-sweet nonfat latte with caramel drizzle* at Starbucks and talks about how much she loves salad all the time. In reality, she wasn't like that at all. But she was still all wrong for Tom somehow. Sure, she was pretty, witty, full of charming anecdotes about her job as a French teacher at a high school on the east side. She was nice enough. She was smart, socially ambitious, and a little shallow, like a human equivalent of one of those glossy magazines with decent feature articles. She was girlfriend material, but she wasn't a partner. She didn't *get* him. She wasn't bone-deep loyal. She wasn't ride-or-die. Or maybe I just didn't want to like her after all. Five minutes after Tom had first introduced us, when he stepped away to get us a round of drinks, Pam leaned over and whispered conspiratorially, "So tell me *everything*. All his secrets," like he was an asset to be secured with the right bit of intel rather than a person, my dear friend.

"I think you should just ask him," I had said, as lightly as I could, "if you want to know his secrets."

She had just laughed, that head-tipped-back kind of laugh that always made things seem funnier than they were. "You're *crazy*," she said. "I knew I would like you."

This proved to be basically how she always acted toward me, like I was her zany, unpredictable, new best friend. Despite the fact that we barely knew each other. There'd been a few awkward get-togethers over drinks with the three of us, then some even more awkward double dates with the rotating lineup of male friends—always male friends—she was trying to pair me off with. Otherwise, I avoided her. Better for everyone that way. But when she asked for my help with Tom's birthday, I caved. A surprise party sounded like the absolute last thing Tom would want for his birthday, but if I couldn't talk her out of it—which I tried first, of course—then I figured at least I could make it suck as little as possible. As it was, she seemed to be doing a pretty good job of planning the worst party ever.

"I was thinking I could call him, like, *I think there's an intruder in the house*," she was saying. "And ask him to come over. Then, when he gets here, everyone is waiting. Surprise!"

I watched her for a second to see if this was a joke, but it did not appear to be a joke. I shook my head. "That's a pretty bad idea, Pam," I said. "He'd be legitimately concerned. He'd probably call it in to the Grandview police to get someone over here faster. I know I already said this, but are you sure that a surprise is the best choice? I mean, it's *his* birthday. We—you should do whatever he's going to like the best. And I don't know that a surprise is it."

She cocked her head, considering this. She had thick, auburn hair pulled up into a messy bun, and ocean-blue eyes behind tortoiseshell smart-girl glasses. Although she was off for the summer, she was still dressed better than I was, in a black-and-white-striped blouse and emerald-green cropped pants, her bare feet recently pedicured with a hot-pink polish. I felt hopelessly shabby in my madras shirt and jeans.

"See, this is why I need your help! You think like he does."

I shook my head. It wasn't that I thought like he did, but rather that I knew him. Really knew him. I drank a little of my sangria, aware that mine was almost gone whereas Pam had barely touched hers.

"But," she continued, "I do want it to be a surprise. If it's not a surprise, he'll just say he doesn't want a party at all. And he has to have a party! This is *forty*." Pam dropped her voice on the last word, as if she didn't want the grim reaper to hear. "Do you know what he did for his birthday last year?" She shifted in her seat on the couch and crossed her legs. "He ate dinner at a Chinese take-out place. Alone."

Last June had been only four months after my father died—four months after Tom killed the kid who shot him—and almost six months before Pam was in the picture. We'd been sleeping together since the night of the funeral but I didn't know when his birthday was; it hadn't come up. He had called me from the Chinese place, told me that he had turned down a bunch of offers of birthday drinks from people who just wanted him to cheer up already, that I was the only person who wouldn't try to make him. We met up downtown and caught the last two-thirds of *Vertigo* at the Ohio Theater summer movie series, got devastatingly drunk on the plastic-cupped champagne they sold at the concession stand, and then fucked in the lounge outside the ladies' room. It had been, from my recollection, one of the better days from the aftermath.

"Well," I said. "That wasn't the only thing."

"Oh, you mean the horror movie?" Pam wrinkled up her nose. "He told me about that. I'm just saying, I want him to have a real celebration this year."

I finished my sangria and poured more from the pitcher. "Well," I said again. "You could get an ice-cream cake from the Dairy Queen—he'd love it, we've talked about that before. How when we were kids that's how you knew someone's birthday party was going to be a good one, if they sprang for an ice-cream cake. You could have them write *I'm sorry for throwing you this party* on it."

Pam laughed. "I will not," she said. "But that's a good idea, an ice-cream cake. I was thinking Pistachia Vera but he'd like that even better. You're good at this, girl. What else you got? Decorations?"

I shook my head. "No decorations. Keep it low-key."

"What about music? Maybe you could make a playlist or something."

"Sure," I said. Why was I taking on more responsibility here? I sighed. "But really, a party is only as good as the guests. Who all is coming? My mother showed me the invitation."

"Oh good! Wasn't it pretty?"

"Very shiny."

She didn't acknowledge the shininess, just got up and disappeared into her kitchen for a second. I used the opportunity to top off my drink. Desperate times. "So here's who has RSVP'd so far, other than you and me, of course. My sister and her husband, and Randy—my next door neighbor, he and Tom are like this." She stood in the doorway to the living room and held up two crossed fingers. Then she rambled off another twenty-five names, all people from her side of the aisle, not his. "Is there anyone else I should send one to? When he was in the shower the other day I looked through the contacts in his phone." She sat back down on the couch and handed me a sheet of paper with a list in her bubbly blue handwriting. "Who are these people?"

I scanned through the list, faintly surprised that she didn't know some of them. "Kim, his sister," I said. "Invite her but I doubt she'll come. She lives in Virginia."

"Duh, I knew that."

"Most of these are cops. Jim Kusarow, invite him. And Lucy

Ohmura, she's cool." Then I frowned. "Frank W, that's my dad." I put the list down on the cushion next to me. It was weird to think of my father's name still in Tom's phone. Weird to think of it still in mine, too.

Pam snatched up the list, horrified. "Oh my God, of course. I wrote these down really fast—I wasn't thinking. I'm sorry."

After I left Pam's house, I checked email on my phone and saw that I had a response from the clock person.

Come by the shop during business hrs HIGH STREET ANTIQUITIES Clintonville

I'd been hoping for an exclamation point or two, but oh well.

I found the shop easily, nestled in a row of vintage stores on High between Weber and North Broadway. Some of them, like the Boomerang Room, specialized in midcentury decor and clothes and had a clearly defined aesthetic. Others specialized in everything, or nothing, for example High Street Antiquities, which was a glorified junk shop, packed wall-to-wall with artifacts spanning the entire breadth of American history—neon signs, furniture, clothing, art, all stacked haphazardly around narrow aisles. It resembled a place about to get burned down for insurance money.

"Hello?" I called, not wanting to venture too far down any of the aisles for fear I'd be buried in an avalanche of crap and never heard from again.

A few seconds later I heard a door open and the muffled sound of something collapsing. "What the fucking fuck," a voice boomed from somewhere back there, "goddamn piece of shit!"

I figured this was the clock person.

"Hi there," I said when he appeared, shoving a mountain of

records out of his path. He was a huge guy in his early forties, both tall and broad, with an unruly beard and collar-length hair. He looked mad.

"Help you?" he barked, jamming a pair of glasses onto his face.

"Uh, yeah, hi." An image of Marin Strasser standing here popped into my head and I struggled to contain an out-of-place laugh. "I emailed, about your Craigslist—"

"What? I can't hear you. Come over here. Just walk on it. Or kick it out of the way. I don't actually give a shit." He motioned me over to the counter, which featured a glass case of Bakelite costume jewelry.

I stepped over the records he'd just knocked down to reach the counter. "I emailed," I said again. "About your post on Craigslist. The woman with the clocks."

He laughed and thrust out a hand. "Rudy Carmichael. She get you too?"

"Almost."

"Bitches," he said sadly, shaking his head. "No offense. I didn't know if I'd get any hits with that post, but I figured why the hell not, nothing to lose. You can imagine my surprise when I called her about the Taylor thermometer and I heard that voice—I've been trying to find this particular bitch for going on ten years. Ha! Joke's on her. So you're a what, a dealer?"

"Yeah, Springfield," I said vaguely, flapping a hand. "I paid her a deposit on another Herschede, this was two months ago, maybe. She said it would be over four hundred bucks to ship it out there, so I said I'd come get it. And she ghosted me. What happened to you?"

He was looking curiously at me. "What kind of Herschede?"

"Uh," I said, racking my brain for some kind of detail from my point-two seconds of research, "turn-of-the-century, with spindle gallery sides?"

He smacked the counter so hard that the jewelry underneath rattled in the case. "Bullshit. Who the fuck are you? I know every dealer in Springfield and not a one of them would describe a Herschede like that. Did she send you here?"

"No, Christ, no," I said, "calm down. I'm a private investigator, and I'm just looking for information about her—"

"You said you had information."

"Well, kind of—can—"

"That's just like her too. You bitches are all alike."

"Hey, now."

"Hey nothing. Get out of here. I'm not telling you anything."

"Have you seen her recently?"

"What? No. Get out of my shop."

"Can you just tell me what happened?"

He reached under the counter and I stumbled backward, certain he was about to produce a weapon. But instead he came up with a grimy cordless phone. "I'll call the police. Get the fuck out."

I held up my hands in defeat and walked back out through the mess, wondering if he was going to write a Craigslist rant about me too.

But at least I'd learned something. Two things. One, his name. And two, the fact that it wasn't much of a stretch to imagine him killing someone.

SEVEN

I met Arthur that evening at his print shop to collect money and information. The money came in a thick envelope with my name written on it in block letters. It made me briefly wonder how many other thick envelopes of cash he was doling out today.

The information was a little harder to get. "No, I don't know who this is," Arthur said, shoving the locket back across the desk to me. We were sitting in his office, which he had partially destroyed that afternoon looking—without success—for his gun. Arthur was pale and sweaty, his eyes desperate. The desk between us, as well as the floor, was covered in thin pink invoice forms that had once occupied a filing cabinet in neat stacks. It was after business hours but Arthur's receptionist was still out front, and the hum of machinery vibrated from somewhere in the back of the suite. He reached into the bottom drawer of his desk and pulled out a bottle of whiskey and two little paper cups, to which I nodded. "And I never heard her talk about this Rudy Carmichael. Or a clock. You're probably laughing at me inside," he said. He poured the whiskey and nudged one of the cups in my direction.

"No, I'm not," I said. Wondering what the hell he was thinking, maybe, but not laughing. Nothing about this was funny. I watched him toss back his drink in one swallow. I wrapped the locket back up in the Hermès scarf and pushed it into my pocket. Then I tossed back my shot too. "I'm just trying to understand. When you met her, where'd she live?"

"Downtown."

Okay, maybe now we were getting someplace. "Downtown where?"

"I don't know."

Or not.

"You never picked her up?"

"We'd always meet, you know, at the restaurant or whatever. She started spending the night pretty quick, and then, I mean, she didn't officially move in till after we got engaged but she was with me all the time almost from the beginning."

"She was staying over."

"Yeah." He leaned back and one of the invoices stuck to his forearm and he snatched it off. "And I liked it that way, right? We were just having so much fun. It'd been a long time since either of us had any fun. We were both married before, and I guess she had a real hard time after her husband left her. She never thought she'd feel so at home with anyone else."

"This ex-husband," I said. "Know anything about him?"

"She didn't talk about him much, but I think they were on good enough terms. She said there was a part of her that would always love him. William, that's his name."

"William Strasser?"

Arthur looked up at me for the first time in a while. "No, I think that's her maiden name." He rubbed a hand over his face. "Christ, I don't even know."

A car rolled slowly past the window, speakers cringing to the blown-out bass of an unidentifiable song. "Is it always this busy here?" I said as the car disappeared.

Arthur looked vaguely over his shoulder. "It's, uh, a busy area," he said. "There's traffic. Listen, are you hot? Because I can hardly breathe."

I studied him. His breathing was a little shallow, his face still pale and slick with sweat. "I'm okay," I said. "Are you feeling all right?"

He stood up shakily. "I think I just need some air. I'm gonna go outside for a minute. I'll be right back."

I stood up too, worried now that he was about to have a heart attack or something. "Arthur—"

"No, I'm fine, I'm fine," he muttered, "just need some air. Please. Let me go."

He walked out of the room and a few seconds later I heard the front door to the suite open and close. I saw him through the window behind his desk as he stood on the sidewalk and looked up at the twilight sky, tears streaming down his cheeks. So not a heart attack. Just mixed-up grief. I sat back down and stared at the sea of pink invoices on the desk, wondering if he'd called the law firm I'd told him to call, or his daughter, if he'd even told any of his employees what had happened, if I was literally the only person who knew what he was going through. Scary, if that was the case. I was good in certain types of crisis, but not exactly ones of emotion. I poured another inch of whiskey into my cup and drank quickly. I was stressed out just by looking at the mess he'd made in here, and my own threshold for chaos was usually high. I squared some of the invoices into a neat stack and glanced up at Arthur again; he was still weeping on the sidewalk, but some of the color was returning to his face. I began collecting invoices from the floor. If I couldn't help him find his gun or explain what the hell Marin had done to him, at least I could organize a bunch of papers.

And that was when the window exploded.

———

I saw it before I even heard the gunshots. The window turned into a mist of splintered glass and time stopped for a second. A bullet lodged in the wall behind me, then another. I dove for the floor, rolling away from the jagged opening as a big gun boomed again outside—one, two, three, four, five, ten times. A deafening rattle that vibrated the filing cabinets. Every part of me tensed up and my hand flew to my hip, but my own gun was locked in my car. So was my phone, I realized.

The shooting stopped and I heard the squeal of tires in the parking lot, doors slamming.

Then an abrupt, piercing silence.

I let out a breath, taking an inventory. I was okay.

Then I remembered where I was.

Arthur.

I hauled myself to my feet and looked out through the hole where the window used to be and saw him lying on the sidewalk, blood spreading across his shirt.

I dashed out of his office, almost running smack into a middle-aged guy with a thick mustache, wiping his hands on a rag. He barely registered me. "Janet? Janet?" he said.

I found the receptionist crouching under her desk, looking stunned. I bent over her, scanning for blood but not seeing any. "Are you okay?" I said. She nodded numbly, her eyes on the carpet. I grabbed the phone off her desk and thrust it into her hands. "Call the police. Is anyone else here?"

"Derek," Janet murmured as she reached for the phone in slow motion.

I left her to it and went to the front door, its glass pane spider-webbed but not broken. I flung it open, and crossed the length of the sidewalk in three long strides as a big white Caddy flew out of the lot and into the street, shocks crunching over the curb. "Arthur," I said as I dropped to my knees. I could see two dark spots in the slick of red that was his shirt, the bullet holes like twin mouths just below his collarbone. His eyes were slitted but they widened a little when I felt along his jaw for a pulse, and he opened his mouth, lips trying for some words that wouldn't come. "Arthur," I said again. I was no doctor, but this was a lot of blood. My own voice was shaky. "It's okay, don't talk." I unbuttoned my shirt. The thin fabric would do little to stanch the bleeding, but little was better than nothing.

"Why is this . . ." Arthur murmured, ". . . happening."

"Arthur, I don't know, I don't know." I tried to force myself to breathe deep, to calm down. But I jumped when I heard footsteps on the bits of window behind me.

"They're coming, the paramedics are coming," the receptionist said. "What can I do, tell me what to do—" She stopped speaking abruptly. My shirt still pressed to Arthur's chest, I looked over my shoulder at her. She was staring, slack-jawed, down the sidewalk, at a bloody hand sticking out of the hole where a side door used to be. "Oh my God."

I stopped her from going toward it, guiding her down next to Arthur and pressing her hands over my blood-sticky shirt. A keening sound was coming from the doorway. I scrambled to my feet and went towards it. My teeth ground together when I reached the doorway. The hand belonged to a young woman. A girl, really. My lungs seized up. The rest of her was splayed on the floor, a massive pool of red fanning out underneath her, soaking the grey carpet and her light brown hair to an inky black, a spray of broken glass around her like a saintly halo in a stained-glass window. A big, youngish guy was crouched over her body, blood spreading through the fabric of the knees of his jeans. The keening sound was coming from him. "No, please, no, no," he was saying, his hands flapping over her in a panic.

"Derek?" I said.

His head snapped around at my voice.

"The bleeding," I added, "do you have a towel?"

He stared at me and moved his mouth soundlessly. I stepped over the glass and looked at the young woman. Her face was a mess of blood and bone, her forehead gone, her mouth slack. She was a teenager, twenty at the most. Her fingers twitched and I heard her take in a faint, wet breath.

"A towel," I said again. "Something, anything."

He sprang to his feet with a swiftness surprising for his size and disappeared through a doorway. I dropped to my knees next to the woman and felt along her jaw for a pulse, already knowing that it was no use.

Heat radiated up from the asphalt surface of the parking lot, but somehow I was still cold. I was stuck in limbo. No one would tell me anything about Arthur's condition, and I wasn't allowed to leave. After repeating my spiel about the car for the fourth time, I sat down on the retaining wall next to the receptionist, Janet.

She was about Arthur's age, a short, wiry black woman in a navy-blue twinset. She seemed like the type who could probably be described as *unflappable* in most circumstances, other than being shot at while sitting in her office. She kept shaking her head as if someone had just told her a very improbable story. The mustached man—a press operator named Bobby Veach—was pacing around the parking lot, talking on his cell. Neither of them knew who the young woman was. Derek, meanwhile, had never returned with that towel, and was nowhere to be seen.

"Are you all right?" I said to Janet.

She said nothing, just stared down the sidewalk at my bloody madras shirt, lying on the curb like a *Law & Order* prop. Then she looked at me and quickly looked away. I'd covered my blood-stained tank top with a random shirt from my trunk, a faded CPD basketball-team tee that Tom had left in my car at some point last fall, but my arms were stained red up the elbows, like gruesome opera-length gloves. Without a word, Janet fumbled with the flap on her handbag and pulled out a package of wet wipes and handed it to me.

I began cleaning myself off. "Thanks."

She nodded and went back to staring at the sidewalk.

Bobby Veach drifted over to us, sat down next to Janet, got back up. "How long do you think they'll make us stay here?" he said.

Janet said to me, "What do you think?"

Veach frowned. "What does she know?"

"I'm a private investigator," I told him, handing him a business card.

His face, already hard with tension, went even tighter. "What? Why?"

I said, "Arthur hired me." But before I could go on, his phone rang and he turned away from us and walked off.

Janet sighed. "Don't mind him. Pressmen are an interesting lot. Do you know what's going on?"

That was a very good question. The police population on the scene only seemed to increase the longer we waited there in the fading twilight, uniforms and plainclothes cops traipsing in and out of the print shop, phones pinging. A coroner's wagon was parked behind my car, its back doors open. I felt sick to my stomach. "No," I said. "I guess it just takes a while."

The cops had stretched crime scene tape around half the parking lot. On the other side of it, a cluster of people dressed in crisp white karate gis looked on, trading their evening martial-arts class for this bit of intrigue. There were nine cruisers parked at odd angles in between, and their blue and red lights turned my view into a demented carnival. A tan unmarked car pulled up behind the group of spectators, and Tom and Sanko both emerged. Tom scanned through the crowd, spotted me, nodded.

"This is bad," Janet said, her eyes on Tom and Sanko as they joined into a conversation with the guy who appeared to be in charge, his badge on a lanyard around his neck, like cops in television shows. Janet produced a pack of cigarettes from her bag, but her hands were trembling too much to work the lighter.

"Here." I dropped the clump of pinkish wet wipes on the wall beside me and took the lighter from her. After flicking my thumb against the spark wheel, I held it out while she passed her cigarette through the steady flame.

"Thank you." She dragged hard on it and tipped the pack in my direction.

I shook my head and resumed wiping off my arms. "I'm good."

"I know I should quit." She exhaled toward the darkening sky. "I always say, but you have to die of something, right?" she said, and winced.

"Have you worked for him long?"

Janet flicked ashes onto the sidewalk. "Oh, yes," she said. "Since the beginning. Since he opened the shop, what was it, thirty years ago. My first job. So I've probably worked for Arthur since before you were born, baby."

Not quite, but I got the point. I said nothing.

She looked back down at the sidewalk. Smoke from her cigarette spiraled up through the air between us. "He gives people credit. Too much credit. He always has."

"Are you talking about Marin?" I said, not following.

"He gets taken advantage of. Because he tries to see the best in people. I know he hasn't taken a salary from the business in years."

"Really." I remembered that Arthur told me they'd just gone through a rough patch, but that things were turning around.

Or maybe that was just wishful thinking, the way a compulsive gambler always feels lucky.

"You should really ask him about it," Janet said, and just then the lanyard guy lumbered over to us, frowning under his grey flat-top. He looked like a bully.

"Janet Morland?" he said to me.

Janet raised her hand like she was giving an oath.

"You work here?"

Janet looked at me, terrified. I stood up and glanced around for Tom, but I didn't see him. "What's going on?" I said. I put my hands on my hips, acutely aware of how ridiculous I looked in this moment: ginormous shirt, clutching a wad of pink-tinged wet wipes.

"We just need to ask you some more questions." The cop put a meaty hand protectively on Janet's shoulder. Then he looked at me. "Don't go anywhere."

I sat back down on the retaining wall and thought about the bottle of whiskey sitting on Arthur's desk, wishing I'd grabbed it. But what kind of person would that make me, if I had? I stared down at my hands. There was blood embedded under my finger-nails, deep. I dug at it with the fraying edge of the wet wipes. Easy enough to pretend it was paint, I told myself. Paint. Red paint. Nail polish. With a name like Blazing Rose or Show Stopper.

Not the blood of a young woman without a face.

I stood up, struck with a sour tug in my throat and an urgent need to get out of there. Then I bent over sideways and puked into the bushes.

"Roxane."

Perfect timing. I coughed and willed my stomach to settle. "Hi," I said as Tom approached me. I wiped my mouth with the back of my hand and nearly gagged at the smell of blood and lemony disinfectant.

His warm brown eyes swept down to the shirt, recognition flashing through them.

I said, "Don't. Please."

"Are you—"

I cut him off. "No, I'm good, I just—" I coughed again. "There's something in my throat, I need a mint or something."

Tom nodded like he understood and produced a linty stick of gum from his pocket and held it out to me. "It's cinnamon," he said, "so I don't know—"

"No, that's great, thank you." I unwrapped it and shoved it into my mouth, chewing hard, waiting for the cinnamon flavor to cover up the taste of bile on my tongue. I took a series of deep breaths and told myself that all of this was helping. "What's going on here?"

"You're the witness—you tell me."

"No, I mean, there're a *lot* of cops here."

His eyes flicked again to the shirt with amusement.

"Come on, I said don't," I told him.

"Hey, I wasn't going to say anything. It's just that I've been wondering where that shirt was."

I nodded calmly. Then, in a melodramatic gesture that made me cringe even as I was doing it, I yanked the shirt over my head and thrust it at him. "Here, take it. I don't want to keep you from your favorite shirt that you haven't seen in six months."

Tom's eyebrows went up in surprise, either at my outburst or at the blood on my tank top. Or both.

"It was the only shirt I could find in the car," I added, lowering my voice a little. "I didn't expect to see you here. Now, please, just tell me what's going on."

He took the shirt as if by reflex, but then pressed it back into my hands. "I think you need it more than I do at the moment," he said. "Are you all right?"

Our eyes met for a long time.

Finally I looked away and pulled his shirt back on. "I told you, I'm good. Now it's your turn."

He didn't say anything for a few seconds. Then he said, "Double shooting in broad daylight? There's going to be a lot of cops on the scene."

I didn't think that explained it but I just nodded, chewing with focus. "I talked to the Craigslist guy this afternoon."

"And?"

"And he lost his shit and almost threw a portable phone at me."

Tom nodded at the scene before us. "You think that's related to this?"

"I don't know," I said, and his eyes winched up.

"It's not. You should just go home, okay?"

I stared at him. "I should just go home."

He touched my shoulder, and I batted his hand away. "What the hell is going on here?"

"It's developing," Tom said, "but suffice it to say it has nothing to do with Craigslist antiques."

"Do you know her name? The victim."

He nodded.

"And?"

"I can't tell you that. Her next of kin hasn't been notified."

I opened my mouth to say I had a right to know, then realized that I didn't. Instead I said, "What about Arthur?"

"Surgery."

The door to the print shop opened and the bully cop emerged. He looked around and made a beeline for where we were standing. The bully's face appeared to be communicating something to Tom in inscrutable cop language, and then he stabbed a finger through the air at me. "You're free to go."

"I'll wait, thanks."

His polo shirt was embroidered with his name: "Lt. S. Chase."

He chuckled without smiling. "No, you don't understand. This is a crime scene, we no longer need you here, so you'll have to go. Freely or not."

"I'd like to talk to Janet before I leave."

He chewed his lip for a second, debating whether or not he wanted to argue with me. Then he looked at Tom and said, "Heitker, get her out of here." He went back into the shop and the door banged closed, the cracked glass sagging.

"Is that your boss?"

"Chase? No. He's from—" He shook his head. "This is a situation you shouldn't be in."

"No kidding. He's from what?"

"Roxane."

"Tom."

We looked at each other. My sinuses were tight.

Finally, he said, "Property Crimes."

None of this was making any sense. "What kind of property?"

"Roxane," he said again. "I can't tell you."

"Why? What's going on?"

"To be determined."

"Is that all you're going to say?"

Tom sighed. "I'm not enjoying this, you know."

I felt like I was going to cry. "Well," I said, "if I'm supposed to leave, you're going to have to move your car."

I headed back to my neighborhood and parked on Main and went into the Westin. The bar was full of solo men in business suits, all gazing without interest at a baseball game on television. I took the only open seat and waited for my brother to notice me. The guy to my left nodded at me in greeting, then gave me a halfhearted once-over. I could see him scoring my attributes—not bad-looking, but a serious case of resting bitch face, plus the weird, oversize T-shirt. All in all a six, maybe six and a half since he was lonely and I was there. Fortunately, I was spared from having to tell him not to talk to me because Andrew swooped in and slid a full shot glass across the bar at me. "Cheers," he said, pouring a shot of his own.

I downed the shot and pushed the glass back to him. The whiskey I'd had with Arthur was a distant memory. "I need a double," I said.

Andrew downed his own shot and swept the small glasses deftly into the plastic bin under the bar. "Rough day?"

He turned around and poured us each a generous whiskey on the rocks as I met his eye in the mirror behind the bar. "Yeah."

When he turned back around, he glanced down at my shirt. "What the hell are you wearing?" he said. "Is that Dad's?"

"It must be."

My brother raised an eyebrow.

I was going to throw this shirt away as soon as I left the hotel. "It's just a fucking shirt, okay?" I said before he had a chance to inquire further.

"What the hell happened to you today?"

I leaned on the bar and drank a little whiskey. "Last week, a client bounced a check to me. I told him to call me later when he had the money to pay me. Now, all of a sudden, his fiancée gets murdered, he gets shot, someone who works next door is dead—I have no idea what happened."

Andrew was multitasking—listening while slicing an orange—but when I said that, he looked up sharply.

"Are you being careful?"

"Why is everyone asking me that all of a sudden?"

"I don't know, because, well." He paused, his eyes on the burn scar on my wrist.

"Change the subject."

"Because you have many, many virtues, Roxane, and caution is not one of them."

"Look, I'm trying, Andrew," I said. I dropped my right hand to my lap. "I'm trying. Honestly, this whole situation started with me trying not to be reckless for a change and taking on what I thought was a boring case. Please, let's change the subject."

Finally, Andrew shrugged. "Guess who I saw in here a few weeks ago." He tipped his head to one side. "Actually, speaking of reckless, I probably shouldn't mention this."

That could only mean one person. "Catherine was here? In the bar?"

"Not her. The husband, whatsisname, Wystan. He was wearing this douchebag hat, a straw one. Like in a barbershop quartet. I think that dude has a problem."

"A problem?"

"He was asking," Andrew said, then dropped his voice to a whisper, "he was looking for oxy."

I raised my eyebrows. "He wanted to buy it?"

My brother nodded.

"From you?"

"I guess. I told him I don't mess with that. Well, actually I told him that neither he nor his succubus wife would be buying anything from me ever again, even if I did mess with stuff like that, which I don't."

I looked into my drink for a while. A ballsy move, for Catherine *or* her husband to show up acting like nothing had happened between us. Even though I was the one she kept on hurting, Andrew took a much harder line with her than I did; he refused to speak to her the last time we were all in the same room together, which was last fall, at a party that I should've known better than to go to. I should've done a lot of things last fall, such as taking my brother's lead on the refuse-to-speak-to-her front, because nothing good ever came from letting my guard down with her. I was trying now, though, I told myself, while wondering at the same time if Catherine's texts had anything to do with her husband attempting to buy drugs from my brother and if that meant she didn't miss me after all. I ran a hand through my hair and felt a few more slivers of glass shake loose. "I think the correct term is a *skimmer*," I said, "a hat like that."

Andrew looked at me for a long time. I knew he could tell something was up. But he didn't press, and I was grateful for that. "My kid sister," he said instead, "too goddamn wise."

EIGHT

Arthur was unconscious when I got to his room at Grant Medical Center. His chest and shoulder were lumpy with bandages under the sheet, and he was hooked up to a full assortment of beeping and clicking hospital machinery. Janet Morland sat next to his bed, pale and drawn in another twinset, this one purple. She clutched Friday's morning newspaper in her hands. When she saw me, she said, "He hasn't woken up yet."

I took a step into the room. "How is he?"

"Serious condition." Her eyes flicked away. "That's all they'll tell me. I called his daughter. She's on the way. But I didn't think he should be alone."

I watched her for a second and understood immediately: She was in love with him. The kind of love that came from proximity, from spending so much time with someone that they became a part of you, whether you wanted them to or not. I leaned against the wall near the doorway so she didn't have to look at me if she didn't want to and said, "I'm sure he'll appreciate it."

Janet said nothing.

"Hey," I added, "can I ask you something?"

Now she turned toward me, her features pinched.

"Last night, when the cops took you inside," I began, but something crumpled in her face and she covered her mouth with her hand, eyes welling. I knew I should say something reassuring and just leave, but I couldn't help myself. I went to the wall directly across from her. "What did they want to talk about?"

"I—" She shook her head.

"It's okay. You can tell me."

She just slumped a bit in her chair and closed her eyes. "They mostly just wanted to know all about Derek."

"What did you say?"

She reached up to fiddle with a gold necklace at her throat. A cross. "I said I didn't know him well. He works in the back on the screen-printing side."

"Do you know his last name?"

"Something with a P. Pomp, I think that's what it is. I hardly ever talked to him. The only time I ever really did was when Arthur had to fire that foreign woman from the art department."

I waited.

"She stole toner for the laser printer. Just walked out with it right under her arm. People saw it happen."

I didn't think stolen toner cartridges were at the heart of this case. But a disgruntled former employee? Maybe. "Her name?"

"Leila. Hassan."

"When was that?"

"Oh, like a year ago."

"And someone saw it?"

"Bobby did. The press operator from last night. I think he felt really bad, but Arthur has a zero-tolerance policy where honesty's concerned."

Right. "What does she have to do with Derek?"

"They were friends," Janet said. "She referred him, got him hired. So when Arthur had to let her go, he asked me to tell Derek, and make sure there wasn't going to be a problem with him still working there."

"And?"

"He was understanding. Very nice kid."

I left a few minutes later when it became clear that she didn't have anything else useful to tell me. Though I knew a bit more than I had last night, I had no idea what I was supposed to do with the information. Mild-mannered, middle-aged, ex-Marine Arthur Ungless, Marin—the victim here, but also not, considering the money she'd stolen. Maybe Arthur and Marin were both just terrible people. I had ten grand in cash sitting on my dining room table at the moment, which constituted something of an ongoing obligation, terrible people or not. When the elevator opened the first person to step out of it was Detective Sanko, and I froze.

"What are you doing here?" he said, with more than a little attitude.

I stepped out of the way of the other people trying to get off the elevator. "Are you the hospital police now?"

Sanko cleared his throat, not cracking a smile. "You have the magic touch, I'll give you that." He folded his arms across his chest, his eyes giving me a once-over. "This case made perfect sense before you got involved."

"Right, because I made all of this happen."

"Like I said yesterday, it's time for you to get uninvolved, okay, sweetheart?"

"Excuse me?"

"You. Uninvolved. I don't know what you think you know," he said, "but this stops, now. You don't need to come back here. He's not your friend. Let us grown-ups do our thing. We don't need anyone playing Veronica Mars in the middle of this."

He nodded, like that settled it.

But it didn't—not by a long shot.

————

There was a black Crown Vic parked in front of my building when I got home. It had chrome rims, shiny ones. So not a cop car. But it still gave me pause. I thought about circling the block until it left, but curiosity got the better of me, as it so often did. As I walked up the sidewalk, the driver's door opened and a muscular buzz cut in a tailored suit got out. He nodded at me. "Roxane Weary?"

I stopped walking. "Yeah."

He took a step back and opened the door behind him. "Please," he said. "Mr. Pomp would like to speak to you."

I stared at him, recalling the name Janet had just told me: Derek Pomp. "I haven't met Mr. Pomp, but if he would like to speak with me, we can do so right here in the open."

The buzz cut casually unbuttoned his suit jacket to reveal a semiauto at his waist. "Please," he said again. "Mr. Pomp would like privacy for this conversation. Get in the car."

With a confidence I did not feel today, I lifted up the hem of my shirt to reveal my own gun holstered to my hip. "Are you for real? I am not getting into a car with a stranger."

Then the rear passenger-side door opened and a shiny double-monk-strap shoe appeared, followed by a charcoal-grey trousered leg. I rested my hand on the handle of my revolver, regretting my decision not to wait till the car was gone. But the man who stepped out of the backseat looked like a lawyer, not a thug. He was mid-forties or so, a vaguely oily-looking fellow with slicked-back black-and-silver hair and a fake tan. Despite good grooming, his face was haggard, his eyes puffy and rimmed in red.

"It's okay, Bo," the man said.

Bo got back into the front seat and closed the door.

The man took a few steps and stuck out his hand. "Vincent Pomp," he said. "I own the Phoenix Group. I apologize for the drama. I lost my daughter last night, and Bo is being overly protective of me."

I thought about that. "Your daughter," I said. I pictured the girl without a face, Derek Pomp weeping over her. "At the print shop."

He looked at me warily. "I understand you were with Tessa when she died. Miss Weary, I do want privacy for this conversation."

"I'm sorry about Tessa," I said, "but you have to understand, showing up at someone's home and demanding she get into a car does not exactly inspire trust and confidence. No woman in her right mind would do that."

Mild surprise flickered through his face. "To be honest, I didn't think of that. But I mean you no harm. I'm just a businessman. I just want to talk to you about what happened. Preferably not on the street."

"A businessman with a driver who carries a gun," I said. But he was clearly in pain. "We can talk inside. You have five minutes. And Bo stays out here."

We went into the building and up the half flight of steps to the first floor. The overhead light in the small lobby was out again, the landing ashy with darkness. I began to question my judgment for bringing him in here. I opened my front door and left it wide open, then leaned against the wall in the entryway, holding my gun against my thigh. My thumb was on the safety. "This is as private as it gets," I said. "Next time you can call first."

He nodded, giving in. "My son said you tried to help Tessa."

I nodded. Although Pomp was on the slight side and the guy from last night wasn't, there was a resemblance in the eyes, dark and wide.

"Derek's grateful. That you were there. I'm grateful. To try to help a stranger. That's something I will remember." Pomp ran a hand over his face. "I know you're a private investigator. I know you're a good one. But what I don't know is why you were there in the first place, and I want you to tell me."

We watched each other. He claimed he meant me no harm, but I wasn't so sure about that. I said, "What was your daughter doing there? Does she work there too?"

Pomp shook his head. "Derek and Tessa were on their way to a concert last night. It would seem they stopped at the print shop first."

"Why?"

"I don't know."

"What's going on there?"

"Nothing, as far as I know."

"So this was some kind of random event?"

"No, I would say this was quite intentional. If you're asking was my daughter involved in anything that could get her killed, the answer is that Tessa was a sweet, generous, innocent, beautiful young woman. Very different from Derek, and very different from me. But I have my enemies, and I will figure out which of them is behind this."

"Why wouldn't they just go after you? Why would someone go after your family at Arthur's print shop?"

His eyes narrowed slightly, like he was growing tired of me. "If I knew exactly what happened, I wouldn't need to ask you questions about it. But generally, Tessa has one of my guards with her. Last night was an exception. We argued over it, actually. Now it's your turn. What were you doing there?"

"I'm working for Arthur Ungless. That's all."

"Why?"

"That's between him and me," I said. "If he pulls through. What is this conversation really about? The very excited police crawling all over the office last night?"

Pomp's mouth twitched. "So you're aware."

"No. I know exactly nothing about it, if that's what you're trying to find out."

He didn't answer that, instead saying, "Did you see who did the shooting?"

"No."

"Anyone who could help me figure out who did this would be well compensated."

I almost laughed. "I don't know, but if I did, you probably wouldn't be the first person I'd tell."

He pressed his mouth into a thin line. "That's unfortunate."

"What are the cops interested in?"

"I don't know," he said, "but if I did, you probably wouldn't be the first person I'd tell."

"Clever. But see, the difference is that I genuinely don't know."

"How much is Ungless paying you?"

"Also between me and him."

"I'll double it," Pomp said. "If you tell me what you saw."

"Mr. Pomp. Vincent. I didn't see anything. I saw a Cadillac driving away, and I saw your son go into the back room to get a towel and then not return. That's it. And even if I saw more than that, I wouldn't be interested. I don't know what the Phoenix Group is, but I try to stay on the other side of illegal, okay? If you know who I am, you probably know my father was a cop. I know a lot of cops. Do you understand what I'm saying?"

"Yes. It means you won't be helping me get justice for my daughter. You're lucky. Because I'm judging your character by what you did last night, and not by what you're doing today."

"Your five minutes are up," I said.

I pointed toward the open doorway with my gun, expecting trouble. But instead he held up his hands and said, "I'm reaching into my coat for a business card." He plucked open his blazer by its exquisite lapel and produced a card printed in gold on textured black stock. "If you have a change of heart."

He walked out of the building and down the sidewalk. Bo

opened the door for him and closed it gently once Pomp was inside, then got behind the wheel and drove away. Only then did I shut my door and lock all three deadbolts with sweaty, shaking hands.

I did a shot of whiskey to calm my nerves, and resisted the profound urge to have another or three. Instead I sat down at my computer. First I quickly pulled some background on Vincent Pomp, which was much easier than my other attempts on backgrounds in this case. He smiled out at me from the website of the Phoenix Group, a firm of nebulous focus of which he was the president. The Phoenix Group offered property management, title loans, structured settlement buyouts, check cashing, tax prep, and notary services, all from a grubby storefront on 161, and Pomp also owned half a dozen other cash businesses: a food truck, two coin Laundromats, a car wash, a nightclub called Shimmy's, and a housecleaning company. It all seemed normal enough on paper, but Pomp's talk about his guards and his enemies told me that there was much more to it. Something that could interest law enforcement in a big way. Money laundering? Cash businesses made that easy. Inflate the register receipts, claim that the coin laundry pulled in hundreds more dollars in quarters per day than it really did, and suddenly that cash looks like legitimate income. But Ungless Printing was wholly owned by my client, and not among the businesses held by the Phoenix Group. And anyway, what could this have to do with Marin? I rubbed the place between my eyebrows, thinking. Tessa was an angel, Arthur's connection to Pomp was tenuous at best— so maybe Derek had been the actual target of the gunman? That would make him lucky, and the person in the Caddy a spectacularly bad shot. But the way Derek had run off in the aftermath, leaving his dead sister in a pool of blood, was deeply strange.

Who the hell were these people?

Pomp had a wife, Ruth, and two sons—Derek, twenty-five, and Simon, twenty-nine. Derek had a series of DUIs and drug-possession busts. Simon was employed by his father's company, no record.

While I was at it, I turned to Leila Hassan. Twenty-six, residing in a converted warehouse loft a block east of High Street near the corner of Prescott and Pearl—but on the opposite end of the Short North from where Marin was killed. Her LinkedIn profile still showed Ungless Printing as her employer. *Electronic publishing specialist,* whatever that was. She was pretty, with olive skin and glossy dark hair and wide, almond-colored eyes. She had twelve hundred Facebook friends—one of whom was mutual. I clicked to see who it was and laughed.

Cat Walsh.

"Of fucking course," I muttered.

I used that as an excuse to click through a month's worth of Catherine's own posts, which were mostly art links and auto-updates from Kickstarters she'd backed. Leila had not interacted with her on any of them.

I looked at my text messages, at the series of dots Catherine had been sending me. It would be so easy to just call her up, ask her how she knew Leila, claim it was for work. Which it was, but I didn't even know if Leila was involved yet. And things always escalated fast between Catherine and me. An innocent phone call could lead to anything. I put that idea aside and dug around for dirt on Rudy Carmichael, finding a restraining order from an ex-girlfriend three years ago, terrible Yelp reviews from customers he'd yelled at, and a public Facebook profile where he posted semi-daily rants about a rich tapestry of subjects, mostly women and, occasionally, the performance of the Cleveland Indians.

I wrote down his home address too, then dropped my pen in disgust. "Aggh," I muttered to the empty room.

I wanted another drink. I got up and paced to the kitchen, contemplated the whiskey bottle again. Over the past few months, I'd been trying to stick to three drinks a day. That had gone out the window yesterday. But today was a new day, I told myself. I didn't need alcohol to cope with stress. I could cope with stress all on my own. It was just that the past twenty-four hours had been *extra* stressful. I grabbed the bottle by its short neck, rubbing my thumb against the grooves in the crown-shaped cap. Put it down and snapped on the burner under my teakettle.

I wasn't that person. I wasn't my father.

After I made a cup of green tea with mint, I returned to my desk and ripped down an old calendar and a page of expired coupons from my corkboard. Then I started scribbling stuff on index cards and pinning them up. Vincent Pomp. Derek Pomp. Tessa Pomp. Arthur Ungless. Marin Strasser. Rudy Carmichael.

It didn't look like anything.

I sat down at my desk and opened the computer again, and then someone knocked on my front door.

NINE

I grabbed my gun off the filing cabinet before I went to see who it was. When I parted the curtains on my front door, though, I let out a long, slow breath. Tom was out there. I set the gun down on an end table, not wanting to get into it.

I opened the door. "Live and in person," I said.

He gave me half of a smile. He looked overheated and dead tired. "I don't know about live," he said. "It's hot as hell out there. Can I have a glass of water?"

"Sure, of course. You sit, I'll get it." I said this last part because my dining room was a disaster zone, not fit for company. But he didn't take the hint and he followed after me down the hall.

"Did you come to spill the beans about what happened last night?"

"Something like that."

I got him a glass of water from the sink. I noticed he was wearing the same light blue shirt and navy tie as yesterday. "You haven't been home," I said.

"No. My body is sixty percent coffee at this point."

"Do you want, I don't know, a sandwich or something?"

He leaned against the doorway, watching me. "Do you even have food here?"

"Funny," I said. "I have bread." I nodded at a loaf of multigrain on my counter, then gave it a surreptitious squeeze to check for freshness. It seemed to be okay. Good enough for a peanut butter sandwich, something I was starting to get creative with. "Do you want a sandwich or what?"

"I can't ask you to make me a sandwich."

"Forget the gender politics," I said. "I just don't want you to die in my kitchen. I haven't had lunch either."

Tom smiled. "Okay then. That would be nice. Thank you."

I opened the cupboard and grabbed a jar of peanut butter and a bottle of sriracha, pushing the Crown to the back of the counter. "Don't watch," I said. "You're going to like it, I promise. Go sit in the other room."

"You're bossy today."

"My house, my rules. I don't need your sandwich judgment."

He disappeared from the doorway. I opened the fridge and pulled out an unopened bag of shredded carrots. "So," I called, slathering two slices of bread with peanut butter, "what do you have to tell me?"

From the other room, I heard a sigh. "Two things, and you aren't going to like either of them," Tom said.

I looked around the doorway at him.

"Sanko called me a bit ago," he continued. "All fired up about you being in the middle of this thing."

"In the middle of it?" I went back to the sandwiches, adding a zigzag of sriracha on top of the peanut butter, then covered both with a layer of shredded carrots. "I wasn't exactly in the middle of anything—I was visiting my client in the hospital." And meeting Vincent Pomp, too, but he'd come to *me*. I kept quiet about that for the moment.

"Here's the thing. If you're in the middle of it, I kind of am too."

I frowned. "Why?"

"Isn't it obvious?"

"Tom, I don't know what this has to do with you at all."

"Are you kidding?"

I frowned harder. "No, actually, I'm not." I sliced both sandwiches on the diagonal and returned to the dining room. "I'm not
even sure what it has to do with *me*."

"Maybe Sanko's overreacting," Tom said. He took a hesitant
bite, chewed, and nodded. "This is weird, but good. Maybe Sanko
is overreacting, but I vouched for you with him yesterday. So if he
doesn't like something, I'm going to hear about it."

"But what doesn't he like?" I said around a mouthful of sandwich. "Come on, I was just at his office to talk to him. It's not like I
jumped in the middle of it after the shooting just for the hell of it.
And I told both of you about the Craigslist guy, and you seem pretty
sure that's nothing. So, I don't know anything."

He didn't respond right away, but his jaw bunched up. Then he
said, "That's good. You need to keep it that way. Your dad—"

But then he stopped and we glared at each other. I could tell
what he was thinking: about what he'd promised Frank before he
died, a topic I'd been clear about not wanting him to bring up
again.

Tom meant well, but it wasn't like my father had been diligent
about looking out for me when he was alive. I could take care of
myself. I'd never done anything other than that. But he didn't look
like he was enjoying this any more than I was. I put my hands on
my hips and said, "Pretty sure my client list isn't up to you."

"I don't want to argue with you, Roxane."

"Then don't."

He let out a sigh. "I shouldn't have said it that way—obviously
who you work for isn't up to me, or anyone else. But this is going to
be big, okay? Your client is in a bad place. So this isn't just about
Marin and Arthur anymore. This is about a dead nineteen-year-old
woman and about ten different jurisdictions. That story's bigger

than both of them. Could be they were involved, or they got caught in the crosshairs of something. We don't know."

"Crosshairs of what?"

"I can't get into it."

"You know I can find out."

Tom closed his eyes for a second. "No, no more *finding out*."

None of this made any sense. I thought about the seventy-five grand and about Marin's lack of ties to the community. That felt like an entirely different story than the shooting at the print shop, or a well-dressed thug confronting me on my street. "So this is you telling me to step back. Officially." I'd relied on him for information a lot over the past year or so, and he'd never told me that before. I wasn't sure if that meant I should be extra grateful for all the freebies, or just extra pissed at him now.

He looked at me with tired eyes. "I know you have some obligation to your client. And I hate having to say this, I really do. But yeah, I need to ask you to take a step back here. Officially."

I felt my molars grinding together. "Tom—"

"Hear me out," he said, holding up a hand.

I bit my tongue for a second, but I thought about all the questions that had yet to be answered. "Did you ever find her car—" I began, but Tom cut me off before I could manage it.

"Roxane."

I waited. A prickly frustration was working down my arms.

"I know yesterday was intense. I know you're a little shaken up and you want to do something. But Marin's car isn't the focus here. So what about her car? That's not the key to this. You really want to stake your whole reputation on it? And mine?"

I stood up, now irritated for real. "I don't think I have to stake anything on anyone. Marin—"

"Marin Strasser is not the one with the secrets here. And yes, we did find her car, we've found out quite a lot, actually, and that's the other thing you aren't going to like."

"What."

He shook his head. "Your client is not as love-struck as he's telling you, that's all I can say." His expression was unreadable, which seemed to be his default state when he looked at me these days. "It's an ongoing investigation, it's not something you should get tangled up in."

"Dammit, Tom, why are you doing this?" I said, with more feeling than I meant to. "You brought it up, but you're not even going to tell me?"

"I just want you to be careful around Ungless."

"He's not even fucking conscious, how careful do I need to be? Spit it out."

"No. I need you to promise me you'll take that step back. Not just stay out of the way. Not just be careful. Step back. I mean, how often do I ask *you* for a favor?"

He was almost smiling when he said it, but it hit me hard. "You're right." I said. I grabbed his empty water glass and took it into the kitchen, exerting all of my willpower not to pitch it, fastball style, into the sink. I waited till the tightness in my sinuses abated before I went back in to face him. "This is a very uneven friendship. I don't even know why you bother now that we aren't fucking, free sandwiches aside."

"Hey, no, that's not what I'm saying, you know that," he began, a hand trailing down my arm.

But I yanked my arm away. "It's fine. Message received. You know, I was in the middle of something when you showed up, so you should probably take off."

He stood up too. "Roxane, you're literally the last person in the world I want to upset—"

"I'm not upset." It came out as a snap, clearly a very upset one. "I'm just busy. I need to get ready."

I escaped to my bedroom, my cheeks burning. A moment or two later, the floorboards creaked in the hallway as he walked toward me, then stopped in the doorway. I opened a dresser drawer in an approximation of getting ready and refused to look at him.

"We'll talk soon," he said eventually, and then he walked out.

"Goddammit," I muttered to the silent apartment. I stalked back to my office and sat down at my desk. My face was hot.

I couldn't stay here.

Rudy Carmichael was behind the counter at High Street Antiquities, yelling into a phone about shipping delays. When I walked in, he scowled at me and held the phone against his collar. "Get out of here. Now."

I stayed where I was, and he reached over the counter to grab my arm, but I stepped out of his reach and unholstered my gun. "Hang up the phone. And don't touch me."

He stared at me, eyes wide, spluttering nonsense.

"You are going to tell me everything you know about the woman with the clock," I said, sounding much calmer than I felt. What I felt like was a rubber band stretched taut and starting to fray. "No talking, unless it's about her. Is that going to be a problem?"

"Who *are* you?"

I gave him a smile. "A friendly antiques dealer from Springfield. Now talk."

Rudy shakily sat down on the stool behind the counter. "You just want to know about her?"

I nodded.

"Are you going to shoot me if I tell you?"

He was terrified. All bark, no bite. Or maybe not. I kept the gun down at my side. "Not if you tell me everything."

He sighed, wiping a sheen of perspiration off his forehead. "Okay. The clock woman."

"Yes. The clock woman."

"I'm sorry for what I wrote, if that's what this is about—"

"Rudy."

"Okay. Okay. I bought a clock from her. On Craigslist. This was a long time ago. Two thousand seven. She was selling this Herschede for four hundred bucks—she didn't know what she had. No clue. Thing was worth four, five grand. I saw the listing go up and got to her a few minutes later. We met up in the parking lot of that Meijer on 23, I gave her cash, boom, done. I buy things all the time this way. Nothing out of the ordinary."

He swallowed. I motioned impatiently.

"No one who comes into a store like this is going to put out five grand for a clock. So I told my assistant—I had this assistant at the time, Jared. I'm not good on the computer. I told him to list it in a couple clock forums for sale, see if we could find a buyer. *Big* mistake."

"Then what happened?"

"Well, it didn't sell right away, but I wasn't in a hurry to sell it since I paid so little. Then a couple months later, guy shows up from the Delaware County sheriff's department. A detective. He says, so about this clock. Turns out, the woman stole it from some rich family, crazy people from the sound of it, and they've been scouring the state for their precious family heirloom."

"Till they found it on your website."

Rudy nodded. "Yeah. So I said, I don't know anything about that, I just bought it from her—and then suddenly I'm in handcuffs for receiving stolen property. And this clock, it's worth enough money to make it a felony. Six to twelve months in jail, that's what they told me the penalty was for this. All because I innocently bought something from this woman."

I wasn't so sure that Rudy Carmichael had ever done anything innocently. I said, "Did you serve time?"

He shook his head. "I gave it back. There weren't any charges. But that wasn't the end of it. Same year, I got audited. By the state." He gestured around the messy shop. "And that was not fun."

"You think that was related?"

"Of course it was related!"

He was about to launch into a rant about the injustices of the tax code, but I interrupted him. "Did you ever see her again?"

"No."

"You didn't try to hurt her?"

"No, come on," he whined.

"Talk to her?"

"Just when I called about the neon sign."

"And that was pure luck."

Another nod.

"You mean to tell me that you nursed this grudge for ten years and took no action?"

Rudy's face fell. "What do you call my Craigslist ad?"

Two women came into the shop, and he looked at me with wide eyes. "Come on. I have customers. Haven't I been through enough?"

"One more question. Do you know the name of this family?"

At that, he finally had something to give me.

Rudy's information on the crazy, rich family who ruined his life was limited to the tax commission employee who cursed him with seven years' bad audits: a man named Barry Caruso, who was related to the family in some way. He was also dead. I sat at my desk with a drink, trying to figure an angle around this one. The Caruso clan were civil servants and electricians, not crazy, rich people in Delaware County who owned expensive clocks.

But were any of them amateur genealogists? I went to a genealogy website and found Barry Caruso's particular branch of the family tree. He'd been one of four kids, two boys and two girls. I opened new tabs for all of them. The ladies Caruso were both married, one to a used-car salesman and the other to a high school gym teacher. The surviving Caruso son was divorced; his wife, Georgette Harlow Caruso, was the daughter of a prominent Delaware County probate attorney.

That seemed promising. I smiled up at the wall of my office, pleased with that bit of information. Compared to the rest of the case so far, it felt easily won—but according to the clock on the wall, almost two hours had passed. I had Elliott Smith on the stereo, loud, but it was still too quiet inside the apartment. That probably meant it was me, and that the quiet was actually in my head. But my head didn't feel quiet at all. I got up and went to the window and looked out at the street, empty except for my car and a green pickup truck with a handwritten For Sale sign on it. Instinctively, my hand went to the patchy burn scar on my wrist, a reminder of my last big case. The green truck. The fire. The two women, including Shelby's best friend, Veronica, whom I'd rescued from the house of horrors, which was what the media called it in the handful of interviews I did at the time. I thought *rescued* was a little melodramatic, and so was *house of horrors,* but there wasn't really a better word to describe it. So maybe it was a rescue after all. Once I was even beamed from the NBC studio on Olentangy into a brief, awkward conversation with Matt Lauer on *The Today Show.* My mother recorded the broadcast and I could only watch about thirty seconds of it. I did not have a future career in TV, there was really no doubt about that. I saw a bit of an uptick in business and fielded two job offers, one from a law firm and the other from a big security agency in town. I didn't take either of them too seriously. The money would have been nice, but I didn't love the idea of someone else telling me what to do, not after being the one in charge of what I did for the past ten years.

As it was, I had a hard enough time listening to myself.

So I rode the wave while it lasted, but eventually business died down again. There were only so many mysteries out there that needed solving, even in a city like Columbus. But I was okay with it. I had medical bills and the scar to remind me of just how messy it could get out there. Not like I needed the reminder, though. Because I couldn't stop thinking about it. Especially when I was alone, which was often. Maybe too often. Maybe that was a problem. As I looked back to my computer, Bluebell slammed a door upstairs. Rationally, I knew that's what it was, but the big, hollow bang of it pushed me up against the wall, heart racing, as if this window might explode on me too.

I slumped back into the desk chair and held a hand over my gun.

A little shaken up, Tom had said.

I pulled up on my computer a *Dispatch* article about the shooting.

> Two people were shot in an apparent drive-by at an
> office building near State Route 161 and Sinclair
> Road on Thursday. Columbus Police said a white
> Cadillac was seen fleeing the area. Tessa Pomp, 19,
> of Upper Arlington, was pronounced dead at the
> scene, and another individual was injured.

There was no mention of whatever had gotten the cops so excited.

I found Tessa Pomp's Facebook page next, took in her smiling face, blue eyes, a silver barbell pierced through her eyebrow. Features that were no longer intact when I saw her. A long list of posts on her timeline from the last twenty-some hours, emojis in memoriam, broken hearts and praying hands.

I clicked around for a few minutes looking for more details on the murder. Her funeral was Tuesday morning at Saint Joseph, which was where my father's had been. Her obit didn't mention her violent end except to say "Tessa left this earth too early for us to understand, but God always has a purpose for us and therefore we all must believe that Tessa is still among us fulfilling hers."

Did that belief bring comfort to anyone? I hoped it did, but I had my doubts.

I pinched the bridge of my nose.

A little shaken up.

I returned to the task at hand and dialed Georgette Harlow Caruso's number.

"This is Georgette," the woman who answered said when I asked for her.

"Hi there," I said. "I apologize for calling so late. My name is Roxane Weary, and I'm a private investigator—"

"Oh, for the love of God," Georgette snapped. "Nice try. You can just tell her to fuck right off, okay?"

I blinked at the phone for a second. "I'm sorry?"

"It'll go through in four more years, and that damned whore can hire all the lawyers and private eyes she wants, but it isn't going to change a thing. They're lucky to be getting anything at all, frankly."

"I'm sorry," I said again, "who are we talking about?"

Georgette went quiet for a second. Then she cleared her throat and started over in a more civil tone. "What is this regarding?"

"Well," I said, "it's kind of a long story, but I'm trying to put together some background about a stolen clock."

She laughed without humor. "Right."

"Look—"

"No, you look. I don't know what she's up to this time, but I am not telling you a thing."

The phone clicked in my ear.

What was Georgette talking about? *What* would go through in four more years? There was only one thing I really knew about the woman who called herself Marin Strasser: People tended to have very strong feelings about her.

TEN

Georgette Harlow Caruso lived in a brick Victorian on a quiet street just north of 36. It boasted a mansard roof and an ornate wrought-iron front porch with a wheelchair ramp running from the side of it. I knocked and heard the barking of a small, angry dog for a few seconds, and then the door opened and a brown-haired woman looked out at me through black-framed glasses. She was short and stocky, mid-middle-aged and dressed in white pants and a black boat-neck shirt with a chunky silver necklace. "Can I help you?"

"I'm Roxane," I said. "We spoke on the phone last night. I thought maybe you'd be open to chatting in person about the clock?"

She narrowed her eyes, but intrigue glimmered in them. She said, "All this about the clock? Ten years later?"

"The clock is only part of it. I'm mostly interested in the woman who took it. Can I come in?"

Georgette's mouth twisted. "This is just like her."

The door closed an inch or two. Before she could shut it on me all the way, I blurted, "Just so you know, she's dead."

Georgette's face went totally blank. Then she said, "Who are we talking about?"

"An interior designer named Marin?"

"Oh, is that what she's calling herself now? An interior designer?"

She let out a harsh laugh. There was an interesting kind of wariness about her: cautious, but the kind of cautious that comes from experience rather than a sheltered life. "Well, isn't that fancy. She's no interior designer. And she's not a Kennedy cousin either. The K stands for Kathleen. How do you know she's dead?"

I withheld my curiosity about her Kennedy-cousin comment and I gave her the oversimplified version by saying, "My client was accused of murdering her."

At that, she practically crowed. "Murder!"

"Um," I said, "yes. And who she was is a bit of a mystery, so I'm just trying to put the pieces together."

Finally, Georgette stepped back and opened the door for me. "Well, plenty of pieces here."

Georgette Harlow had dropped the Caruso from her name. She had lived in the Delaware County house with her brother Paul since William Harlow passed away. "More or less," she said now, shooting a glance over at Paul. They were fraternal twins, fiftyish, bespectacled, attractive in that way that money made you attractive, whether you were or not. We were sitting in the living room, or one of them. The house was massive, done up in smooth dark woods and plush upholstery. I was on the couch with Georgette, and Paul was in his power chair next to the end table. He was, he'd told me, a diversity poster in action: he had MS, and he was gay. "Once we got the miserable slattern and her brat kid out of here, anyway."

"Slattern," I said. "Not every day you hear that one. She has a kid?"

"It's not every day you *encounter* a slattern, honey," Paul said. "Although I suppose it's bad form to say so now that she's dead, right?" He didn't look like he felt the least bit bad about this fact. Neither of them did. "And yes," he added. "She has a son."

"Nate," Georgette chimed in.

I showed them the picture from Marin's locket, and they both nodded.

"The baby Jesus," Paul said, and his sister laughed.

"So who is she?"

"Our ex-stepmother, technically. She married Dad a few years after our mother died. He was close to fifty. And she—Marin—was twenty-five."

Georgette added, "For reference, we were also twenty-five."

"Ouch."

The twins nodded.

"You have to understand," Paul said. "Dad was always a practical, reasonable person. Upstanding. He sat on the board at Ohio Wesleyan, for chrissakes. He and Mother made one hell of a couple, before she got sick. Then, after she died, he met Marin and he turned into somebody else. That's not just a thing to say, either. Married in Vegas, of all places. And the way he spent money on her—it was insane. Furs, trips, anything she wanted."

"Bail, too, let's not forget."

"Oh, how could we."

They glanced at each other, nearly giggling.

I said, "Bail?"

"Drunk driving, shoplifting. Petty, trashy stuff. I don't even know how many times she got arrested," Georgette said. "The wife of William Harlow, shoplifting earrings from Macy's? Ridiculous. They both drank too much, got into these big, ugly fights in restaurants—"

"Like the time we were all at the Refectory for his birthday, and we got *asked to leave,* they were bitching at each other so much," Paul said.

That sounded familiar.

"I always hoped they were on the brink of ending it," his sister said. "She was always threatening to take Nate and leave, and Dad adored that kid. The baby Jesus."

They both cracked up again. Paul caught me looking confused and said, "Nate was a holy terror. Truly. A nightmare child. But in their eyes, he could do no wrong. He could be writing on the walls in blood and Marin would be talking about what a precious angel he was. Thank God we never had to live with the kid."

"Interesting way to talk about your half brother," I said.

"Well," Georgette said, "who knows if it was even true."

"That William was Nate's father?"

They nodded in unison. "Nothing would surprise me," Paul said.

"And we know she wasn't faithful to him. Especially right before he died."

"But that's another story."

"And even if Nate really was Dad's, biologically, Marin did everything she could to keep us from getting close to the kid anyway. She'd tell him lies about us—that we'd tried to kill her, that we wanted to send him away. You probably think we're pulling your leg. But this is the God's-honest truth. The woman was pathological."

I looked down at the blank page in my notebook. All of this sounded a bit too much like the plot of a Lifetime movie, and the way they finished each other's sentences was frankly a little creepy. But then again, Marin had stolen seventy-five thousand dollars from Arthur while living in his house and pretending to plan their wedding. So pathology might very well factor into it. I figured I could decide later on whether or not I believed this bit of family history. I nodded for the twins to continue.

"Where was I?" Paul said. "Oh, right. The baby Jesus. He kept getting kicked out of schools. The Chase Academy, St. Matthew's, this paramilitary school, on and on. They tried to bribe him to behave: karate classes, archery classes, art, dance, nothing worked. Holy terror."

"This was middle school, probably."

"He was, what, eleven when it happened?"

"Ten, I thought."

"Well, what year was he born?"

"It was the year we went to the Virgin Islands for our birthday—"

They might have quibbled over this detail forever, so I interrupted. "Can you just tell me what happened?"

Georgette and Paul looked at me in unison. "She slept with one of Nate's karate teachers," Paul said. "And Dad found out. Sweating up the sheets in every motel between here and Powell. Motels my father paid for, by the way." Paul's eyes were practically gleaming with delight. "Which was how he caught her. Credit-card bills."

"Uh-oh," I said.

"Uh-oh is right. He started divorce proceedings that week."

"But then he had the heart attack," Georgette finished. "Playing a round of golf."

Paul said, "Dead at the fourteenth green."

Good Lifetime movie title. I waited for one of them to claim that Marin had murdered him with antifreeze in his iced tea.

But instead, Georgette said, "He had a history of heart problems, Dad did. Which only got worse once he took up with Marin, because she wasn't helping him take care of himself. Anyway, it was a shock, and also, it wasn't. But after that, things got *really* bad."

"Because of the will. Or lack thereof."

"Your dad didn't have a will?" I said. "Even though he was an estate planner?"

Paul gave a flat little smile. "Well, that's just it. Of course he would've had a will. But Eugene—his business partner at the law firm—he said that Dad didn't. He was very kind to Marin in those days, and not so nice to us. So we assumed he was fucking her."

Georgette nodded. "Or was hoping to fuck her."

"Either way," Paul said, polishing his glasses on the edge of his shirt, "we still don't know exactly what happened there. But even though Dad had filed for divorce, they were still married at the time of his death—or so we thought—and under Ohio law, if someone dies intestate, the spouse inherits exactly half of the estate."

"Which was considerable," Georgette said.

Her brother said, "Quite."

"And her getting half meant that each of us was only getting one-sixth."

"A third of the remaining half to me, Georgette, and Nate. Plus Dad had set up a trust for Nate already. Something he couldn't access till he turned thirty."

"Which wasn't fair. The extra sixth to him. That's what I was talking about on the phone. The trust. I thought it was just another one of her ploys. But we'll get to that."

"It just wasn't what Dad wanted. We knew it. Even before the divorce stuff started, he wouldn't have given her half, wouldn't have given Nate more than he gave us."

The more I looked at them, the more they looked the same. Even the timbre of their voices was similar. "Okay," I said, "so she destroyed your dad's will so she would get half of the estate."

"More than half, with the money Nate was getting. Not to mention the life insurance."

"Which wasn't fair," Paul said again. Or maybe Georgette had said it the first time. "And she wanted to stay in the house. Meanwhile, she was selling off everything that wasn't bolted to the wall."

"And we were *not* going to stand for that."

"Not a chance. Dad would've wanted the house to come to us."

"So we hired a private investigator."

That was unexpected. I put down my pen. "And here I thought I was your first," I said.

Paul laughed. "In this family, we hire private investigators like most families hire nannies. But you *are* the first lady detective I've ever talked to."

I did not mention to him that most families didn't hire nannies either. I said, "Okay, so you hired an investigator to track down the missing property that she'd sold."

Paul nodded. "That was one of the angles. But—oh, it gets better. This guy went *deep*."

"*Richland* County," Georgette said, with more than a little distaste. "Some godforsaken place called Bellville."

"That was the clincher."

"Bellville?" I said.

"She was from there. Born and raised. And married, it turns out."

"She was already married to some backwater HVAC technician when she and Dad had their little ceremony!"

The siblings sat back and looked at me, pleased. Easy to figure why. I said, "Which nullified the marriage."

"Bingo," Paul said. "And therefore the intestate law giving her half the estate. Of course, there was nothing we could do about the life insurance money—the policy listed her by name, so she got that. Seven-fifty, that's how much she walked away with. We had her over a barrel about the marriage though, honestly, so in the end she took it without much of a fight."

"Well, I wouldn't say that, exactly," Georgette said. "We had to file eviction proceedings in court and get the sheriff to physically remove them from the property. Oh, and she did not go quiet into the good night. Screaming in the yard like we were the ones who did something to *her*."

I couldn't shake the image of Marin Strasser calmly flipping through her magazine in Stauf's the other day. The picture of elegance. She'd looked like someone who had never screamed at anyone over anything. "Know where she went after that?"

"We got a restraining order against her during the eviction, preventing her from coming here. So at least she knew enough not to do that. But she called all the fucking time, different numbers, different tactics. She moved all over. Miami. Nashville. And so on." The corner of Paul's mouth twitched.

"That's why I was so, you know," Georgette said, "brusque with you on the phone."

"So much for over a barrel," I said. "What did she want?"

"Over a barrel with the will," Paul said. "But remember, the trust for the baby Jesus. Locked down till he turns thirty. She was just bound and determined to get around that."

"Is that even possible?"

He held out a hand and tilted it back and forth. "Sometimes, in very specific circumstances. Not in this one. But she sure did try. She'd call and say hey, your half brother needs a bone marrow transplant—oh, and money to pay for it, preferably in cash. She'd say they've got robbed at gunpoint, she'd say their new house burned down and they're homeless, she'd say Nate was having psychological problems because *he missed us.*"

"Which," Georgette said, "I mean, come on. He didn't."

Her brother went on, "The last time was, what, five years ago? She said Nate had been arrested and she needed money for a lawyer." He paused briefly, one eyebrow raised. "As for why she thought that would compel us to act when the threat of a bone-marrow transplant didn't, I have no idea."

"Maybe he really did have legal trouble this time."

Georgette and Paul shrugged.

"Do you have a more recent picture of him? More recent than

this, anyway," I said, holding up the tarnished locket. "Assuming you didn't burn them all."

"Burning photographs, how gauche," Paul said.

Georgette got up and rummaged around a bookcase for a while before pulling out a burgundy photo album. "I wouldn't turn my nose up at burning some of these." She sat back down and flipped through pages, the album spine cracking. "This looks like a school picture. From high school. He'd be twenty-five or so now."

She handed me a five-by-seven print of the little boy from the locket all grown up. Sandy blond hair, blue eyes, and cheekbones that could cut glass, just like his mother. He was sharply good-looking, the baby fat and youthful innocence gone. His features had an intensity, even smiling in front of a swirly blue backdrop on picture day. "Mind if I keep this?"

"Knock yourself out." Georgette continued flipping pages in the photo album. "Oh, God. Here. Look. This is classic Marin. This was Easter dinner, for God's sake." She passed the album over to me, tapping a page with her fingernail.

The image showed Marin in a strapless black dress and stilettos, her hair nineties-puffy and platinum blond. She stood with a portly guy in a tweed jacket. He looked happy, the kind of happy you feel when you get away with something. Marin smiled seductively, though it wasn't clear at whom. They were standing on a familiar-looking sidewalk with a brick arch in the background.

"Where was this taken?" I said.

Georgette glanced over my shoulder. "Oh, that's Grandmother's house. Or was. Down in the city, Victorian Village. Aunt Agnes got it when she died. Dad's sister. Crazy Aunt Agnes."

I stared at the setting some more. "On Dennison?" I guessed. Where Marin had been shot. I'd seen that house recently—I knew it.

Georgette nodded, her eyebrows going up. "Yes. How did you know that?"

"Lucky guess. She still lives there?"

Another nod. "Unless the Martians in her shower got her, since our obligatory Christmas visit," Georgette said, and she and her brother laughed. "You must think we're just awful," she added, in a way that said she didn't feel the least bit bad about it.

ELEVEN

Every time I walked into Grant Medical Center, I tried to hold my breath from the door to the elevator. The hospital smell in the air— sanitized linens and rubber gloves—was like a time capsule that opened itself up and unleashed the memory of the night my father died.

I'd been in New York for ten days on a case when it happened. Three in the morning and I was dreaming about him: a wren had flown into the picture window on the front of the house, and we were burying it in a Crown Royal bag. And then the girl from the bar was shaking my arm. "Hey, um, hey you," she was saying. She didn't know my name, but I didn't know hers either. So we were probably even. "Your phone's been ringing nonstop."

I opened my eyes to her messy-chic Williamsburg loft, pink and white Christmas lights crosshatching the ceiling. I hadn't been asleep long enough to be hungover. "What?"

"Your phone," she said. "It keeps ringing."

"Sorry." I heard it then, the muffled sound of crickets chirping. I got out of her bed, held an arm over my tits as I looked for my stuff. What had I been wearing? There—my leather jacket on the back of a desk chair. I fumbled through the pockets as the chirping stopped, then started up again a few seconds later. When I finally got the phone out, I saw that it was Andrew and I knew. I knew what it was going to be. Even though there were any number of emergencies Andrew might be calling me about, I knew it was only one.

My father had been shot twice, once in the arm and once at the base of the throat, just above the collar of his Kevlar vest. A third bullet had glanced off the vest but it didn't matter. He and Tom were helping a gang task force in the housing projects at Poindexter Village and had chased a guy from the row houses over to the playground, when the suspect stopped, turned, and fired. He was in surgery. The prognosis was grave. I flew back on the earliest flight I could get, drank a Bloody Mary on the plane while paging through the seat-pocket magazine without seeing it, the fingers of my right hand crossed and balled into a fist—my version of praying.

The flight was only ninety minutes but time had stopped passing. When I landed, I ran through the airport and spent fifteen minutes waiting for and then riding the parking shuttle, thumbing my phone for updates, and then I couldn't remember where I had parked my car. The lot seemed to stretch on to the horizon. It was February and bitterly cold and I almost gave up and called a cab. But then I found it, and for a split second I felt a surge of complete happiness, like *this* was what I had come to do.

Then I remembered, and I threw up on my own fender.

At the hospital, everyone was still waiting. My mother was surrounded by my father's friends, a pale, drawn figure in a sea of broad shoulders and CPD jackets. I went to her and reached out but she was overwhelmed, everyone reaching out to her all at once. Andrew grabbed my arm, told me there was no news yet. We looked at each other and neither of us knew what to say. The inside of my mouth was on fire from chewing two handfuls of Altoids in the car to cover up the taste of vodka and vomit. Matt hugged me halfheartedly and then, gripping my shoulders at arm's length, said, "Jesus Christ, Roxane, it's seven in the morning."

"Hey, leave her alone," Andrew said. "She had to get on a plane to get here."

Matt shook his head and walked away.

"Self-righteous fuck," Andrew said. He looked tired but his eyes were clear. I thought of the drink I had on the plane and clenched my jaw so tight my sinuses throbbed. "Here," my brother added, steering me toward an empty seat amid the people waiting in Grant's emergency room. "Why don't you sit. I'll get you a cup of tea. Or"—dropping his voice to a whisper—"if you want to straighten out—"

"No," I said. "Just tea."

Andrew squeezed my arm and walked away.

I stared at the dirty industrial carpet between my feet for a long time. Then I glanced up and saw Tom on the other side of the room. He met my eyes, his face full of guilt. There was blood on his shirt. My father's blood. We were looking at each other like that when a sliding glass door opened and the doctor came out and walked grimly past me, and the *before* part of our lives was over, just like that.

Today, I made it nearly to Arthur's room before I had to take a breath. When I got to his doorway, I looked in and saw him still unconscious, still hooked up to a symphony of beeping machinery. Bobby Veach—the pressman who'd been in the office the night of the shooting—was sitting at his bedside. When Veach saw me, he immediately got up.

"I was just leaving," he said. He was wearing a polo shirt with the same nylon gym shorts. He was probably one of those guys who wore shorts even in the winter.

"You can stay."

"No, I should go."

He brushed past me into the hall and I followed him. "I'd like to talk to you, actually," I said. "We didn't really have a chance the other night."

"Sorry." He looked at me over his shoulder but kept walking. He was in a curious hurry to get away from me. "I gotta get home. Sorry. Later, maybe."

We'd made it back to the elevator, which stood open as if waiting for him. I thrust another business card at him before he stepped in. "Call me," I said, "later."

He nodded vaguely and shoved the card into his pocket and didn't say anything else.

I went back down the hall to Arthur's room and sat down in one of the chairs next to his bed. I wanted to think that his color looked better than it had the other night. But he kind of looked the same. "Arthur," I whispered.

His eyes fluttered, stopped, and then finally one opened.

I let out a breath I hadn't realized I was holding and said, "Hi."

He closed his eyes for a second. "Roxane." After clearing his throat, he added, "Janet told me . . . what you did. My daughter . . ."

I waited to see if he would finish that thought.

". . . Somewhere."

"Your daughter's here somewhere?"

Nod.

"Well, good," I said. "I'm glad someone is around for you. Bobby was just here too, from the print shop."

He nodded faintly. "Good guy, Bobby . . . hard worker. Been with me a long time."

"Listen, are you up to answering a couple questions?"

His eyes closed halfway and for a second I thought he'd gone back to sleep. But then he nodded.

"The police were telling me about something they found. Something that makes it look bad for you. What didn't you tell me?"

"I didn't." He cleared his throat. "Why would I. I told you everything."

"Please think, what are they talking about?"

"No idea."

I changed tactics. "Arthur, did Marin know Derek, the guy who works for you?"

He didn't answer.

"What's going on at the shop that the police are so interested in?"

"I told . . . them. Everything."

"But tell me, Arthur. What's going on?"

He looked away from me, his gaze settling on the wall. "They wanted to buy the print shop." A tear squeezed out of the corner of his eye. He whispered, "Now that poor girl died."

My stomach twisted. "I know. Who wanted to buy the print shop?"

"It's not for sale."

His voice was going fuzzy, and I knew I needed to hurry up and ask the rest of my questions before he passed out again. "Did Marin ever talk about someone named Agnes Harlow?"

He swallowed wetly, shaking his head.

"William? Nate?"

"Who . . . no."

"Did she ever mention having a son?"

Here, Arthur's mouth pressed into a thin line. "No . . . no family. Don't you believe me?"

"I'm just trying to figure out what happened."

"The police don't believe me. Marin. Everything."

Based on what I'd learned about Marin in the last two days, I believed Arthur more than ever. I just wished I knew what *everything* referred to. "I'm going to figure this out. Why this happened, just a few days apart. Can you tell me anything? About the print shop, about Derek, or Leila Hassan, maybe?"

He gripped my hand, then let go as his breathing began to slow. "Leila . . . Marin liked her. Friends . . ."

"Arthur, tell me about Leila."

But he didn't respond. Not then, and not at any point in the ten minutes I continued to sit there.

I left the hospital with something needling me, like an itchy tag sewn into the back of a shirt.

I checked.

That wasn't it. I'd already cut the tag out of my shirt.

After I got back in the car, I consulted my list of scribbled notes and drove to Leila Hassan's corner of the Short North, parked illegally, rang the buzzer, no response. A UPS notice with her name on it was stuck to the building's front door, dated Wednesday.

So she hadn't been home in a while.

Inconclusive.

I could fill the rest of my notebook with questions: What was going on at the print shop, and who had wanted to buy it, and why; what did any of it have to do with Marin; was my own client even telling me the truth?

Victorian Village was alive on this sunny Saturday afternoon, the park full of joggers and people lounging on the grass. I parked by the tennis courts and walked up to the house in the picture Georgette gave me. Crazy Aunt Agnes's house. It was a shingle-style Victorian, like most of the homes on the street. Hunter green, with a hulking brick arch over the front porch. I realized I'd knocked on the door on Wednesday to no response, also like most of the homes on the street. I sauntered casually around the house, counting the rooms. It was a massive property. Eight bedrooms, maybe more. There was a two-story garage in back, space for three cars plus maybe an apartment upstairs. *A carriage house.* It was that kind of neighborhood.

This place was likely worth more than half a million dollars.

No lights on, no cars in the garage, no signs of life.

Not even when I abandoned my casual search and walked right up to the front windows and squinted through a gap in the heavy drapes into what looked like a sitting room. Despite the darkness inside the house, I could make out the buxom curves of a vintage divan, the horn of an actual Victrola, a brass lamp with a fringed shade. It was like peering into a display at a historical museum.

Frozen in time.

I knocked on the door again but didn't get a response this time either. The house sounded hollow and empty, decidedly unlived-in.

Next I tried to see into the back of the property through the locked gate that sealed it off from the street. There wasn't much yard to speak of back there, and what was there was a landscaping project gone to seed: a scummy pond with a dried-up waterfall; several square planters filled with medium-size hardy palms and the dead remains of tall exotic grasses; a wrought-iron patio set given over entirely to rust, its table umbrella fallen over and stuck under the legs of a chair. I stepped back over a bush and checked through the windows on the other side of the porch, taking in a dining room with a table that would seat twelve people. There was a china cabinet off to the side, its shelves stacked with ruby Depression glass.

I walked back to Buttles and strolled through the alley toward the house, pretending I was Marin Strasser, a con artist full of booze and duck confit or whatever they served at the Guild House, pissed off about the fact that my fiancé-slash-easy-mark had discovered my scam. Marin's blood was still visible in the gaps between the cobblestones, just slightly, four or five yards from the carriage house.

This couldn't be a coincidence—Marin being shot less than twenty feet away from the former home of her former sister-in-law? Unlikely, but then again, if Agnes Harlow's actual blood relatives weren't fond of her, it was hard to imagine an enduring connection between Agnes and her brother's second, contested wife.

A house full of antiques did seem like something Marin would like, though.

Out of the corner of my eye, I noticed curtains rustling in one of the apartments on the other side of the alley. Edward Bennett Wilkington, who had rustled curtains at me the last time I was back here.

I knocked on his door again. "Hi," I said. "Remember me?"

He nodded, uneasy.

"You're pretty attentive to this alley."

Another nod.

"Are you sure you didn't see or hear anything?"

The big man's eyes were wide. "I told you, I didn't. I'm just vigilant now that something happened back there."

I stared at him for a while. He seemed like a class-A weirdo, but that alone didn't mean anything. Still, my hackles were up. "Vigilant."

"Yes."

"Good. I have a question for you. Do you know your neighbors? Especially the ones in the houses that face the park."

Edward Bennett Wilkington shrugged.

"How about the green house down there?"

I pointed.

His eyes said both yes and no. "I know her to see her. But she's weird. Always muttering about stuff in the alley."

"Who's *she*?"

"Agnes. The lady. Who lives there. Lived. I haven't seen her in a few weeks. Months."

"She lives alone?"

He nodded.

"Has anyone been in the house?"

"Not that I saw. She might know more," he said, pointing across the courtyard to Meredith Burns's apartment. "The other neighborhood cat lady."

Meredith Burns told me where to find Agnes: a convalescent home called Brighton Lake, where she'd been since early April. "It was the Sunday after Easter," she said. We were sitting on her porch, an annoying wind chime clanging over my shoulder. "That's when it happened. I remember because I fed the cats the last of my leftover Easter ham. She usually fed them, the strays in the alley, that is. She kept her garage half open so they had a warm, dry place to go, and she'd put out the kibble every morning. I knew something was wrong when I saw the cats prowling around one day, begging for food. Agnes has her problems, but she always takes care of the cats."

"That's sweet."

She nodded. "So I went in through the garage and up to the house, and she'd fallen. In her basement. I have no idea how long she'd been down there. But it was a frightening scene."

Agnes had been trapped at the bottom of her basement steps for days, Meredith told me—hip broken, no food or water. And no antipsychotic medication, which she used to manage her paranoid schizophrenia. "I thought she was dead. She wasn't moving. But I turned on a light and she started shrieking." Meredith's eyebrows knit together. "About Salome."

"Salome."

Another nod.

"Like, the Oscar Wilde play? Dance of the seven veils?"

"I don't know. That's just what she kept saying. I called 911 right away, of course. I tried to calm her down but I don't—I had no idea what to do. She was very deep into something, in her mind."

"Calling 911 seems to be your role here in the neighborhood."

Meredith smiled. "Maybe you're right."

"So you and Agnes are friends?"

"Yes, I guess we are," she said. "We sit out here in the evenings sometimes, when the weather is nice. My cats—I have three—they love Agnes. You can always tell that there's something different about her, from her mannerisms. She doesn't say a lot—the medication makes her feel fuzzy, she told me once. But she's witty, very smart. It's terrifying, frankly, how so many things can go wrong in the brain. And so quickly, too."

She was right. I didn't like thinking about that, the brain's potential to betray us. "Since it happened, have you seen anyone at her house?"

"No."

"Not even family?"

She pursed her lips. "Well, a few days after it happened, her daughter Suzy stopped by here. To thank me, for getting Agnes help. When I asked her if I could visit Agnes at Brighton Lake, she looked at me like I was an alien. Like why in the world would someone want to visit Agnes. They didn't have much of a relationship. I'd never even seen her before."

"So Agnes is just alone all the time."

"Well, there's a case manager from OHMH who checks on her. Once a week, I think."

"OHMH?"

"Ohio Hospital for Mental Health. I drove her to appointments a couple times, but usually he takes her—A.J., that's his name. A real nice young guy. He built the cat shelter in the garage. And I know she liked him. She even gave me his card once—she said, if anything ever happens to me, call A.J. first. He'll know what to do."

I raised an eyebrow. "Was she expecting something to happen to her?"

"She meant here," Meredith said, tapping a temple. "And I thought she was just being sort of self-deprecating—I had no idea what was really going on under the surface. But when I saw the cats, that morning—I did call him, only he didn't answer. That's why I went into the house. I didn't know what else to do."

"It's probably good that you did," I said. "She might not be alive otherwise."

Her expression told me that she wasn't so sure she'd done Agnes any favors.

I showed her a picture of Marin, but she didn't recognize her.

"If you go see Agnes," she said as I went down the porch steps, "would you tell her that I'm feeding the cats?"

TWELVE

I added the names of the Harlow family to my corkboard and leaned back in my desk chair, staring at them. Rather than narrowing my focus, what I'd learned about Crazy Aunt Agnes and the stray cats had actually only broadened it.

I pulled some background information on Nate Harlow and saw that Marin might have been telling the truth about one thing: Her son *had* been in legal trouble. Seven years ago, in the Cincinnati area, he'd been convicted of grand larceny. There was little detail available online, but I got the names of the arresting officer and the prosecuting attorney from the clerk of courts website, and left a pair of voice mails—which I gave twenty percent odds on actually getting returned.

Armed with the knowledge that at one point in her life, his mother had been Marin Harlow, I finally got somewhere on *her* background: a few misdemeanors in Delaware County, just like Georgette and Paul had said. Shoplifting, shoplifting, passing a bad check to a department store.

I wondered which had come first, the shoplifting or the check?

The eternal question.

None of these crimes sounded like the type of thing to require bail money, as the Harlows had said, but maybe that was a slight exaggeration on their part.

I got a drink and opened the balcony door and stood there looking out at the street while I sipped. Whiskey didn't have magical properties. But sometimes it shook something loose. I thought back over what I'd done for the past few days.

Got shot at.

Got lied to.

Got into arguments with the cops who could help untangle this mess.

I wanted to know what the hell the police had found that made things look worse for my client. But if Tom hadn't been willing to tell me that yesterday, there was probably no chance that he'd be into it after I kicked him out of my house. I remembered a conversation we'd had in bed late last year, about my tendency to stop an argument in its tracks by suggesting sexy times. He'd said something like *If we weren't doing this, what would happen if I said something you didn't want to hear? Would you just throw me out?* Apparently that was exactly what I would do. A curious response, considering that Tom was one of the only people I could stand half the time.

While I was puzzling over that, I heard footsteps on the landing and a quiet knock at my door.

Spontaneous visits to my apartment hadn't been going that well as of late. Gun in hand, I parted the curtains for a peek at who was out there.

Shelby.

She offered a sad little smile and my heart sank. My thoughts raced over my mental calendar—did we have plans? I couldn't remember anything like that. I covered the gun with a stack of mail and unlocked the deadbolts.

"Shel, were we supposed to meet? Did I stand you up?"

"No," she said, "no, I'm just, I needed somewhere to go and I, um, I need to talk to you. I hope it's okay."

I was relieved, but not that relieved. "Come in, of course it's okay."

Shelby sat down on one end of my sofa and I sat on the other end. She sighed. "This is going to sound so stupid."

"Don't worry about how it sounds. Just tell me."

She looked at me. "So, you know that girl, Miriam."

"Tori Amos. Right."

"Yeah. We were talking today and she said she and some friends are going to this cabin next week, in Hocking Hills—it's her aunt's and it's usually rented on the weekends but Mir can stay there during the week. Whatever, the point is, she's going there with some friends on Tuesday and she invited me."

"Nice."

"Yeah, well. So I was telling my dad tonight, that I was going. And he was just, he said no way could I go to a cabin with a bunch of strangers, especially not some girl. And he asked," she said, her eyes welling, "he said, are they all gays too, like that made the trip some kind of twisted orgy or something."

Heat rose to my face. "Dammit, Joshua," I said. "Shel—"

"No, before you say he didn't mean it, after he said that, I told him Dad, I'm just telling you where I'm going, not asking if I can go, I'm eighteen, and he went well, you're still living in my house and it just—I don't even *want* to live in that stupid house. So I said fine, I don't live here anymore and I left." Her voice shook. Her eyes were on the floor a few feet in front of us.

I could tell that she'd never left her house that angry before. When I first met them, Joshua and Shelby were very close. I wanted them to be close. I wanted that for her—to have a good relationship with her dad, something I never had, and never would.

She continued, "And it was like he was saying that, because I'm, you know, that nothing would ever be normal, going camping with some people is like automatically deviant or something. I know you're going to say that he's just trying to protect me from the world but that's crap, he doesn't even care, he just wants to control me. If he wanted to protect me, he wouldn't expect me to stay in that house. If he had his way, I'd live there till I was thirty and never go farther than the front porch."

"Shelby, does he know where you are right now?"

She shook her head.

I turned to her. "I hear everything you're saying. But you do know that he's worried out of his mind right now."

"I don't care! He doesn't get it. At all. God, why can't I just live with you? You get it. I could pay you rent, I mean, you have all this space, and it would just be for a while, till I find a place—"

I opened my mouth, momentarily speechless. The thought of another person witnessing my day-to-day life filled me with spontaneous panic that had basically nothing to do with Shelby and everything to do with me.

She got up and went over to the screen door, where the soft sounds of early evening drifted in. "I'm such an idiot," she muttered. "I'm not kidding when I say I have no friends. Not friends you go to in a crisis. Veronica wouldn't even have been my friend if she didn't live next door. I couldn't really have friends, not with all his rules, him wanting to keep track of me all the time. And I'm never going to make friends at this rate, either." Eyes still on the street, she folded her arms tightly across her chest. "But you know what, if I hadn't had that stupid curfew, if I'd just gone with Veronica that night, none of this ever would have even happened."

She covered her face with her hands, thin shoulders shaking.

"Shel," I said. But then I didn't know what else to say.

What had happened to Veronica Cruz wasn't Shelby's fault, or Joshua's. But I could see her point, could see why she was so desperate to get away from Belmont, why Joshua's *my house, my rules* was the very last thing she needed. "It's not that I don't want you here."

"No. Forget I said anything." Even though she didn't look up at me, I could see the tension and embarrassment on her face and hear it in her voice. "It was a dumb idea, sorry, we don't have to talk about it."

"No, it's not dumb, you just surprised me. But Shel, I know I probably need a role model more than you do, and I know you're not a kid—but, well," I paused, my stomach twisting as I tried to think of how to say it, "I'm kind of a mess. You know?"

She shook her head, still not looking at me.

I thought about my own teenage years, how my dad had kicked me out a few months shy of my high school graduation. If my brother Andrew hadn't taken me in, there was no telling what would have become of me. And Shelby didn't have siblings. I heard myself sigh. "You can stay here tonight."

She finally turned to face me, her green eyes hopeful. "Really?"

"Really. What's a cool surrogate aunt for?"

Shelby smiled and wiped her face.

"But you have to call your dad first so he knows where you are. And tell him that we need to talk."

THIRTEEN

The door to my guest bedroom was half open when I woke on Sunday morning, Shelby still asleep in that dramatic teenager way with one foot hanging off the mattress and the blankets over her head. I fished a spare key out of my desk drawer and left Shelby a note on the bulletin board in the hallway: *Lock up, and come back if you need to.* Then I grabbed a spoonful of peanut butter by way of breakfast and headed out into the world to see about some loose ends.

As I walked up the sidewalk, I called Shelby's house. "Hi, it's Roxane Weary," I said when Joshua Evans answered.

"Roxane," he said, his voice tense, "oh God, is everything okay?"

"Hey, relax," I said. He sighed audibly. "Everything's fine. Shelby's still asleep. Listen, how about we get together this week?"

A beat passed before he answered, and when he did, his voice had turned hopeful. "The three of us?"

"No. You and me. We can get a drink, have dinner, and catch up."

"That—yeah, that would be nice."

"Great," I said. Last fall I'd promised myself I wasn't going to meddle in their lives any more than I already had, but that seemed unavoidable at this point. We made plans to meet up that night at Taverna Athena, whose melitzanosalata was literally the only good thing Belmont had going for it.

After another drive by Agnes's house—where exactly nothing was happening yet—I tried Leila's building again. The UPS notice remained on the door, but today that door was propped open while two deliverymen carried in a mattress and box springs.

I parked on a side street and went in behind them.

Leila's apartment was on the second floor. When I knocked I heard nothing, not the hopeful unlatching of a chain lock, nor the less promising—but better than nothing—scuffle of somebody trying to escape out the window.

Nothing.

I knocked on the other three apartment doors on the floor. Only one person answered, a harried woman in hospital scrubs.

"Yeah, hi," I said, "I need your neighbor's signature, have you seen her—"

"Maybe try knocking on her door then," the woman barked at me. "I need to go."

She bustled out of the apartment and into the stairwell.

It made me feel almost fond of my neighbor Birdsong for a second.

Back in the narrow lobby, the deliverymen were bringing in a bed frame. I pressed myself against the wall to let them by, taking the opportunity to examine the row of—locked—mailboxes. Leila's was bursting at the seams; a wrinkled white envelope was sticking out from the bottom corner.

Once the bed frame was gone and I was alone in the lobby, I tugged on the edge of the envelope. It came free easily, but it was only an American Express solicitation. I opened it anyway, in case it contained some previously unknown bit of information about the woman. But it didn't.

Hardly worth the federal crime now on my conscience.

I ripped it into eighths and tucked it into a coffee cup on the top of an almost-full trash can by the door, then shoved the entire thing deep into the rest of the garbage, delicately avoiding drips of coffee and whatever else was in there. The maneuvering caused me to shift the balance of stuff that had been thrown away, and something interesting displayed itself on the top of the pile.

A flyer, featuring a photo of the building in which I now stood.

AVAILABLE!
1 and 2 bedroom modern lofts
Secure parking
24/7 fitness center access at Snap
Some units fully furnished
Possible short term lease
$1295-$2195

The exorbitant rent wasn't what interested me. It was the logo at the bottom right of the sheet:

THE PHOENIX GROUP

Vincent Pomp's company.

I plucked the flyer out of the trash and gave it a shake, then sat down on the modular sofa by the window and smoothed out the flyer.

So Pomp owned or managed the building where Leila lived, and his daughter was murdered at Leila's former place of employment.

I could make excuses for one coincidence, but not two.

While I was making connections left and right, I decided to follow up on Arthur's other employee. Bobby Veach lived in the end unit of a row of town houses north of Crosswoods—or *had* lived, anyway. The door to his unit stood open as I approached it and I could see an expanse of beige carpet and a pile of boxes and hear the hum of a vacuum. I knocked on the doorframe and waited. I'd hesitated before coming up here, since I had just seen the man yesterday and he didn't seem keen on talking to me. But in fairness I'd given him two business cards and four days during which to call me, and he hadn't.

And I wanted to see what other connections I could make.

The vacuum turned off and a young woman leaned into my line of sight. She wore denim short-shorts and a hot-pink tank top, no bra. "Um, can I *help* you?" she said, like she really, really did not want to help.

"I'm looking for Bobby," I said. "He around?"

She shook her head. "He's gone, dude."

"Gone?"

"This is my place now," she said protectively. "Bobby moved out."

"Where'd he move to?"

"He got this boat or something. Gonna sail the world, I guess."

"Wow."

"Right? It's wild. Totally off the grid."

"Did he say why?"

"Uh," she said, like it should've been obvious, "because the world is *fucked*?"

"Oh. That. Well, do you know how I could get in touch with him?"

"Off. The. Grid," she said. "Helloooo. No one can get in touch with him."

She was getting on my nerves. "Can I ask how you know him?"

She put her hands on her hips. "How the fuck do *you* know him?"

"I just really need to talk to him. It's, um," I said, stalling while I tried to come up with something good, "it's just that I'm . . .

pregnant. And Bobby's the . . ." I trailed off, folding my arms over my midsection in what I hoped was a frightened, maternal sort of gesture.

Her eyes went wide. "Oh. Fuck."

I nodded.

"I mean," she said, "I don't really know him that well. He was my stepdad, but my mom divorced him a long time ago. She just died."

"I'm sorry."

She nodded. "But Bobby knew I needed a place to live. So he called the other day. I'm renting it from him while he's gone. He left me these weird instructions to pay him with Bitcoin."

"Weird how?"

She unfolded a piece of paper from her pocket and handed it to me.

On it, a messy blue scrawl explaining how to use the Bitcoin ATM at a cell-phone store in Franklinton to send him money anonymously. I wouldn't have guessed that Bobby Veach was so tech-savvy. Then again, I obviously wouldn't have guessed that he was going to run, either.

"When is he coming back?"

"I don't know."

"*Is* he coming back?"

"I guess that depends on how much he likes being off the grid."

I said, "I suppose that's true."

Brighton Lake was really more of a pond, a man-made kidney-shaped thing with a cadre of overfed ducks floating near a small fountain. The care home itself comprised three buildings: two brick towers in the rear of the property that housed the active seniors, according to the website, and a white single-story building in the front that housed the common areas and the skilled-nursing wing. It looked nice enough, but I didn't want to go in. I was reminded of my grandmother, who'd died in a place like this when I was fifteen. I hadn't wanted to go in that time, either. But it wasn't about me then, and it wasn't about me now.

I walked into the lobby, signed in, and asked the receptionist where I could find Agnes Harlow's room. She told me and pointed down a long hallway, past a circle of old ladies in a community lounge area. They were knitting and laughing. Maybe it wasn't so bad here. They seemed to be having a good time, anyway.

I went to the end of the hall and found Agnes's room, my resolve cracking with every step. This was the type of place I remembered: the small rooms, the hospital smell, the greying figures propped in their adjustable beds. Agnes was one such figure, small and still, a long, grey braid draped over one shoulder. Eyes open but gazing at the ceiling. Her cheekbone was bruised, and she wore a tan brace on one arm. She had a visitor, an elderly man slouching in a chair beside her bed, reading out loud from a Bible.

"'For the Lord knoweth the ways of the righteous,'" he said. "'But the way of the ungodly shall perish.'"

I lingered in the doorway for a moment before deciding to come back later. But the man sensed my presence and put the Bible down, eyes flicking to mine under heavy, still-dark eyebrows. His hair was a gradient of black to white and longish on top, held out of his eyes by a pair of tortoiseshell glasses. His face was craggy and expressive. With his baggy white Oxford sleeves rolled up to the elbow, he looked like an eccentric professor. "Hello, young lady."

"Not that young," I said. Agnes didn't react; her eyes stayed on the ceiling. "I didn't mean to intrude."

"Younger than me, at least by half. Are you here to see Agnes? You can come in."

I took one step into the room. "Is she . . ." I started.

"Awake?"

I nodded.

"Yeah, she's just bored with me. Are you a volunteer or what?"

I pushed down my natural instinct to lie. Instead, I told him, "No. I was just hoping to ask Agnes a few questions. I'm an investigator."

"A cop?"

"No, private."

"Oh, a Mike Hammer type? Agnes, things are getting interesting now." The man flipped his glasses down onto his nose and he squinted at me. "But what's a private investigator want with a little old lady?"

I sat down in the other bedside chair. "It's about family, actually. Are *you* family?"

"We used to be married. Samuel J. Kinnaman," he said, shaking my hand. "Sam."

"Roxane."

"Must be the Harlow side of the family," he said softly, "because my side, we're not the type to require, ah, intrigue." Then he looked up, almost embarrassed. "Sorry, Agnes, I don't mean to pry into your business."

The woman in the bed glanced over at me, her eyes fierce.

"Those things which you have seen," she whispered urgently, "and the things which are, and the things which will take place after these things, and the things which you have seen. . . ."

I had a sinking feeling.

"She doesn't like strangers much," he said. "And she's not having a good day. Some days, they're better. Other days, she goes pretty far into herself. Schizophrenia. This place, it's no good for her. It's tough, seeing how she ended up. She doesn't say much. And what she does say, it doesn't make a lot of sense. Not to us, anyway."

"I'm sorry," I said. I kept my voice gentle. "Listen, maybe you can help me."

He shrugged. "If I can, why not."

"When were you and Agnes married?"

"Oh, goodness. A hundred years ago. The end of the eighties."

"And you stayed close, even after you split?"

"Not so much *split*. She left me, me and my girls, in one of her fits. Nineteen eighty-nine. Just walked out."

"Wow."

"In some ways, that was a relief. Things were hard. She would go through periods of not taking her pills, and it made her difficult to be around. But I never stopped caring about her. Never stopped trying. And now, well, she's got nobody. She chased everyone away. Except me, even after everything. The last few years, I guess they've been hard on her. Till recently I was out in California with my older daughter, but I came back when Agnes had her fall. Didn't want Suze to have to deal with it all on her own." He shook his head quickly. "Sorry. That wasn't what you asked. Yeah, we stayed close enough."

"Do you ever remember meeting her brother's second wife? Marin. And her son, Nate. Agnes's nephew. Do you know them?"

Sam thought for a second and said, "No."

Agnes said, "Herodias." She dragged out the "s" into a long, tense hiss. Then she turned and faced the wall, again muttering, "Those things which you have seen . . ."

Sam said, "The Harlows were unrelentingly Catholic. I think it's from the book of Revelation. I don't know what it means. If it means anything at all."

Then I showed him Marin's picture, but there was no reaction in his eyes.

Ditto for Nate's.

"Agnes never went in for the blood-is-thicker stuff. So we didn't see a lot of Bill and his people, even when Agnes was doing well, when we were still together. He had some bratty kids, five, ten years older than ours. They weren't the most, you know, empathetic people. When it came to Agnes's diagnosis. Like it was some kind of affront, for a rich person's brain to go bad. It's simply not done." This last phrase he said like it was a direct quote.

It was easy enough to imagine Georgette Harlow saying it just like that.

Sam added, "Of course, maybe they got closer later on, Agnes and them. But I'd be surprised."

I drove back toward the city, detoured up to the OSU campus for a bribe from Buckeye Donuts, and then stopped at my brother's. Andrew opened the door of his Italian Village loft looking aggrieved. "It's ten in the damn morning," he said, rubbing his eyes.

"Ten thirty, actually. And I came bearing breakfast." I held up a drink carrier and a greasy bag. "I thought you didn't get hungover, anyway."

"I still get tired, though." He snatched the bag away from me and let me in. "Crullers. What is wrong with you? Nobody likes crullers."

"There's long johns too," I said. I followed him into the loft, which bore evidence of a lady visitor: a fancy purse and a pair of Louboutins next to the door.

"Don't ask." My brother carried the doughnuts over to the granite kitchen island. His place was nicer than what one might expect a thirty-seven-year-old bachelor to own, although he and I shared the same shitty housekeeping skills. He grabbed a jug from the fridge and doctored his coffee with milk and a slug of whiskey. "So what do you want?"

"I have a question," I said. "Vincent Pomp. Do you know him?"

"What makes you think I would?"

"You know about a lot of things. And you know a lot of people, too."

He dragged a hand through his collar-length hair. "I know the name."

I splashed a drop of whiskey in my tea—for flavor—and bit into a cruller. "And?"

"And, he's a real-estate guy on paper, but he's also a lender."

"Payday loans, I know that."

"Well, I'd probably go with loan shark, but okay."

I raised an eyebrow. "Are we talking small time, or big time?"

He shrugged. "Big enough, I guess. He's got a lot of money. And he's paranoid, from what I hear. Or maybe just loaded. He's got a driver, a gated guard shack at his place, all that."

"Why?"

"Who knows. Like I said, I know the name, but I don't really know the man."

"What about his family?"

My brother shook his head. "I don't know his family either."

The bedroom door opened and a woman scuttled out, head down. Without looking at either of us, she grabbed her bag and shoes and escaped from the apartment.

My eyes met Andrew's, and we both laughed.

"You could have at least offered her a cruller," I said.

Andrew finished his coffee. "I told you, no one likes crullers. So why are you asking about Pomp?" He squinted at the trash can and pitched his cup toward it, missing badly.

"You need glasses."

"I need practice. *You* need glasses."

"I have glasses. I just don't wear them."

"You're such a brat," Andrew said.

"But you love me."

"I do. Which is why I *don't* love the sound of you involved with somebody like that. Now, if you were to ask me for a reco on a tattoo artist, then I could help. But this so-called underworld stuff—not really. I just sell weed to out-of-towners."

I sipped my tea, thinking. I didn't need a tattoo artist. "Okay, what about Bitcoin?"

He bit into his second long john. "What about Bitcoin?"

"Do you know what it is?"

My brother raised an eyebrow. "Planning to put your money in alternative currencies?"

"Would you just tell me how it works?"

He opened the balcony door and motioned for me to join him. "I need to smoke."

My father's strict rules against smoking in the house had clearly made a major impression on both Andrew and my mother.

Andrew lit a cigarette, squinting in the bright sun. "Bitcoin is a digital currency. It's like cash that you use online, basically. So if you want to pay for something online, anonymously, that's the way to do it. It's also popular with a certain brand of antiestablishment doomsday prepper."

I wondered if that applied to Bobby Veach and his off-the-grid living, or if there was more to it than that. "What are people buying anonymously?"

"You know, Silk Road shit. Dark net. People sell drugs that way, weapons, porn, counterfeit green cards, bootleg DVDs—you'd be surprised how much of a market there is for bootleg DVDs."

"Copier toner?"

"What the fuck is that?"

"Like, office supplies?"

"Ha. No."

"Have you ever seen one?"

"A copier toner?"

"No. A bitcoin."

Andrew exhaled a stream of smoke at the sky. "No. It's not a physical thing."

"You're losing me."

"It's not like a dollar bill. It exists only in cyberspace. If anything, it's a sheet of paper with a serial number written on it."

I thought of the weird slips of paper from Marin's nightstand. "With QR codes?"

He shrugged. "It sounds like you're asking about something specific now."

I explained about the slips, and my brother nodded. "That sounds like ATM receipts. Maybe. I'm not an expert—this shit is way too complicated for me." He stubbed out his cigarette against the brick facade of the building. "These questions today—are they about the same case? Because it sounds a little . . . I don't know."

"It's nothing. I promise. I'm leaving. You're welcome for breakfast."

My brother laughed and caught me in a one-armed hug. "Be careful."

"Oh, shut up," I said.

FOURTEEN

As I drove back downtown, I thought about things.

Bobby Veach was on the run.

Vincent Pomp's daughter had been shot to death outside of Arthur's print shop, while one of its employees was living in a building that Pomp owned.

Marin was dead too, murdered behind her ex-sister-in-law's house.

Maybe this was the world's most complicated stolen-copier-toner ring, but I had my doubts about that.

I told myself I was doing what Tom had asked and staying out of his case as I took another drive past Leila's house. I was doing a lot of driving past people's homes so far. I wasn't sure this counted as progress.

But it did count as billable miles, which was almost the same thing. At least on paper.

I parked on her street and reclined my seat. On one hand, she had to come home sometime. On the other hand, there was only one of me, so twenty-four/seven surveillance wasn't possible. It would take at least three people to pull that off, and there was no guarantee it would go anywhere. And on the third, imaginary hand, even though she had to come home eventually, "eventually" meant any time between the present moment and the inevitable heat death of the universe.

I scrolled through my phone, looked at Catherine's number, shook my head, looked at it again. Calling was a bad idea. That was probably why she'd resorted to texting me punctuation. I quickly typed out a message to her:

> . . . Hi. I have a work thing I could use your help on.
> Would you be up for that?

Five minutes later, I got a response from Catherine: *she lives!* Then a separate message: *and sure.*

Half an hour later, I was sitting along the back wall at Upper Cup with my laptop and a glass of iced tea when the door opened and the atmosphere changed. I didn't need to look up to see who it was. I knew the smell of her, the way the air moved around her. But I looked anyway. Catherine wore a plain black tank and tight white jeans. Her pale green eyes were rimmed in navy eyeliner and I noticed her ring finger was currently unadorned.

I hated myself for noticing that.

She didn't walk over right away, just got in line at the counter to order a dirty chai, standing with her back to me while the barista made it. I kept my eyes on my screen, but I could no longer concentrate on anything. Finally, she doctored her tea with a dash of cinnamon at the condiment station and sat down across from me.

"That thing is like a thousand years old," she said by way of greeting, with a nod at my computer. "Crime doesn't pay?"

"Crime occasionally pays, but this still works, so what's the difference?"

"It looks like it's being held together by muffin crumbs."

Despite myself, I laughed out loud.

"So," she said, "you're not returning my texts, and you're drinking iced tea. What's happened to you?"

"I don't have that much to say to *dot dot dot*," I said, "and, not that I have to explain my tea temperature to you, but it's hot outside."

She shrugged. "You know I'm always cold."

"I do."

We looked at each other for a while.

"I was surprised," she said after a pause, "that you didn't respond. That isn't like you."

That, I thought, was very telling. "Just taking a page from your playbook," I said.

"Which is?"

"Radio silence to drive somebody crazy. Is it working?"

She laughed that big laugh of hers, dirty and sexy and joyful all at once. It always made my chest hurt, like my heart was too big for my rib cage. "I thought you were mad at me."

I drank some tea. "I'm not anything at you. But it's finally dawning on me that you aren't good for me, Catherine, so I'm just keeping to myself."

She arched an eyebrow. "And yet, here we are."

"I told you, I have a work thing."

The corner of her mouth tipped up. Then she lifted her left hand. "I saw you clock this the second I sat down."

I took a second before responding. "I'm a detective. It's what I do."

"I'm sure that's it."

"Is it over?"

"Probably."

"What happened?"

She blew on the foamy surface of her chai. "What didn't happen is a shorter list. We didn't love each other, for instance. Or even like each other very much."

"Why get married, then?"

"I don't know," she said, her voice going far away. "I found him interesting. That's where it starts for me, you know that. Then I didn't anymore."

"So it had nothing to do with her."

"Who's *her*?"

"Your girlfriend. The photographer," I said. "Thao."

A slight flare of her nostrils. "That's over. No."

"Or me."

"No. Just me, and him, and his endless supply of ironic hats."

It wasn't funny, but we both laughed anyway.

Then her expression darkened. "And his oxy habit," she added. "It doesn't get any less interesting than that, does it."

"My brother mentioned something about that the other day. He saw him, at the hotel."

"Looking to score?"

"That's what it sounded like."

She shook her head. "At least I got a beautiful house out of the deal." She sipped her tea. "He'll never get that house from me."

"It is a beautiful house."

Catherine raised her mug and clinked it against my glass. "So let's hear about this work thing."

I opened a new browser tab and navigated to Leila Hassan's Facebook page and flipped the computer around so Catherine could see. "Do you know her?"

Catherine looked at the screen, her expression blank at first. But then her eyes narrowed. "I—kind of, yeah. How in the world did you figure that out?"

I tapped the edge of the screen. "Mutual friends."

"Oh. Right. I forgot that you even have Facebook. You never use it."

"So how do you know her?"

Catherine clicked through Leila's profile. "She was a student. At a workshop I taught at this little letterpress studio in Worthington."

"What kind of workshop?"

She bit her lip. "She came to two. Intaglio. Both levels. She was good, too. More advanced than the first-level class, and I told her that, but she said she needed a refresher. She's a designer, I believe, but she studied printmaking in art school."

"Intaglio," I said. "Why do I know that word?"

"It's a medieval printing technique. You engrave a metal plate, either by hand or using acid. It's kind of like a stamp, except the materials give you the capability to do astounding detail. It's how money is printed, for example. The portraits?"

I nodded.

"That's intaglio."

"There's a demand for workshops about this?"

Amusement flared in her pale green eyes. "Old-school technique is always in demand. Letterpress, stuff like that. Wedding invitations and stationery, especially."

"Right, wedding invitations," I said as it hit me, where I'd recently heard about intaglio. From Arthur, one of many specialty production and finishing options on offer at Ungless Printing.

"How long ago was this?"

She leaned on one hand. "The workshop was, oh, last year. February, I think." She pulled a bulky flip phone from her pocket and clicked some buttons. "Yeah, February."

"Talk about a thousand years old," I said. "*That's* the cell phone? I thought you said twenty-first century."

Both corners of her mouth tipped up this time. "Baby steps. As it is, this thing annoys me to no end. Why would anyone want to be accessible all the time? Anyway, so that's that. I met your lady friend two times over a year ago. Does that help?"

"Not really."

"Sad."

I chewed my lip and clicked back to Leila's profile. "Do you think she'd be willing to meet up with you?"

"Um, why would I need to meet with her?"

"You don't, *I* do. And she seems to be hiding out somewhere."

"Oh." Catherine sipped her tea. "Maybe. What's this all about?"

"I'm not sure yet, but I know she's involved," I said. "You don't mind?"

"If this is how the universe delivers you to me," she said in a way that made heat rise to my face, "who am I to complain?"

I was late to Taverna Athena, but fortunately Joshua was later. I got a booth near the window and ordered a drink and the melitzano-salata. It was a quarter past seven when he arrived, his face nervous. "Sorry I'm late," he said as he sat down across from me, "there was an accident on 270 and then I had to stop at home to change. I hate keeping somebody waiting, especially you. I'm lucky some other guy didn't take my spot." He gave an awkward laugh and looked around desperately for a waiter.

"No worries," I said. "And hey, Joshua, relax, we're just catching up."

He let out a long sigh. He was a handful of years older than me, a big teddy bear of a guy with a scruffy salt-and-pepper buzz cut and stubble to match. He had a good heart, and he'd been through a lot. Supportive over Shelby coming out this year, but since then he'd gotten a little weird around me. I couldn't figure out if it was because Shelby had confided in me long before she opened up to him, or because he'd assumed I was straight and was embarrassed for low-key flirting with me the first time we met, or if there was something else to it.

We made small talk until he had ordered and received a beer. Then I said, "Listen, Shelby is fine."

"I know she's fine. Like what could happen to her in a day, right?"

We looked at each other, each fully aware of what could happen in a day.

"I just, Roxane, I don't want to have that kind of relationship with her. Us at odds all the time."

"I know. So you have to listen to her."

"But she's only eighteen, for God's sake. She thinks she's all grown up, but she isn't. She's still a baby. Would I let her go to some cabin with a boy? No way. So why would I let her go with a girl?"

"You do know that being gay doesn't mean she wants to have sex with every other girl she meets, right?"

He blushed bright red and went quiet.

"She's not having sex with anyone," I added, "and when you tell her she's not allowed to make friends, she feels really, really isolated. And she's already isolated, because of everything that's happened."

"I never said she's not allowed to make friends."

"No, you're just telling her that she's only allowed to see her friends on your terms while she's living in your house."

"I know I shouldn't have said that. It just came out." He looked down at the table. "But how am I supposed to just let her go off with people I don't know?"

He didn't say *after everything*, but I heard it anyway. He added, "If you're going to let her go, at least can you get the address for this cabin? In case anything goes wrong or whatever."

I finished my drink, my chest aching for him. "Nothing is going to go wrong," I said. "But sure, I'll ask her. I'm not letting her do anything—she's an adult. She can go if she wants and that's all. I know I have no business giving parenting advice, okay, but as a former teenaged girl, I can tell you that you treating her like a child now is only going to make her want to leave faster, and she already wants to leave."

"She's too young. I mean, come on. How old were you when you moved out of your house?"

I almost laughed. "I was seventeen," I said. "I wasn't even finished with high school. My dad kicked me out, actually, because I was dating a girl and he didn't like it. I lived with my brother until I graduated."

As I said it, I watched Joshua's expression morph into a kind of confused horror. "But that's—I don't want her to leave. I want her to stay."

"Well, you asked," I said. "So I moved out when I was young, and I turned out all right, relatively speaking. And the thing is, it's not a matter of Shelby moving out or staying in Belmont. It's between her moving into a good situation, or a bad one. She can't stay in that house. You both deserve a fresh start. Have you thought about looking for a new place together?"

He took a long pull of his beer. "Well," he said, "to be honest, I owe money on that house. A lot. I took out a second mortgage six, seven years ago—terrible interest rate, but I didn't have a choice. I was out of work and got behind on stuff." He looked down at the beer bottle in his callused hands. "So I can't get a new place."

"Shit."

"Yeah."

"Joshua, I'm sorry."

"It's my own fault. I know that. Too much debt, not enough money. I couldn't cover two houses, and God knows the house would never sell anyway. There's already three houses on the market on our street. Nobody is touching any of them."

He finished his beer and motioned to the waiter for another. I tossed back the rest of my drink and nodded for a refill too.

"So that's why I can't move, even though I'd love to get a new place for me and Shel." He rubbed a hand over his face. "And when she says she can't stay there, and I can't fix it, I feel like I'm failing her. And I guess I didn't really get it till this week, that trying to make her stop talking about it is just pushing her out faster."

"It is." I touched his hand. "She doesn't want to get away from you—that's not what she wants at all. Last night she was really rattled from the fight you had."

The waiter brought our second round and we sat in silence for a while.

Finally, Joshua said, "So what am I supposed to do?"

I felt like an idiot for thinking that I was in a position to give Joshua advice. My big plan was to convince him to move. It hadn't occurred to me that he literally could not. "I don't know," I said. "But step one is trusting her. That you raised a good kid. Because she is. She's a really good kid. Smart. But she needs her space, so give her that space. She wants to go to Hocking Hills with some friends, let her."

His face fell.

"And when it comes to the apartment thing, give her some credit. She's being very smart about this, she's looking at a lot of places. Olde Towne East is a great neighborhood. I've lived there for years." Besides, I thought but did not say, the reason we were even having this conversation was that far worse had happened down here in Belmont.

Joshua sighed again. "But what if something goes wrong? She's just a kid."

"Come on, you know that Shelby's more responsible than either of us," I said, and we both laughed. "She can stay with me for a few days while things cool off between you. Maybe then you could show her some support, maybe look at some places with her?"

"Yes." He nodded. "Okay. That sounds good." He finished his beer and touched my arm. "Why do you always know exactly what to do?"

"That couldn't be further from the truth, but thanks for saying so," I told him.

When I let myself into the apartment, I saw the faint blue glow of the television. Shelby was on the sofa, watching an episode of *Law & Order,* the one where Claire Kincaid tries to quit her job. "Hiya," I said. "I see you're embracing the bachelor lifestyle in the same way I do."

"I never heard of this show before. But it's good."

I sat down on the other end of the sofa. "Just when I think I'm over it, you go and make me feel old again. This show was in its prime when I was your age."

Shelby smiled. "You aren't old. You just feel like that because the world makes you feel bad sometimes. Can I tell you something?"

I nodded.

"Sometimes I feel that way too."

Out of nowhere, my eyes welled up in the dark. "A lot of stuff has happened to you already, girl."

"What did you talk to my dad about tonight?"

"That's between us old people," I said. I would never tell her about Joshua's mortgage problem. "I think I got him to understand why you don't want to live in Belmont anymore, at least."

"Not that he'll do anything about it."

"Maybe he won't. But understanding is something, at least. So when are you heading to the cabin?"

She perked up at that. "Tomorrow morning. I think we're staying till Friday, as long as the weather isn't gross and rainy."

"Are you excited?"

"For sure. Miriam's cool, and I love Hocking Hills. It's so pretty. I'm going to grill veggie dogs for everyone—hopefully it will make them like me."

"I'm sure you don't have to purchase anyone's affection with veggie dogs, but even if you did, that's guaranteed to work. So you haven't met the other people yet?"

"There's Miriam, and her sister Abby, and Abby's boyfriend, and their cousin, I think. I haven't met them but we have a group text and they seem cool."

"One thing your dad and I talked about," I said, "is that he wanted me to ask you for the address of the cabin. Just so someone knows where you are."

"What, for the police report? When I disappear too?" Shelby made a frustrated groan. "Fine. Whatever."

"Hey, it's a not a bad idea. Someday, when you're old too, you'll *wish* people cared about where you were."

She pulled out her phone and tapped at the screen, her face illuminated in a pale white glow. "I'll text it to you when Miriam finds out," she said.

"Thank you."

She gave me a small smile. "Is he going to be like this for the rest of my life?"

"Probably."

She sighed again. "When I say I live in Belmont, people are like, *OMG, did you ever see the guy, do you know where it happened?* And I don't want to talk about it. I don't want that to be the one thing about me, you know?"

"Yeah. I know." I touched the rubbery scar on my wrist. I didn't want Belmont to be the one thing about me, either. The one case I solved. The one time I made a difference. "Look, Shelby," I said, "I know it's hard right now. I don't want this situation to define either of us. And I really don't want you to have to come of age thinking you hate your father. That's what happened to me, and it screwed me up, a lot. So you can stay with me as long as you want. Not an official *move in here* situation, but you don't have to go home when you get back from Hocking Hills, if you aren't ready."

Shelby covered her mouth with her hand.

"But you can't cry," I added. I fanned at my face. "Because I will too."

"Okay," she said quickly, nodding, blinking fast.

"It's just that everyone should have somebody who makes things easier and not harder." I unfolded myself from the couch. I didn't have a person like that at the moment. Tom used to be it, but that wasn't the case anymore, it seemed. I felt a full-blown tantrum building behind my eyes and I needed to escape to the privacy of my bedroom before it happened.

Shelby was still nodding.

I held out my hand for a fist bump as I walked out of the room, and she tapped her knuckles lightly on mine.

FIFTEEN

The UPS notice was still on the door of Leila's building, and the neighbors still didn't want to talk to me when I checked on her place again in the morning. I hoped Catherine would come through soon with a means of getting to Leila, but antiquated printing processes might not be high on Leila's list of priorities at the moment. So I switched gears and decided to see if there was anything else I could learn about Agnes Harlow's potential relationship with Marin.

Sam Kinnaman lived with his daughter and her wife and kid in a twisty subdivision on the far outskirts of Dublin. I got lost back there for nearly ten minutes before realizing that there were somehow two streets with the exact same name, and eventually found my way to a medium brown gable-front with an open garage full of crap. I walked up to the house and heard a woman saying, with no small degree of frustration, "Brandy, please, those things *do not spark joy* and we're getting rid of them."

A little blond girl in a polka-dot sundress was sitting on the cement floor, flinging things out of a giant pile. "But this is mine and this is mine and I still want it," she whined. Then she saw me walking up the driveway and gave me a big smile. "Are you here for the yard sale?"

A woman poked her head around the corner, holding a dusty

French press and a strip of price stickers. "Can I help you?" She was about thirty, blond, clad head to toe in a lululemon outfit that probably cost more than my whole wardrobe. She looked wary of me.

"My name is Roxane, and I'm a private investigator," I started.

"Oh." She smiled and set down the coffeemaker. "I've had people coming up all morning, asking if they can shop. The sale isn't till Friday! You're the one he was telling us all about."

"I promise I won't even look at anything," I said. "Are you Sam's daughter?"

"Daughter-in-law," the woman said. "Molly. Sam's at his rehearsal—he's playing piano for a community-theater musical this summer. You look familiar. Have you been on TV?"

I shook my head, not wanting to get into it. "I just have one of those faces."

"Let me grab Suzy real quick. I'm sure Sam will be back in a few minutes but I know Suze will want to talk to you. Brandy, come with me, sweetheart."

Molly took her daughter's hand and they disappeared into the house through the garage. I perused a table stacked high with seventies-era cookbooks, touting the benefits of microwave ovens. One of them showed a whole turkey on the cover. Despite my firm lack of interest in cooking, I flipped it open, curious to see how exactly a whole turkey could be cooked in a microwave. Then the garage door opened again and a tall, short-haired woman in a chambray shirt came out. She had Sam's thick eyebrows and the Harlows' square jaw and she looked about ten or so years older than her wife. "The sale isn't till Friday," she said, then quickly added, "I'm kidding. Molly's very concerned about people trying to shop early."

I patted the cover of the cookbook. "I promise you, I wouldn't know what to do with a cookbook if my life depended on it."

Suzy Kinnaman led me over to the front porch, where we sat in those plastic Adirondack chairs that make you lean back awkwardly. A few seconds later, the garage door closed. It did not escape my notice that Sam's family did not seem to want me in their home or around their stuff, even the items that no longer sparked joy. "So Dad was telling us that you came by Brighton Lake yesterday," Suzy said eventually. "Can I ask, what about?"

"I'm looking into your mother's family. Your uncle's second wife, to be specific. Marin."

"Marin," Suzy said. She looked out at the lawn, chewing on her lip. "Yeah, I barely remember her. I went to college shortly after Bill married her."

"What do you remember?"

"I remember at Bill's funeral, she was wearing sunglasses. She and her kid, both in sunglasses. *Identical* sunglasses. It was so weird."

I waited, but that seemed to be all she was going to say. "So you didn't think much of her."

"She was fake. That's mostly what I remember about her. Fake. But also, I had other things to think about, back then. Like my mother being insane. My dull uncle's trash-bag trophy wife didn't really concern me much."

She said it with a bit of an edge, like her family was something she preferred to keep firmly in the past. "Of course," I said. "And your mother wasn't close with her either?"

Suzy kept her eyes on the grass. "No, but Agnes isn't close with anyone, really. Except the cats, maybe, and those cats weren't even hers. Why are you asking about Marin?"

"Well," I said, "she was killed last week."

"Killed?"

"Murdered."

"Whoa." She finally looked at me, her eyes going wide. "That's . . . awful. Wh—wow, that's crazy. She was murdered. What happened?"

"I'm not too sure yet, but the reason I'm here is that it took place in Victorian Village, near your mother's house."

"And you think—what?"

"I don't know. That's why I'm asking questions. As far as I can tell, she didn't have any other ties to the area. So I'm trying to figure out what might've happened. It could very well be a coincidence, and she was there for some other reason that I haven't come up with yet."

Suzy shrugged. "I'm not sure what to tell you. The house is empty. And I doubt my mother was in touch with anyone from Bill's family. She thought Marin was a shrew, just out to steal the Harlow family money. Which wound up being true, from what I remember hearing, but all of that was so long ago. I haven't even thought about her in years. The thing about Agnes," she said, "is you never know what's the illness and what's her. She can be so funny, so smart. But she can be really nasty. Even when she's taking her meds. So it's always been hard to have a relationship with her, for anyone."

"Including you."

"Including me. We're not close. I don't blame her for being sick, nothing like that. I just have to protect myself."

I nodded. "How often do you speak with her?"

She didn't answer for a while. "I saw her at Christmas," she said, looking away. "If you'll excuse me now, I have to get to work."

When I left the Kinnaman house, I rustled up a phone number for the Ohio Hospital for Mental Health and went through the prompts for the alphabetical staff directory to leave a message for A.J. Watson, Agnes's case manager. I asked him to call me back but figured he wouldn't, on account of patient privacy; still, it was worth a try. It seemed like he'd been in close contact with her when no one else had.

Then I called Georgette Harlow and asked if she could meet me for lunch, and an hour later we got together at 1808 on Winter Street. Paul, she told me, was at work, and was very sorry to miss another opportunity to dish about Marin, which didn't surprise me in the least. "But I told him, pettiness is my specialty, so I figure I can handle it," she said, plucking the olive out of her dirty martini. "So what's the latest?"

"Well," I said, "it's about your aunt."

Georgette's features twisted. "Agnes?"

"You sound disappointed."

"Not disappointed. Just . . . a person's slightly estranged, schizo aunt doesn't make for much of a story. What about her?"

I sliced into my salmon. "I think Marin had been in recent contact with her. There are still a lot of questions. And I know you aren't close with Agnes anymore, but you should probably know that she broke her hip in April. She's not doing well."

Georgette finished the martini, not her first. "Unfortunate."

"She's at a home called Brighton Lake in Upper Arlington, if you'd want to go see her."

"Goodness," she said, almost chuckling. "You know, it runs in the family. Mental illness. Dad said it's very likely his mother had it, but back then they just decided you were hysterical and that was that. He could get a bit blue himself, Dad could. He said Mother's genes must have had a stabilizing influence on Paul and me, thank heavens. Agnes probably gave Marin money. Probably didn't even know any better."

"Well, there's no evidence of that," I said. "But Marin was murdered behind Agnes's house."

"Grandmother's house."

"Uh—right. Anyway, Marin had no other ties to the area, and I don't think it was a coincidence."

"Agnes loathed Marin, is the thing. It was her idea to hire that private investigator who found out about her previous marriage. I think it was just because of the house. She didn't want Marin to get the house. Agnes wanted it, even though she already had Grandmother's. She was pretty stable at that time. She was between crackups. Speaking in sentences, at least, and not the John the Baptist and Herodias nonsense she says now."

I recalled the eerie way Agnes had hissed that word—*Herodias*—and wondered what it meant.

"Did Marin know? That Agnes was responsible for her being cut off?"

"I'm sure. It wasn't a secret or anything. God, I've been in such a good mood since the other day. Murdered." She shook her head, gleeful.

I was definitely starting to prefer the Kinnaman side of Agnes's family. "So Christmas was the last time you saw your aunt?"

Georgette flagged down a waiter for another martini. "Yes. We took her a plant, a poinsettia. She said she didn't want it, because of the cats. It's apparently poison for cats. But the cats live outside. She insisted that we take it with us because the cats might get the poison through the air. That's what she said. For the love of God, she's weird. Even before we found out she was actually crazy, she was always a little odd. Crazy is fun, for a while. I used to love it when Agnes came to visit. Of course, that was before Marin, before Mother died. She was strict, Mother was. No makeup, no drinking, no smoking. Agnes always smoked. And she'd curse like a sailor, goodness." She was starting to ramble now. "Then she started to get strange. The Pope was communing with her through her car's radio. It's almost funny."

I definitely liked the Kinnaman side better. I said, "Um."

"Oh, come on, like you'd take a claim like that seriously? She would say the wildest things. The pope! John the Baptist! At first everyone just thought that she was reconnecting with it. *The Church*—did you ever notice how Catholics say it like that? *The Church*. Agnes *loathed* Marin. Such a liar. Like her whole shtick about being John Junior's cousin—talk about a Catholic family, right? But we'd go to Mass for Christmas and it was like Marin had never even *heard* of the Bible . . ."

Something had been needling at me since Saturday, and now whatever it was gave me a sharp little twinge. "I'm sorry," I interrupted, setting my knife on the edge of my plate, "John Junior's cousin?"

Georgette finished her current martini and looked at me, a little wobbly. "You remember him. The airplane situation, his poor girlfriend, what a mess. You know, I always thought—"

"What are you talking about?"

"He was a pilot too, you know. Dad was." She reached for her drink and frowned at it when she saw that it was empty.

"Georgette. What does JFK Junior have to do with Marin?"

She blinked a few times. "Oh, didn't I tell you? She said she was a cousin. She said the 'K' in her name stood for Kennedy, when we all knew it was Kathleen. Right there on her driver's license. But no, she claimed she was part of the Kennedy clan. On the Lawford side. Which didn't even make any sense, because if that was true, why wouldn't she have *Lawford* in her name? Even her stories didn't make sense. Like I said, she was a shit liar, but people just want to believe you. I swear to God, that's all there is to life."

Pushing aside Agnes Harlow for a second, I tossed two twenties on the table to cover my lunch. "I have to go."

SIXTEEN

I ran into my apartment, almost tripping over the wheels of my desk chair in the process of lunging for the cigar box I'd found in Marin's dresser.

Her passport.

STRASSER, MARIN KENNEDY

I sat down heavily on the edge of my desk. "It's a fake," I said to the empty room. It had to be. Her name was Marin Kathleen. Kennedy was a dream, an aspiration. I briefly considered whether she might have had her name legally changed, but no—there would have been a paper trail for that.

I flipped on a light and squinted at the detail on the booklet's printed pages.

Intaglio, a printing technique used to get the fine line detail on money, Catherine had said.

Counterfeit green cards, my brother had said.

The passport was fake, someone in Arthur's print shop had made it, and I was willing to bet I knew who.

———

"Look at you," Catherine said when I got to her house. "Identifying medieval printmaking techniques on sight."

We were standing over her kitchen counter, Marin's fake passport and Catherine's real one on the granite surface between us. Up close, and in comparison to the genuine article, the counterfeit was easy to spot—the materials were a little too shiny, the colors were off, the patterns weren't as intricate. But in passing, it was damn good.

"Aside from the part where they swipe it, right? I don't know anything about fake passports but I have to imagine there's no way to fake that part. So what's the point?"

"I have no idea," I said. "But I bet people are willing to pay for something like this. I bet it would fool somebody."

Catherine picked it up and looked at Marin's picture. "In high school I had a fake ID. My neighbor made it in his basement. I was fifteen years old, buying beer, getting into shows. Nobody ever looked twice at it. There is no doubt in my mind that this would be able to fool somebody."

I sighed. Things were starting to make sense—not everything, but a lot of it. The police at Ungless Printing last week. Tom's insistence that I stay out of it. If passports were being manufactured at Arthur's shop, it was probably a federal case at the minimum, and a tangle of multiple jurisdictions at the most. It was easy to see how that was bad for Arthur. His business, his problem.

"I really need to talk to her," I said.

Catherine shrugged. "I sent her a Facebook message, but she didn't respond. It says she read it, though. Why does that feature exist? What I want to know is who invented *that*."

I had wondered such things myself, but that didn't matter at the moment. "What did your message say?"

"It just said *Hi, how are you?*"

I laughed. "You're terrible at modern life."

She elbowed me in the side, her eyes flashing. "I've never denied that. Anyway, I was trying to start a conversation first, rather than just drop an invitation on her out of the blue."

"Can you try again? Tell her . . . say you're trying to get rid of some supplies. Something to do with this intaglio crap. Ask her if she wants them."

Catherine lifted the lid of her laptop. "Okay, I can see how that's better than hi."

I watched over her shoulder as she typed a new message. *Hi again—sorry to bug you again—I have a huge box of aluminum plates and Charbonnel inks that I need to get rid of TODAY. No space in new studio. Reaching out to old students to see if there are any takers?*

She hit Enter and the message blooped across cyberspace. A second later, the message showed as *seen.*

And a few seconds after that, Leila Hassan responded.

Catherine set up the meeting for later that afternoon, to take place in front of Hopkins Hall, where her office was. "You can park in front of the building," she told me, "there's usually spots during the summer. I'll give her the box and then you can follow her or whatever you intend to do."

"You don't actually have to be there," I said, "I just need to get *her* to be there."

"I don't want her to think I'm some kind of asshole, what if she goes in the building and starts yelling about me?"

"She's a criminal. I don't think you need to worry about what she thinks of you. Also, I have never heard you express concern that someone might think you're an asshole."

Her eyebrows went up. "Hey, I'm helping you here."

"I know that, and I appreciate it immensely. But you don't have to actually give her anything."

But it turned out that Catherine did have a box of etching inks that she was trying to get rid of, so she packed it up and we drove up to campus in my car. I couldn't remember the last time I'd driven her around—the last time I'd had her in my car, we had been doing something other than driving—and I loved the way she looked to the right of me, her long blond hair whipping in the breeze from the open window, her delicate features in profile.

I shook my head at myself.

"What?" She glanced over at me, smiling coyly.

"Nothing. I'm just grateful for your help."

"Right."

"Really, I am."

I looked back to the road but I felt her eyes on me.

"Will you let me know what happens?"

I nodded as I pulled up alongside Hopkins Hall and parked behind a van. There were several open spots in front of the van— hopefully they'd stay that way, so Leila would park there and allow me to follow her easily. Catherine got her box out of the trunk and leaned down next to the door to say, "I mean it, I want to hear about what happens later."

She hefted the box onto one slim hip and disappeared into the building.

Twenty minutes later, a silver Audi with tinted windows pulled into the parking lane, and a woman got out. Her hair was curly, glossy, and dark, pulled back from her face in a low ponytail. Her left deltoid was tattooed with an ornate hamsa. She looked about five-six, fit, and very attractive. She was dressed in jeans and a sleeveless blue blouse, her eyes hidden behind oversize sunglasses. Someone sat in the passenger seat, but I couldn't make out anything beyond a person shape. Leila looked up at the building, then at her phone, repeating this gesture every few seconds until Catherine pushed open the door to the building and came out with the box.

It was almost absurd how well this ruse had worked. I couldn't hear their exchange but Leila looked pleased with the box as she smiled and nodded at Catherine and said what looked like *yes, totally* several times. Then she loaded the box into her trunk and got into the car.

I shot Catherine a thumbs-up through my open window and, after giving Leila a head start of a few seconds, I followed.

We drove to a furniture consignment store in Clintonville, where Leila went in for a few minutes and returned with a modest wad of cash. Then a jewelry store, where she came out empty-handed. I still couldn't see into the car well enough to identify who she was riding with.

From there, we went north on High Street, past Morse, past my mother's street, and up to 161. Toward Arthur's office.

No, *to* Arthur's office.

Leila turned into the stucco office park, but instead of driving straight back to the building that housed the print shop, she turned right and went to the far end of a building that ran perpendicular to Arthur's. I kept going north, not wanting to out myself as a tail by following her into the lot.

Instead, I turned in to the next driveway—a water-treatment plant—and rolled slowly up to a fence so I could see the stucco building through the rusty chain-link. I felt around in my backseat for a pair of binoculars and found them tangled in a bra that I did not think was mine. But that mystery would have to wait. I hopped out of the car and peered at the stucco building. There were three vehicles parked directly in front of it—Leila's, a white delivery van, and Vincent Pomp's shiny Crown Vic. Leila's trunk was open. Dropping off the intaglio supplies? I focused on the door to the suite, which bore the residue of vinyl letters that had been recently removed. I watched for a few seconds, sweat pooling at the small of my back in the afternoon sun. Then Leila came back out of the office, with Pomp behind her. He looked bad, his face pale, shirt wrinkled. He skimmed a hand down her upper arm but she shook him off, inclining her head toward the car.

That was interesting.

Then she slammed the trunk closed and climbed into the vehicle, while Pomp stood in the lot, looking lost.

I followed Leila out of the maze of offices and we merged onto 71 going north, Leila and her mystery passenger in the passing lane, me in the center lane a bit behind her. With the AC cranking, my body temperature began to come down from hyperthermic levels. I leaned back, put Emily Haines on my aftermarket sound system, and nonchalantly kept an eye on her car.

The silver Audi went west on 270 and made a quick exit onto High Street, southbound.

When we reached 161 and headed east again, I sat up straighter.

We were sort of going back the way we came.

Leila kept driving past Arthur's print shop and got back on 71, going south this time.

I hung back a quarter mile at first, unsure of what was happening. Had she noticed me? Not likely, unless she really had an eye out for a tail. Sure, my car was distinct, but not in heavy midday traffic. And though caution might not have been one of my virtues, I was pretty good at following people.

Leila's car maintained a steady speed rather than zooming away from me. So maybe she hadn't noticed me. Maybe she was just an absent-minded driver. I gave it five miles before I got any closer. I kept to the outside lane, several cars and two lanes between the silver Audi and me.

Then Leila merged right so she was in the lane beside me and braked suddenly.

I shot ahead a few car lengths.

The silver Audi eased over one more time. Right behind me.

Now *I* had the tail.

I looked to the rearview mirror. Leila's eyes were concealed behind the sunglasses. She was smiling, gesturing mildly, the way you do when you chat with a friend. She didn't look like she was paying attention to me at all.

Through the less tinted glass of the windshield, I could finally make out her passenger.

Cheekbones that could cut glass.

It was Nate Harlow.

A twisty feeling of dread wound through my torso. Even though I was in front, I was no longer in charge of this situation.

I exited the freeway at Eleventh.

They exited too.

"Okay," I muttered. I flipped off the radio. I needed the silence so I could concentrate. I drove west toward campus for a while, then left on Summit. So did the Audi. But I stayed in the inside lane, while the Audi sped up in the center lane. Pedal to the floor, like we were drag racing. I sped up too because I didn't want to lose her.

Sixty.

Seventy.

Too fast for this street.

I let up off the gas a bit, crying uncle.

Then it happened.

The Audi swerved in front of me without warning, braking hard. I slammed on my own brakes but there was nowhere to go, no way to avoid it at that speed, barely even time to brace myself as I plowed into the right half of the Audi's bumper. The impact was deafening—metal crunching and groaning, my windshield spiderwebbing up the side—but the sound was nothing compared to the jolt of it, the seat belt biting into my throat as it yoked me back.

For a second I couldn't get any air into my lungs, couldn't move. The collision spun the Audi ninety degrees and into the next lane. I sat there with a hand over my chest, trying to relax the muscles in my throat enough to allow a breath.

Meanwhile, a station wagon with a ladder tied to the roof rack had stopped behind me. I fumbled with the buckle on my seat belt as a pair of young guys in hipster attire—white tees, skinny jeans—ran toward me.

"Oh my God, are you okay?" one of them said.

The passenger door of Leila's car opened and Nate got out, rubbing his shoulder. "Is everybody okay here?" he said. He was taller than I would have guessed, six-two or so, lanky but strong. His hair was short on the sides and longer on top, like a fifties heartthrob's. He was clean-cut, good-looking, his eyes muddy brown like a roadside ditch, hard and shallow.

Leila emerged too, shaken. "I am so sorry," she said, "there was a cat, a small white cat, did you see it?"

"I saw it, babe," Nate said. "It got away. Don't worry. And don't say you're sorry."

He looped an arm around her waist.

What the hell was going on here? I finally got in a breath and opened my door and struggled out of the car. I said, "I just want to talk to you."

They both blinked at me like they were innocent as lambs.

"I called the police," one of the hipsters said. "That made the loudest fucking sound. How fast were you going?"

"No—" I wheezed.

"You're bleeding, you need a doctor," Leila said. Her accent was soft and I couldn't place it; something like Beirut by way of

London. Her eyes went to the base of my throat. I touched the area, found a wide gash and a slick of blood, courtesy of the seat belt. "Here," she continued, thrusting a wad of tissues at me. "I'm really sorry. So, so sorry."

Nate said, "It wasn't your fault, babe. She was speeding. Don't say anything else."

"You were in an accident," the other hipster kid said to me, his eyes wide with concern. "Do you know where you are?"

I pressed the tissues to my neck and glanced at the front end of my car: broken headlights and some damage to the fender and hood, but it in no way looked like it had been through the same accident it felt like I had. I was dizzy, and I balanced with my hand against the doorframe.

"That old German craftsmanship," Nate said. "It's why you drive a car like that, right? If you're gonna be reckless, I guess you should."

"Hey, dude, chill out. She's hurt. Maybe you should sit down, ma'am," the first kid said.

"Who are you?"

He looked at me, alarmed now. "Brian Peters?" he said.

I heard sirens wailing toward us. It wouldn't be much longer.

I looked at his friend next. "Austin O'Neil."

"I am so sorry, really," Leila said. Tears welled up in her eyes, and Nate made a sympathetic noise. I started to wonder if I was losing my mind. "The cat—I was only thinking of the cat. I didn't even know you were behind me."

The hipsters nodded assent. "It happened so fast."

"Did *you* see a cat?" I demanded of them.

"Maybe she hit her head or something."

"No, I did not hit my head—"

"Just try to stay calm, hon," Leila said, patting my shoulder.

SEVENTEEN

A paramedic listened to my lungs and looked down my throat and into my eyes with a penlight and then she pronounced me A-okay. "You'll be sore for a few days, but that's it. Good thing you didn't hit your head."

Jesus, everyone was awfully concerned with my head.

"Lucky girl," Officer Stan Kelly was saying. "Those old European imports are built like tanks. Plus you got your guardian angel looking out for you, Roxie—your dad."

I nodded, impatient. Stan Kelly had known my father—like every other cop in the city—and I supposed I should've been grateful to be dealing with a semi-familiar face. But I was barely able to restrain myself from telling him to shut up. One, I wasn't in the mood for his patriarchal condescension, and two, I was trying to hear what Leila and Nate were saying to the other uniform down the block.

It wasn't going well.

They were standing up the sidewalk in front of a row of town houses. Leila glanced over at me a few times, but she didn't look nervous, anxious, or impatient—just friendly, happy to help, moderately concerned. I squinted at her, half wondering if the crash had wiped my memory clean somehow. Maybe this woman wasn't the one I'd followed at all. Because she certainly wasn't acting like someone who'd made me as a tail and then staged an elaborate intervention.

"I'll tell you what, they don't make them like they used to," Stan Kelly went on. "Even a brand-new Benz wouldn't hold up like this, but some of these new little subcompact rice burners you see on the road? Forget about it—we'd be picking you out of a ball of tin foil after that."

"Okay," I said, having heard enough at that point. "Listen, is this going to take much longer? I'd really like to—"

"Aw, no you don't. There's nothing more important than your safety, Roxie." He was talking to me like I was a silly twelve-year-old. "Now just sit tight for one second, okay?"

I leaned against the busted hood of my car and watched as Kelly chatted with his partner. I closed my eyes and tried to come up with a way to breathe that didn't hurt my whole body.

I opened my eyes when I heard a jangle of keys approaching me.

"Hello," Nate said.

He wasn't smiling anymore. Without the all-American smile, his features turned cold.

Especially when I noticed that he was holding a small switchblade.

I barely had time to react before he plunged it into my driver's-side rear tire and sliced a jagged hole in the wall of it as the Audi rolled up beside us, its busted bumper trailing dangerously close to the ground.

Nate said, "Good luck following this time."

He got into the car, and they drove away.

"Fuck," I muttered, slapping my hood. A bad idea. It sent a jolt of pain through my chest and down my arm.

"Everything okay?" Kelly called as he walked back over to me.

"Yeah, great," I said. I reached into the car to pop the trunk for my spare. "I might need a hand with this, though."

Kelly took in my tire. "Well, how the heck did that happen?"

I shook my head and tried to extract information about Leila and Nate from him, but he wouldn't play. Then he explained that the hipsters had seen me speeding, so it was impossible to tell who was at fault here: Leila for cutting me off, or me for failing to yield.

"But it really is your lucky day," he said, heaving a jack out of my trunk and onto the pavement. "Any other cop and you probably woulda got a citation, Frank Weary's kid or not."

Strangely enough, I didn't feel so lucky.

As I walked into my apartment I called out Shelby's name, mostly to determine if she was there so I could strip in the hallway and pour a drink immediately. I was dirty and sweaty from changing the tire, and I also looked like someone had tried to slit my throat.

"In the kitchen," she called back.

I stopped in the bedroom to swap out my shirt for a tank top. As I got closer to the kitchen, I smelled freshly baked bread and rosemary. I said hey and stood in the doorway, taking in Shelby's expression of abject horror as she brandished a small canister of garlic powder. "This expired *nine years* ago."

"Shit."

"Seriously, how does someone who owns a brand-new bread maker not even have spices bought in this decade?"

I toed the now-open bread maker box. "It was a gift." I wasn't even sure who'd given me the bread maker, or when. I had a number of similar appliances stacked in one corner of my kitchen, gifts from someone who mistakenly believed I had interest in food preparation beyond guessing the correct amount of water to make a bowl of instant oatmeal. Measuring cups might have been a better gift, come to think of it. I tried to ignore the siren song of the liquor cabinet and added, "I'm more curious about what happened nine years ago that made me buy garlic powder in the first place."

"It was probably left over from whoever lived here before."

We both laughed.

"I'm making pasta, if you want me to—" She stopped as she finally looked up at me. "OMG, Roxane! What happened?"

I touched my neck. I wasn't used to having someone in my house to observe what condition I was in when I returned. "Fender bender," I said. "It's okay, the car is mostly okay, I'm fine."

Hands on her hips, she studied me. "Is that true?"

"Yeah, it's just," I said as I leaned against the doorway, "it hurts, but it isn't the end of the world. I see you figured out how to use the gas stove."

She nodded. "YouTube. You should go rest or something. And I can make you up a plate when this is done. Okay?"

I nodded, though I didn't particularly want spaghetti.

I wanted a drink.

Shelby was here.

So I shouldn't.

But I wanted one. It was like an itch, but in my brain. An itch with a very specific remedy.

I brushed my teeth—a sorry excuse for whiskey, but at least a minty-fresh flavor to enjoy for a while—and sat down at my desk, forcing myself to ignore the itch.

I opened my laptop and looked over the info I'd pulled the other day on Leila Hassan. It revealed no new information. I didn't know what to make of her. Especially now that I knew she was willing to wreck her own car to keep me from following her further.

Unless there really was a small white cat.

I gingerly touched my collarbone.

There hadn't been a cat.

I tried the hipster boys next—Brian and Austin, both of whom had a completely normal digital life. Facebook, Change.org petitions, swim-team results, a gaming forum. Too normal to be anything other than normal. So they probably *were* just Good Samaritans.

I was furious at myself, though I didn't know how I could've avoided it. Hang back further, maybe. Not follow in the first place.

I opened a new browser tab and tried to figure out whose office Leila and Vincent Pomp had been in, turning up a website for a defunct restaurant furniture sales catalog.

That probably wasn't it.

I stared aimlessly at the internet for another few minutes, until Shelby appeared with two plates of spaghetti.

"It's nothing special," she said, "but I saw from the dishes in your sink that you usually eat peanut butter for dinner."

"Not just peanut butter," I said. I moved to the couch, trying not to wince with every step. "Sometimes I have a piece of cheese."

She cracked up. "You do need a role model."

"Well, here you are."

"I would've had us eat in the dining room, but you have stuff all over the table and I wasn't sure if it was clues."

I laughed. "I wish it was clues. Pretty sure it's just laundry. Clean, I think. Thank you for making dinner. I'll move the crap on the table." I looked over at my computer. "Eventually. Definitely by tomorrow."

"Well, take your time. I'm going to that cabin tomorrow. And I know you're a total workaholic and you're going to look for clues on your computer all night, not put away your laundry."

I spun a hank of spaghetti onto my fork and chewed. I wouldn't have described myself as a workaholic, not exactly. Just a person with an obsessive need to resolve the things that I got paid to resolve. "I'm pretty boring," I said. "When I have a case, all I do is work. When I don't have a case, I mostly just sleep."

"Is that why people hire you? Because you can solve their cases in two days?"

"Sometimes. Or sometimes it's because they want a detective who isn't a jerk. There are a lot of jerks in the business. People assume because I'm a lady that I won't be a jerk. Fools them every time."

"Very funny."

We chewed in silence for a while. Then she said, "Do you like being a detective?"

I thought about that. It was an oddly complicated question. It almost didn't matter if I liked it, because it was the only thing I could do. I needed to do it, whether I wanted to or not. It was impossible to imagine being anything else. But I said, "I think so. It's satisfying, to figure things out. And some of the time I help people. And that's good too."

"But it's dangerous."

"It's honestly not usually dangerous. It's usually just Googling stuff."

"What kind of case are you working on now?"

"I'm not sure yet. You're nosy enough to be a detective yourself." I set down my fork. "But don't do that. Real job security is in being a dental hygienist. People are always gonna need their teeth cleaned." She looked at me blankly, so I added, "That's what my dad used to tell me. He was deeply disappointed when I showed zero aptitude for hygiene."

"My dad wants me to be a chef," Shelby said. "And I thought I wanted that too, I mean, I do like cooking. But cooking doesn't help people. And there are a lot of people who need help."

"It can help people. Anything can."

"I guess that's true."

I wondered if I was actually helping anyone right now, though.

———

I couldn't sleep. Part of it was the bruise blooming across my sternum. But most of it was my brain. Tessa Pomp's funeral was at ten in the morning, and I was planning to go—whatever I had witnessed between Vincent and Leila that afternoon made me think she might be there, and I didn't know how else to get back on her trail. That was hours away, though, and didn't do anything about right now.

Shortly after three, I gave up. Usually when I couldn't sleep, I'd just put on some music and start the day early. But Shelby was the next room over. I didn't want to wake her up, and I also didn't want her to worry. I crept out of my bedroom and made myself a cup of tea, snatching the kettle off the burner just before it started to make noise. I poured the hot water over a chamomile teabag, added the smallest splash of whiskey, and took my computer out to the porch. The night air was almost cool, but not quite. The street was dark and quiet. Everyone was sleeping, even Bluebird upstairs.

That, at least, was a blessing.

I lay down on my porch swing, knees bent over the armrest. Disorienting, but if I tilted my head backward, my torso stopped aching and I could almost see actual stars above downtown. I was frustrated. Usually, case-related frustration stemmed from being unable to find out anything. But here, I'd uncovered quite a lot—I just didn't know what it meant, or how it fit. On one hand, there was Marin Strasser—shot to death behind her ex-sister-in-law's house—some long-standing family resentment, and contested legal documents galore. On the other hand, there was the shooting at the print shop, where a document-forging operation had probably been taking place right under my client's nose. I knew I should ask him about it, but at the same time, I didn't want to talk to him. I knew what he'd say. He'd say he didn't know, which wouldn't mean anything. The only thing linking these two separate paths seemed to be Leila. She was in the middle of everything—she was Marin's friend, according to Arthur, though he originally told me his fiancée didn't have any friends; she lived in Vincent Pomp's building and delivered supplies to a secret office; she was in some sort of a relationship with Nate.

Among the many question marks peppered through what I knew so far was Agnes Harlow. Marin's death had taken place near her home—but why? I was deep in the weeds with Agnes's family, but they seemed pretty certain that Marin hadn't been in Agnes's life since her brother died.

I closed my eyes as I rocked slowly back and forth, thinking.

Marin had already shown aptitude for selling off antiques owned by the Harlow family, and from what I could tell, Agnes's house was full of them. I wondered if the neon thermometer that Rudy Carmichael posted about had come from Agnes, somehow.

I yawned, and told myself to get up and go back to bed so I didn't fall asleep on the porch.

EIGHTEEN

Of course I fell asleep on the porch. I woke up shortly after seven, the rising sun directly in my face. My spine was stiff and my feet were numb from hanging off the armrest for a few hours. For a moment I was confused. Then I remembered why I'd come out here—to solve my case with my computer and a cup of tea. At the thought of my computer I jerked upright, terrified that it had been stolen because I didn't see it on the ledge. Then I spotted it on the small plastic table next to the swing. Shelby must have seen me asleep out here and moved it; if she hadn't, then I'd been visited by a ghost or an unusually considerate thief.

After I took a quick shower, I dropped the car off at Joshua's garage and let them arrange a loaner for me, a white Ford Focus that smelled like new car and old ketchup. Joshua wasn't in yet, which was just as well because one, I still felt guilty, and two, I was wearing a bit of a disguise and I didn't want to explain myself. I had on a sleeveless turtleneck to cover the bruise on my throat, with a grey pencil skirt and black heels. I'd put on eyeliner, located a pair of glasses, and pulled my hair back into a twist secured by all of the bobby pins I could find in my bathroom. The effect was, I had to admit, a little jarring. I looked like an important lady on her way to work at Jones Day. Between my getup and the new car, I thought I might stand half a chance of staying incognito at the funeral.

I hadn't been inside Saint Joseph since my father died. Then, the rows of the cathedral behind us were all filled. Today, though, it felt the way I remembered it from being a kid, cavernous and cold— impossibly empty with its dramatically vaulted ceilings, its arched concrete pillars hulking along the length of the nave. I slipped in a few minutes before the service was supposed to start and took a seat in a pew at the back of the crowd, looking around for Leila as discreetly as I could.

The organ swelled up with "Amazing Grace" and everyone turned to face the altar. As Tessa's casket was carried forward and her family filed in somberly, I hoped they found more comfort in the ritual than I had at Frank's funeral. But it was hard to say. Vincent and his wife, both impeccably dressed in black, walked rigidly next to each other, a conspicuous gap between them. Two young men followed behind, mid-twenties, tall and thick, uncomfortable in suits. As they passed, I recognized one of them from the night of the shooting. Derek. He'd shaved and gotten a haircut, but it was clearly the same person. The other guy was a little older, a little more put together, but they had the same features—I figured this was Simon. Tessa's other brother. The crowd of people in attendance ran the gamut from churchy ladies, to uneasy middle-aged dudes who looked like they were worried about their souls, to a handful of young women in a group near my spot in the back. Tessa's friends, maybe. I saw two men who looked like cops—the haircut, the suits. None of them noticed me as I sat there with my nose in a hymnal, discreetly scanning faces.

Nothing happened till a woman a few rows in front of me went up to the lectern to do the first reading. As people shifted to let her out into the aisle, I caught the profile of someone sitting at the end of the pew. Shiny black hair, pulled away from her face with a wide, flat barrette. She turned her head enough for me to be able to tell it was Leila. Her features were pinched with real pain. It seemed real, anyway. She turned back to the front of the church.

At the lectern, the reader's voice was clipped and tight as she struggled through Wisdom 3:1–9—*And their departure was thought to be a disaster, and their going from us to be their destruction; but they are at peace.* I kept my face hidden behind the songbook and continued to watch Leila. She appeared to be alone, with the nearest person a respectful distance away.

When the service was over, I lingered outside, pretending to read a *Rite of Christian Initiation of Adults* pamphlet from a table near the door. I kept my nose down but watched Leila to see what she'd do, which turned out to be nodding somberly at one of the brothers, brushing past Ruth Pomp without looking at her, touching Vincent Pomp on the sleeve and murmuring something, to which he nodded, his hand lingering at her hip.

I lurked in a corner of the small, dark lobby, watching the exchange. Pomp shook his head, cupped her shoulder. Ruth Pomp stood in the doorway with her sons, her features stunned. The guys who looked like cops were outside the church by now, eyes on the Pomp brothers. Leila wore a black sheath dress and a grey cardigan with tiny pearl buttons. Her eyes were caramel-colored and rimmed in kohl. She was beautiful. I'd noticed that yesterday but it was even more apparent now, in this intimate moment they clearly thought no one else was going to see.

Finally, Pomp broke away from Leila, glanced at his wife, then looked up at me, a bit surprised. He gave me a somber, funereal nod but didn't come over. Instead he joined Ruth and they filed out onto the steps, still not touching or even acknowledging each other. Leila watched them, then looked at the floor, then just started walking over to me.

Her arms were folded over her chest. At first she didn't say anything. She looked mad and scared at the same time. "You have no idea what you're doing," she told me finally. "We need to go somewhere else."

We went across the street to SuperChef's and got a table by the wall. She hadn't said a word since we left the church and as we sat there, she seemed like she might not say anything now either. Her features had a current of energy in them. I said, "So do you want to tell me what we're doing here?"

She squeezed a lemon wedge into her iced tea. "You work for Arthur."

I nodded. "How did you know?"

"I Googled you. You're a private detective. Marin was all worked up about a private detective Arthur hired to follow her. And now you're following *me*. Context clues."

"Maybe *you* should be a detective."

"I already have a vocation."

"Which is?"

"I am a problem solver. An efficiency expert. The shortest distance between two points is a straight line, and all that."

"Archimedes."

She smiled faintly. "Smart girl."

"Sometimes. But what does Archimedes have to do with you?"

"I would rather have a conversation than follow somebody around, trying to guess what they're about."

"Touché."

"Not everyone shares this vocation, though. And I'm not just talking about you, but about many people I know. This makes them impatient, which makes them dangerous. So here is what we'll do: You tell me what it is you are trying to accomplish by showing up at this funeral, and I will see if I can help."

This wasn't what I had been expecting. I took a bite of my croissant and used the time to think about what to say. After a brief silence, I said, "Now you want to help me?"

She gave me that smile again. "I'm trying to get rid of you. I need you to stay away from me, and I suspect that only happens if I throw you a bone. I could just lie to you, send you off in the wrong direction altogether, chasing shadows. But I like efficiency. So I'm just being honest to save us both time. Tell me what you want."

I didn't trust a single thing about her. But I was curious where this would go. "Who are all these people you know?"

"I have many associates. Many friends," she said. I still couldn't place the accent.

"Like Vincent Pomp."

"Sure."

"You're involved with him."

A perfectly arched eyebrow went up a fraction of an inch. "You know more than you let on."

"I know that he owns your condo," I said, "and that you shared a tender moment back there a few minutes ago."

"So you're interested in Vincent. Something like this?"

I watched her for a few seconds, debating whether I should give up any ground to her. She had a point. Having a conversation did save time, especially if she could fill in some gaps for me. "Like you said, I work for Arthur. The police think he shot Marin, and I want to prove he didn't."

Leila sipped her tea. "That is too bad," she said.

"Why?"

"This is not something I can help you with. I don't know who shot Marin."

"One of your many friends, maybe?"

"Marin was among my friends. We're all reeling from what

happened. But I don't know why she's dead. Is there anything else you want?"

I nodded at the church across the street. "I want to know who killed Tessa Pomp and put Arthur in the hospital."

Leila's eyebrows went together. "You're hurting my feelings," she said, "only wanting things I can't give you. Knowing this is what *I* want. But I don't know who killed Tessa. It would be very lucrative for me if I knew. But I don't."

"Lucrative," I said.

"Vincent is grieving the death of his only daughter. He wants to know who has done this, so this person can be dealt with. If I knew, he would be dealt with already and you would not need to look for him."

"Or her."

"Or her," Leila said. She smiled again. There was no warmth in it, but it was not entirely cold somehow. "So let's try once more, see if we can find something you want that I can give you."

"Let's talk about the passports, then."

"I have nothing to do with that."

"Is that right."

"What, because I'm brown you assume I'm a terrorist?"

"No, not at all," I said, "but somebody over there is making passports. And you're the intaglio expert."

"This is what you want to know about?"

"Among other things, yes."

She studied her nails, which were painted blood red. "Here's a little story. One of Arthur's clients is the local UFCW. That's United Food and Commercial Workers. We were to make membership ID cards for them, on card stock. Hundreds a week, because turnover is high. Print, cut, laminate. So Arthur bought this machine. The Datacard. It prints on PVC, it does magnetic keycard access, holograms. Like what they have at your bureau of motor vehicles. I found it to be an inspiring device, so I began to play with it. Driver licenses and whatnot. There is a market for this, you see. Harmless, mostly. Kids who want to buy beer."

I thought about that. "You started out selling counterfeit driver's licenses," I said. I grasped for one of the terms my brother had thrown out yesterday. "Tor. Dark net. Bitcoin."

She smiled. "Yes. A nice girl like me, if you can imagine! Taking money from Reddit-obsessed seventeen-year-old boys, and the occasional person with a secret. It was an okay gig. Good money. I made the mistake of telling my lover about how well this was going."

"Mistake?"

"Vincent sent me some business, here and there. Marin, for example. Before he was with me, he was with her. But eventually he suggested I cut his younger son in, and for some reason, I listened. Derek, a boy in need of a vocation."

"So you got him a job at Ungless Printing."

She nodded. "To help me produce these things. Everything was going fine, but Derek wanted more, more, more. Before long he wanted to make OSU IDs, security badges, he wanted to do every state in the country, he knew people in Windsor and wanted to do Ontario driver licenses, he wanted to do green cards. Things escalated. I told him passports were a bad idea. Much too difficult. I'm an artist, but Derek—not an artist. I said no."

"You did?"

"In your spy movies, you've heard of honor among thieves? There are lines you can cross, and there are lines you don't. This far and no further. The people in the market for a fake passport are not good people. And the risk was much greater."

"But the intaglio class," I said. "You tried."

Her eyes narrowed slightly. She didn't know that I knew about that. "I tried. I was curious. But I was right. Too difficult. So Derek found someone else to help."

I thought for a second about what I knew of Arthur's business. "Bobby Veach."

She nodded.

"And then he and Derek figured out a way to get rid of you."

She nodded.

"By making up a story about copier toner."

Another nod.

"And then what?"

She tapped the screen of her phone, checking the time. "My ride will be here any minute. You're running out of questions."

I paused and took another bite of croissant so I could think. Then I said, "Tell me about Nate."

Instead of answering, she glanced up at the window behind me.

I turned around to see a white Cadillac parking at one of the meters on Broad Street.

The same white Cadillac that had been at Arthur's office the night of the shooting.

And Nate Harlow got out of the driver's side.

I felt my heart speed up. "I thought you didn't know who shot Tessa," I said, staring at the car.

"I don't."

"That car was there that night," I said, "I saw it. I was there too."

Leila didn't react at all. "Nice try. But no."

"Oh, so you really didn't know that."

Now she pressed her mouth into a thin line. "It's time for me to go."

Nate strode into the restaurant and dragged a chair from an empty table over to ours. He leaned in and kissed Leila long and deep, and it seemed more like an exchange of power than a romantic gesture. They had a very different dynamic than Leila did with Vincent Pomp. That had been intimate. This was not. Finally Nate pulled away and said, "So what's good here."

"Nate, baby," Leila said, discreetly wiping her mouth, "we're not staying."

"That's quite a car," I said. I stole a glance at Leila, who was staring down at her nails, rattled. "Looks like a Coupe de Ville, '61?"

Nate gave me a big grin. "Close. A Series 60. You know your cars."

"In my line of work, you learn a little bit about a lot of things. Get really good at recognizing something you've seen before. I saw a car very much like that the other night, in fact, when I was trying to stop your mother's fiancé from bleeding to death."

Leila opened her mouth to say something, but Nate beat her to it, laughing as if I'd told a real knee-slapper. "That seems unlikely, doesn't it," he said, "that you'd see two different Series 60s in the space of a couple days. But I suppose stranger things have happened. We live in a crazy world. Crazy. But don't talk about my mother."

He threw the last part in almost as an aside, but his eyes went even darker.

"Excuse me?"

"She was *terrified* of you," he hissed, his smile disappearing.

"What? She had no idea I was there."

He watched me coldly. "You're a liar, too, then. You *don't* get to talk about her."

"Okay, listen, I only want to figure out who killed her—"

"I said, *you don't talk about her.*" He raised his voice enough that the other people in the restaurant glanced over at us, eyebrows raised.

"Nate, baby, we should go," Leila said, her voice going syrupy-sweet as she slipped her arm through his, "we should go."

Nate allowed her to pull him to his feet. His eyes never left mine, and the contrast between his earnest good looks and the dead-inside hollowness of his gaze gave me chills. He leaned in as if he was going to kiss me on the cheek, but instead he grabbed my shoulder. He knew exactly where to dig his thumb in, just above my collarbone where the bruise was its most colorful. The air rushed out of my lungs for a second. "You'll see how it feels," he whispered, "how about that?"

Leila said, "Now, Nate."

She pulled him out of the restaurant. I sat there, a hand over my chest, a tight band of pain humming across my sternum. My rental car was parked across the street and there was no way I could get to it in time to follow them to wherever they were going. But before they reached the Caddy, I got to my feet and took a picture of Leila through the window. She saw me but didn't react, just turned to face me, almost posing, her mouth pressed into a thin, sad line.

NINETEEN

When I got to my apartment, Shelby was in the front room, folding a stack of towels. "You look fancy," she said.

I dropped my computer bag next to the table in my entryway and ditched my high heels and shook my hair out of its elaborate twist. "A failed attempt at going undercover." I nodded at the towels. "You didn't have to do that."

"I also washed the sheets from the bed. I didn't want to leave you without any clean linens."

I sat down on the edge of my desk, watching her do a complicated thing with a fitted sheet so it folded up neatly. "So do you know where this cabin is and all that? I promised your dad I'd get the address."

"Oh, right." She placed the folded sheet on top of the basket and took her phone out of her back pocket. "I tried to be, like, chill about it. When I asked. I thought Miriam was way cooler than me, but she was just like oh yeah, my mom is super overprotective too. So she gets it." She tapped the screen a few times and my own phone buzzed a few seconds later. "There you go."

"Thanks."

She tossed her phone onto the couch next to the laundry. "It's near Logan so it's on the close part of Hocking Hills. It's only like an hour away."

"Shel, you're eighteen years old. You don't have to convince me. If you want to go to the *far* side of Hocking Hills, you can. And should. Just know that if you're ever in a situation that doesn't feel right to you, just call me, that's all you have to do."

Shelby's phone chimed and she looked down at it, grinning.

"That's her. She's here. Roxane, thank you for, you know. For listening. For getting it."

I waved a hand. "We can do the emotional thank-you later. You have a date. So go. Have fun. Lots of kissing."

She rolled her eyes, but she couldn't hide how excited she was. "Okay. Bye."

"Let me know how it goes," I called as she grabbed her phone and backpack and dashed out.

I stood there in my silent, empty apartment for a while, not sure what to do. I could peel my shirt off with abandon, at least, but I couldn't help but feel lonely. I grabbed a whiskey bottle and a coffee mug from the kitchen and lay on my bed in my skirt and bra for a few minutes. Then I sat up and splashed a little whiskey into my cup and swallowed half of it.

It was hot going down. For a second, it made me forget about everything. I tossed back the rest and put the bottle on my nightstand instead of pouring another. I wanted to forget about everything, but I shouldn't.

Leila confused me. Nate alarmed me. I had no idea what I was supposed to make of any of it. She insisted that Nate wasn't involved in Marin's death—and, in fact, he thought *I* might have been—but she seemed rattled by the idea that he might have been involved in Tessa's. If nothing else, his car was. The circumstances were already hard to follow, and I hadn't even gotten to the matter of Agnes Harlow yet.

I changed into jeans and a tank top and sat down at my desk for the illusion of productivity. There was no proof of anything here, not really. Even Marin's passport didn't count, since the object itself didn't prove where it came from. And none of it explained why she was dead.

Could Nate have killed her?

He was obviously capable of it. I knew that much. But why would he?

"Why were you there, dammit?" I asked the apartment.

I got up and paced the length of my hallway, twice. I could have another drink, but I didn't really want one. No, that wasn't true. I wanted another drink, but only as a stand-in for what I actually wanted, which was to solve my case.

I sat down again and Googled Herodias.

A princess of the Herodian Dynasty of Judaea during the time of the Roman Empire.

Not terribly relevant to my case.

I kept reading.

Herodias is most famous for her role in having John the Baptist beheaded after he criticized the illegality of her marriage.

I leaned forward. Illegality of her marriage. That did seem relevant. Some mix of mandatory theology classes in high school and English in college gave me a partial narrative of that story: Salome and her dance, the king offering her anything her heart desired. So she talked to her mother about what she should ask for, settling on the head of John the Baptist, on a platter. Her mother, Herodias.

I rubbed the place between my eyebrows. Agnes had hissed *Herodias* when I first mentioned Marin. Did that mean anything at all? Was Marin Herodias?

The garage door of the Kinnaman house was up again, with Molly and her daughter still hard at work on the garage sale. "Hi again.

Suzy isn't home. But Sam's around back," Molly said, pointing toward the rear of the house with a ski pole.

I thanked her and walked over the bristly grass between the houses. Sam was sitting at a table on the deck, listening to something through white earbuds. He saw me approaching and pulled one out. "Hello there."

I climbed the steps and took a seat across from him. "Got a few more questions for you."

He hit pause on his music player and removed the other earbud. "Shoot."

"Agnes said something, the other day."

One of his bushy eyebrows went up but he didn't say anything.

"Herodias, that's what she said. When I mentioned Marin. Do you know why she said that?"

"Why?" Sam said. He looked at me a bit incredulously. "She's— it's a thought disorder. Schizophrenia is. It means her thoughts are not like our thoughts. They're all jumbled up. No, I have no clue why she said that."

"Have you ever heard her say it before?"

He paused for a second before saying, "Yes."

"Do you know when?"

"When I first got back to town, after her accident—she was talking a lot more then. But she said a lot of things. She'll recite the entire book of Revelation to you if you let her."

"Listen," I said, "I'd really like to ask her about it. But I don't want to do anything that would upset her, or be bad for her recovery."

He kept quiet again for a while. "She doesn't talk much in front of strangers," he said, "but maybe if I go with you. Maybe that would show her you're not the bad kind of stranger. We'll clear it with the staff first."

When we walked into the community center at Brighton Lake, several nurses greeted Sam by name. He responded warmly but muttered to me, "They just want my business. Ha! The joke's on them. I'm broke. Suze'll just put me on a raft and shove me out into the ocean when I can't take care of myself anymore."

"Oh, I'm sure that's not true."

He flapped a hand at me. "You're young. You don't know anything. Now, look here, it's Miss Zahra." He took my arm and pulled me toward a woman in a batik-print scrub top, who turned and beamed at us. "Nothing happens here that Miss Zahra doesn't know about, isn't that so."

They embraced. "Oh I don't know about that," Zahra said, smiling down at the older man. She was tall, dark-skinned, her hair woven into French-braid pigtails. She spoke with a lilting Ethiopian accent. "But I try, I try. Who's your friend, Sammy?"

"Zahra, Roxane, Roxane, Zahra. She's the nurse-manager in this joint. How's my girl doing today?"

"Oh, she went outside for a bit this morning, to watch the birds. She said she misses her cats. She's calm today, a little more lucid than she was when you were here last."

"Think she's up for a new visitor? I want to introduce her to my buddy Roxane."

Zahra nodded. "I think so." Her eyes flicked over to mine. "Ten or fifteen minutes at the most, though. Our Agnes gets overwhelmed easy."

I followed Sam down the hall to Agnes's room. Today she was holding the bible Sam had been reading from on Monday, running the thumb of her good hand over the edge of the pages. She looked up when we entered, her mouth folding into a distrustful grimace at the sight of me.

"It's okay," Sam said, "Agnes, I brought my friend with me. She's nice. Her name is Roxane. She'd really like to talk to you."

"Talk," Agnes said. She stared at me silently for a while. Then, her eyes flicking back and forth between Sam and me, she added, "You can talk to anyone."

I didn't know what to say. "I'd like to talk to you, though."

"It doesn't need to and shouldn't be me, not when there are spirits with poison darts in every corner of the fortress. I could talk about that, but I won't."

Sam took a seat beside her bed. "No, who needs to talk about that? Nobody."

"That's right. Nobody." She went quiet again, but her hands were still fiddling with the book, and her eyes were bouncing around the room. Her demeanor was very different from the other day. "Will you look at this?" she asked, pushing the book toward Sam. "I looked but I think it happened again. The words. They came loose. I can't read them when they're loose. Are you fucking her?"

"What—Agnes, Lord have mercy, no. We're friends. Roxane, come, sit down."

I didn't want to do that. But I sat on the edge of the other chair.

"You should fuck her. Or someone. Before you die. Not that you'll die until five thousand years but there's no sense in wasting the now." She looked at me. "Do you speak? Because for someone who wants to talk, you aren't."

My heart was hammering in my ears. "Hi," I said. "Can I ask you a few questions?"

Agnes picked up the book and resumed running her fingers over the pages. "That's already a question. So if I say no, you already got away with it. But I'll say yes, because I owe a debt only I can repay, not that I ever will but I *owe* it, is what I am saying. Ask me your questions. What are we questioning now?"

I took a deep breath. "Could we talk about Herodias?"

Agnes dropped the book, and it slid off the bed. Her eyes narrowed to slits. "You know about her?"

"Who is she?"

"The whore wife who got me killed in the dungeon, of course."

"Your brother's wife?"

"Brother. I don't have any siblings. Why would you come here and ask that? Herodias. This is a trick, isn't it? You tell me I have it wrong and then I just lay my head on the platter for you, is that right? I've told everyone already. Herodias will steal the kingdom again, you have to watch her like a hawk but no one is watching, because they're watching me. I told A.J. all about it, and she silenced him too, there is no other explanation. He wouldn't leave me to languish here, waiting to repeat that night over and over and over and over and over and over—"

"Agnes, honey, it's okay," Sam said, but she stabbed a finger in his direction.

"Like you would know what all went on." She folded her arms over her chest, her eyes up on the ceiling again.

"Maybe this was a bad idea," I said. "I'm sorry if I upset you, Agnes."

"Not upset," she hissed. "Just tired of this bullshit all the time. I've explained it again and again. She will steal it, and everyone will have nothing."

I thought about what she was saying. She'll steal the kingdom *again*. That didn't sound like part of the story of Herodias and Salome, but possibly of Marin and the Harlow family home. I said, "Are you talking about your house?"

Agnes looked at me sharply. "Not *my* house."

"I want to help you," I whispered. "How is she going to steal it?"

"A.J. knows. Ask him. I'm not good with the details of such things, the certified copies and all that. He knows how to walk the walk. To get the optimal results. I told them about the quetiapine here, but I don't think they have an endorsement deal. The special notebook and the clicky pen that I thought would write pink but it's just regular old black. Oh, who cares, that's the stuff that shuts me up. I didn't want to talk anyway."

She turned on her side and faced away from us, and she didn't say anything else.

Sam looked at me and shrugged, the kind of shrug that said *I told you so.*

On the ride back to his house, I asked Sam if he knew Agnes's case manager, A.J. He said, "Yeah, I met him once or twice, a couple years ago. Come to think of it, he never called back. When Suzy contacted him after it happened. That's . . . odd."

I chewed my lip. He hadn't returned *my* call, though I hadn't expected him to. But he didn't call Meredith Burns back either. Did that mean something? I said, "Do you have a cell-phone number for him or anything?"

"At the house, sure."

When we reached his house, his daughter-in-law was in still in the garage, sorting baby clothes into two piles that were in danger of merging together as one. Sam shuffled inside to get A.J.'s info, and Molly held up a tiny seersucker jacket. I almost laughed out loud at the thought of a baby wearing it.

She smiled at me pleasantly. "Do you have little ones at home? Because I have a small fortune's worth of Janie and Jack right here."

"No, I don't."

"Not yet, anyway," she said, sly.

"No, not ever."

She looked put out, the way people got sometimes when you expressed no desire to have what they have. "You think that now, but just wait," she said.

TWENTY

When I left the Kinnaman house, I saw that I had eight missed calls. I went through them on speaker as I drove home, and groaned. Ambulance-chasing law firms and auto-body shops, calling to wish me a speedy recovery and offer their services. Thanks to the police report, I would probably be getting these calls for the rest of the month. Solicitations in the mail, too.

Their concern was touching.

The second-to-last voice mail was from a Cincinnati area code. A man brusquely said, "Yeah, Jerry Pauwels here, Hamilton prosecutor's office, returning a call from you regarding Nathan Harlow's larceny conviction."

I quickly called him back, eager to hear what he had to say.

"Well, I gotta tell you, I normally wouldn't bother with a private eye, no offense, but I'm delighted and not surprised to hear that Mr. Harlow has popped up on somebody else's radar."

"Especially because he's out of your jurisdiction."

Pauwels chuckled. "Not least, that."

"So can you tell me about the case? I couldn't find out much online."

"I can send you over the transcripts, but the long and short of it is, a family by the name of Colberg hired Harlow and his *mother*, if you can believe it, to redecorate their living room. Harlow was involved with the Colbergs' daughter, I guess. They all said that mother and son seemed like the warmest, kindest, most trustworthy people you could hope to find."

"Famous last words."

"I'll say." Pauwels cleared his throat. "This is not a cute mother-son team. Nice-looking, but this is a woman with a criminal record going back thirty years, drunk driving, possession, shoplifting, check kiting. And Harlow, he's nineteen, Mr. All-American, polite. So the family went out of town during part of the renovation, and when they got back, the house had been cleaned out. Top to bottom. Art, antiques, jewelry, guns, electronics, even some fancy chair, a what was it, an Eames chair."

I laughed out loud.

"Funny?"

"Not funny," I said. "Kind of familiar, though. What happened then?"

"Well, the house had a security camera on the garage. Caught the two of them going in and out of the house with all this crap. Dead to rights, basically. Harlow tried to pawn some of the jewelry and for once the broker actually read the notice the police faxed over, specifying in exquisite detail the stolen items. Harlow was real convincing, and there was one girl on the jury who looked at him like she had the hots. But that videotape made an easy conviction, let me tell you. I remember all of this because Harlow scared the hell out of me. One minute he's charming, or crying these big crocodile tears, but convincing. He'd tell you exactly what you wanted to hear, get you on his side. Then he could just turn it off like a switch and he looks at you with these dead eyes. I thought it was a miracle that larceny was all he'd done."

Not anymore. "What about Marin?"

Pauwels paused for a moment before answering. "Ah, you know about her already. Don't believe I mentioned her name."

"She's what started all of this for me," I said. "Was she charged?"

"Sure was, but she was in the wind. And since she had that record, too, I doubt she would've gotten off as light as her son did. And after we started looking for her, it turned out there were a bunch of other individuals she'd scammed with this interior-decorator bit. She'd get a retainer, take some property under the guise of getting it appraised, or maybe to match a color, and then disappear with the money and the goods. By all accounts she was very knowledgeable about antiques and whatnot. People were shocked that she was a crook. I would've loved to get her. I used to check the visitor logs at the prison he did his time in, to see if she'd been by to see her son. But she never came."

"Cold."

He chuckled again. "So yeah, the saying is true, like mother, like son."

"Do you know when he got out?"

"Last fall. September."

"Parole?"

"No, he served every minute and then some of his sentence. Young Nate could not behave behind bars. I gotta ask you. What's your interest in Harlow?"

"Well, I'm not sure about the extent of it yet. But Marin is dead—I can tell you that much."

"Huh," Pauwels said. "Well, may she rest in peace, though I suspect not."

A woman answered A.J. Watson's phone when I called the mobile number on his dog-eared business card. "Hi, this is Emily," she said pleasantly.

I frowned. "I'm trying to reach A.J. Watson?"

There was a ruffling of papers and a concerned throat-clearing. "Are you a client?"

"No, I'm just trying to reach him. I was told this number is his."

"Yes," Emily said simply. "I supervise the case managers. Is there something I can help you with?"

This was odd. I leaned back in my desk chair and propped my feet up. "Does A.J. have new contact information?"

She sighed. "I'm sorry to have to tell you this, but he's no longer . . . with us."

"Oh."

"I'm sorry."

"Did he leave recently?"

"Leave?" She cleared her throat again. "No, that's not—A.J. died, recently."

"*Oh.*"

"Yes. Quite a shock. But all of his cases have been reassigned, so if you have a care-related issue . . ."

"No. I don't. Um, can you tell me what happened?"

More ruffling pages. "No, I—no, I'm not comfortable discussing that."

I winced. "Right, of course. I'm sorry. Take care."

I hung up and lifted the lid of my laptop, quickly pulling up A.J.'s obituary on the *Dispatch* website. It showed a photo of a thirtyish black man with a wide, bright smile, hair worn long in dreadlocks and pulled back at the nape of his neck.

Anwar James "A.J." Watson departed this life much too soon on Sunday, April 10, 2017. He was born to Stella Watson on May 3, 1987 in Cleveland, Ohio, and attended Cleveland State University, the first of his family to do so, where he earned a Bachelor of Social Work

degree with a minor in psychology. He went on to gradu-
ate school at Ohio State and was expecting to complete
his masters degree next year. He spent most of his
professional life as a mental health case manager and
counselor. A.J. worked at Ohio Hospital for Mental
Health, where he was instrumental in coordinating care
for Central Ohio individuals struggling with mental
health issues, enabling them to return to society. A.J.'s
infectious smile and huge, loving heart will be missed
by everyone he touched. Those left to cherish his mem-
ory include his wife, Alecia; his mother, Stella; his half
brother, Darius (Lucille) Porter; cousins Danny, Aisha,
and Sonya; aunts, uncles, and other family members
and friends. In lieu of flowers, please consider dona-
tions to Mental Health America of Franklin County.

That didn't tell me much—"departed this life much too soon"
could mean anything. I deleted "obit" from my search query and
tried again.

Homicide detectives say A.J. Watson was found shot
in the street in the 500 block of Lilley Ave, on the Near
East Side, Sunday night. The 29-year-old was pro-
nounced dead at the scene, homicide unit Sgt. Jessica
Lopez said. Police do not have any known suspects or
motives at this time. . . .

"Christ," I muttered. There was a streak of bad luck a mile
wide through Agnes Harlow's circle of acquaintances. Lilley Avenue wasn't far from my apartment, but may as well have been on
the other side of the world from her stately Victorian Village house.

Shot in the street.

Could this be related to Marin's death? She'd also been shot in the street.

I squinted at the screen and clicked on the next search result, a blog called *Justice for A.J.*

A post dated four days ago read:

> Living as a Black woman in this political climate means I am no stranger to discrimination and racist behavior. But I have never experienced anything as blatant and inexcusable as the treatment that I have received from the Columbus police in the wake of my husband's murder. It has been made clear to me time and time again that the police believe a Black man murdered on the street in a socioeconomically depressed area of town had to be involved in gang-related activity, which could not be further from the truth. Repeatedly I have been told that I "must not know [my] husband as well as [I] thought," despite an overwhelming lack of evidence that any such involvement exists. I have been called "uppity" and "sassy" for pushing back on the lazy investigation into A.J.'s death. We live in a neighborhood that has gang activity. There are many people who live here that are not involved. Being active in the BLM movement online does not equal gang activity. Blackness does not equal gang activity.

There were pages and pages of posts, chronicling the aftermath of her husband's death and the lackluster police investigation. The sidebar showed a picture of A.J. with his arms around a woman, presumably Alecia, his wife and the author of the blog. Below the image it said, "A.J. Watson was gunned down in front of our home on Easter Sunday. There are no suspects. If you have information, please contact me."

Easter Sunday.

Meredith Burns told me that it had been the week after Easter when she found Agnes at the bottom of her basement steps, where she'd been for at least several days.

Agnes had mentioned A.J. that afternoon, too. That Herodias had silenced him. That he knew the details of how she was going to steal the kingdom, that he knew about the certified copies.

I was afraid to take what she said as any sort of fact. But I was also afraid not to.

I wandered into the kitchen and ate the remains of Shelby's bread with peanut butter. I wasn't hungry so much as I needed food as a vehicle for more painkillers. I chased the bread with three aspirins and looked out the window into the alley, where a plastic bag and a flattened soda bottle were being whipped into a miniature urban tornado. Rain was coming, and I wanted a drink.

I quickly poured a shot and downed it, annoyed at myself but so, so happy.

I liked whiskey. I liked the taste of it, the burn, the way it muffled the edges of things. I didn't have a problem with *drinking*, I told myself, but with everything else. I had an unhappiness problem. A loneliness one. I stood in my silent kitchen, shot glass in hand, as I had too many times before. "I'm lonely," I said, trying it on for size.

I didn't like it.

I dropped the glass in the sink harder than I intended to, and it shattered.

After I cleaned up the broken glass and collected myself, I went back to the computer.

So, assuming Herodias was Agnes's name for Marin, maybe she was saying that Marin was trying to do what she did before, when

Bill Harlow died—take something that didn't rightfully belong to her. Steal a kingdom. Steal a house. You couldn't really steal a house, though. Well, that wasn't quite true. Ownership of a house was both complex and bizarrely simple. Underneath all the mortgage and loan stuff, ownership, by law, was a matter of whose name was on the deed on file with the county recorder's office. I'd heard stories of fraud perpetrated this way—steal a house right out from under someone, even if they currently live in it, just by filing a few documents.

I opened a new browser tab and pulled up the county auditor's site, typing in Agnes's address, just to see.

If Marin's name showed up anywhere on the document, I'd know I was on the right track. If it didn't, I could release the Herodias idea and quit thinking about it.

When the result popped up, I said, "Holy shit."

The current owner of the property was not Marin, but Nate.

I needed a change of scenery. I walked over to the Olde Towne Tavern, where I sat at a table on the patio with a drink, a basket of nachos, and the county property databases, like the party animal I was.

Under the most recent transfer heading I saw:

Transfer Date	Feb-11-2017
Transfer Price	$1
Instrument Type	QC

So Agnes had transferred her house, for one dollar, in February, via a quitclaim deed, which meant that the rights to the property weren't guaranteed to be free of liens or encumbrances the way a warranty deed would certify. There was nothing unusual about quitclaim transfers within a family. But to Nate? When Agnes had children of her own?

I switched databases and pulled up the deed itself on the county recorder's site.

> *Know all men by these presents, that*
> *AGNES LEIGH HARLOW*
> *the designated Grantor herein, for consideration of*
> *ONE dollar, to their satisfaction received, hereby give,*
> *grant, bargain, sell, and convey unto the said Grantee,*
> *NATHAN KENNEDY HARLOW*
> *whose tax-bill mailing address will be 862 NORTH*
> *PEARL STREET #2B, all interest in the following real*
> *property:*
>
> *Situated in the State of Ohio, County of Franklin and*
> *in the City of Columbus, and bounded and described*
> *as follows:*
>
> *Being Lot Number Six (6) of DENNISON PLACE*
> *ADDITION, as the same is numbered and delineated*
> *upon the recorded plat thereof, of record in Plat Book*
> *17, Pages 42 and 43, Recorder's Office, Franklin*
> *County, Ohio.*
>
> *Property Address: 2140 DENNISON AVE*
>
> *Parcel No. : 100-XX55X55X57*
>
> *The foregoing real property is granted by the Grantor*
> *and accepted by the Grantee subject to all the*
> *recorded reservations, conditions, limitations,*

highways, public roads, rights-of-way, leases,
easements, restrictions, zoning ordinances, and any
mineral rights severances, as well as real estate taxes
and assessments both general and special . . .

It was the sort of dull paper trail that usually made my eyes glaze over, but this one was riveting.

I studied each page of the document carefully. It was a crappy scanned copy, but legible enough. It had been signed by Nate—his name dashed off in an angular scrawl—and Agnes—a shaky, over-size cursive—in the presence of a notary whose name and stamp were unreadable.

Of course it was unreadable.

I leaned against my hand, feeling bad about the world. A theory was finally taking shape, and I didn't like it: that Nate Harlow somehow conned his schizophrenic aunt out of her house and then—what—pushed her down the stairs and murdered her case manager? It was a theory I wouldn't want to share with anybody, not yet.

I rubbed the scar on my wrist, remembering another theory I had that was too crazy to be real. Remembering how that had turned out.

I needed to talk to A.J. Watson's wife. I went back to her blog and skimmed some of the entries in chronological order:

Crime Stoppers is offering a $5K reward for information.
Thanks to the generosity of A.J.'s coworkers, we are
able to set up our own tip line and offer $20K for
information about A.J.'s murder.

A NOTE ABOUT THE TIP LINE: Please do not call to
leave condolences. Every time I get a message, my heart

just races, thinking this is the one that will solve the
murder of my husband. I appreciate the sentiment but
please, reserve the tip line for tips. Feel free to comment
on this page instead.

To those of you asking how many tips we are getting,
the answer is none that are viable.

Ordinarily, I'd call Tom and ask for background on the case
before bothering the victim's family, but it sounded like Alecia
Watson would probably be eager to talk to me. That, and Tom
probably wouldn't. I'd been out of line with him. But also, I'd been
right: There *was* more to Marin than it had appeared last week.

That didn't make the prospect of calling him any more appealing.

I ordered another drink and wished I could skip ahead to tomorrow morning, since it was after nine now and too late to visit
A.J.'s wife. But that left me with several hours of solitude to fill. I
wasn't sure when I'd started minding that—or maybe it wasn't so
much that I minded solitude, but that I didn't have anyone to
keep me company anyway. Forced solitude. I thought about going
to see my mother—she could always be counted on to be happy to
see me, even when no one else could—but family dinner night was
tomorrow and I'd surely get my fill of her then. A year ago, Tom
would've kept me company. I shoved a nacho into my mouth. I was
glad he'd met Pam. I was glad he was better.

I wasn't better, though, and it sucked.

I could pretend I was for a while, and even fool myself into believing it. When things were going well—for example, when I was
solving my cases and not watching nineteen-year-old women die
in front of me—it really seemed true. But in times like this, frustrated and stressed, I knew it wasn't. I grabbed my phone and dialed Tom's number. As I listened to his voice explain how to leave

a message, I tried to think about what I might say to him if he were here, in person. Maybe something like, *I know I'm an asshole, I'm sorry for throwing you out of my apartment, we really need to talk about Marin Strasser, and I kind of miss you.* But after the beep, instead of saying anything, I just hung up.

I scrolled through my texts, pausing on one from Catherine that she'd sent last night while I was asleep on my porch. *So . . .*

Quickly, as if I could outsmart myself by doing it fast, I texted her back:

I'm at the Tavern.

TWENTY-ONE

Forty minutes later, Catherine walked in. She saw me and didn't smile, but the light in her eyes changed in that way she had that was better than a smile any day.

"Are you *working*?" she said as she walked up to me.

I looked at her. She hadn't responded to my text. I'd already closed my tab and sent the nachos away in preparation to make a discouraged exit. "Crime never sleeps."

"I thought it was *crime doesn't pay.*" She caught the bartender's eye and pointed at my drink and flashed two fingers.

"Crime doesn't sleep *or* pay." I got out my wallet but she dropped her hand over mine, pushing my wallet away until her fingers grazed my thigh.

"I'll get it," she said.

The bartender brought over two whiskeys and Catherine slipped him a twenty. "So," she said, "you didn't tell me what happened."

"A car accident."

Concern flared in her pale green eyes. "Oh no."

"Yes."

"Related to Leila?"

I explained what had happened after the meeting with Leila yesterday afternoon.

"I had no idea that she was so *treacherous*," Catherine said.

"Does it make you like her more?"

"Eh. Mostly I'm just mad that she hurt you."

"It's fine."

"Does that mean you don't want to talk about it?"

"I don't know."

She watched me for a while. "On Sunday you said I'm not good for you. So what prompted you to pass along information about your whereabouts tonight? Hopelessly lonely?"

I tried to think of something clever to say in response, but I couldn't. "Yeah."

She nodded and didn't say anything. Then she set down her glass and leaned her head on her hand. "Sometimes I think I'm not so good for myself. And before you say anything about the sudden bout of self-awareness, don't. Do you remember a conversation we had, like, a million years ago, about the brain and when it stops developing?"

I did remember that. "Sure, about when the brain's adolescence actually ends."

"And you said," she went on, gesturing for me to fill in the blank.

"I said the reason that so many people seem to have a quote, *quarter-life crisis,* end quote, around age twenty-five or so is that, finally, the brain is developed enough to understand that your life isn't actually how you thought it would be," I said. "It was right before you went to London."

She nodded. "And I was, what, twenty-six at the time. Very much having a quarter-life crisis. And yet you *swore* up and down you weren't talking about me." The corner of her mouth twitched. "I should've listened."

"I should've done everything I could think of to keep you from going."

"Didn't you?"

"Short of physically restraining you, I kind of did." I finished my drink and pushed my glass away. "And—"

"And I didn't. Even. Write," Catherine said, correctly guessing what I was about to say. "Sometimes I look back at things I've done and I just don't understand why. Not in a *holy shit, that's so fucked up* way, but like I genuinely don't get it. Things that hurt me too, things no one is making me do, things I don't even want in the first place. Who does that?"

"It's like the scorpion and the frog," I said. "The fable. Know that one?"

Her pale green eyes were sparkling. "No, enlighten me."

"So there's a scorpion and a frog, chilling next to the river. The scorpion decides she wants to go across to the other side. But she can't swim." As I spoke, she laced her fingers through mine and I got that roller-coaster feeling in my stomach. I continued, "She asks the frog to take her across and the frog says, *How do I know you won't sting me?* The scorpion says, *Because if I sting you, we'd both drown.* So the frog lets the scorpion climb on her back and they start out across the river. Halfway through the trip, the scorpion stings the frog, who says, *Now we're both going to die! Why did you do this?* And as they both slip under the water, the scorpion shrugs and says, *It's in my nature.*"

"Ooh, ouch," Catherine said. "Let me guess. I'm the scorpion here, and you're the frog."

I shrugged. "Interpretation is up to you. I'm the scorpion in my own story."

She brought my hand up to her mouth and pressed her lips against my knuckles. "If I had one hour left to live, and I could do anything I wanted—anything, okay—I could go skydiving, I could do ecstasy and swim naked, I could eat a hundred oysters . . ."

"If you're going to die anyway, why *not* eat a hundred oysters?"

"Exactly," she said, "but I'm saying, if I could do anything I wanted to make my last hour on earth as enjoyable as possible, I think I'd pick listening to you talk."

I stared at her.

"I wouldn't even want to kiss you. I'd just want to listen to you, Roxane, because you're the only person I've ever met who isn't capable of boring me to tears."

"High praise, coming from you," I said, but I felt an electric heat spreading through my body, like someone had flipped on my seldom-used happiness switch.

"I guess what I'm saying is I'm sorry," she finished. "Don't make a joke. Just let me say it. I'm sorry. For always acting like I never owed you anything and expecting you to put up with it, just for the thrill of my company. These last couple of months, you *keeping to yourself*, as you say, I've been lonely a lot too."

I didn't respond, just watched her instead. Even when she was acting her worst, she was lovely. Now, repentant and open, she was irresistible to me. I said, "Are you sure you wouldn't want to kiss me?"

The air was cooler as we slowly walked the five blocks south and four east to my apartment, like the approaching storm was almost here. I was still carrying my computer bag, so there was some urgency to get home before the skies opened up on the device that was responsible for most of my income, but that didn't stop me from pausing under a streetlight to kiss her. Catherine's mouth was full and soft, slightly minty from the lip gloss she had applied as we walked out of the bar. Her hands gripped my shoulders, thumbs trailing across my clavicles. I drew in a sharp breath and stepped back. I'd actually forgotten about the pain for the last hour. "Sorry," I said, peeling down the edge of my turtleneck to show her the damage, "I wasn't kidding about the car accident."

Her lips pursed with concern. "That looks awful. Are you sure this is a good idea—"

"Yes, God, yes," I said, maybe a little too fast. "But you might have to be gentle. If you can handle that."

We resumed walking, her arm linked through mine again, her long blond hair brushing my elbow. "I think I can handle it," she said.

When I opened the front door to my building, the lobby was pitch black again. "That's not scary or anything," Catherine murmured.

"I keep meaning to call the landlord," I said, but then I heard a sound: there was a faint whimper, a fluttery breath. I held an arm in front of Catherine so she wouldn't go any farther into the darkness.

I pulled my gun out of my bag, listening hard. "Who's there?" I said.

"I'm sorry to show up here," a voice said, low but feminine.

"Leila?" I said. I fumbled for my phone with my other hand and turned on the flashlight.

In the pale glow of the screen, I saw that she was sitting on the top step outside my door, knees to her chest. She had blood on her—a lot of blood. On her face, her neck, her arm, her shirt. She was clutching a wad of brown paper towels to her shoulder, blood running between her fingers.

Catherine let out a choked cry.

I rushed up the steps. "Jesus Christ, what happened?"

"This is the one place he would not expect me to come," she murmured.

Catherine came up to the landing, bumping into me in the dark. "Leila, oh my God." She dropped to a crouch next to Leila and moved her hands away from the paper towel. "Let me take a look at this."

"It's bleeding less now," Leila said. Her voice was weak, unsteady.

"Oh, fuck," Catherine said. Her hand gripped my ankle. "Roxane, I think she's been shot. This is bad. She needs to go to a hospital—"

"*No.*" Leila cleared her throat. "I can't. No. The police."

I abandoned my efforts with the door and crouched down, shining my flashlight over her. "Let me see," I said, knowing the instant I peeled away the paper towel that this was beyond any bathroom patch-up job I was capable of. There was a slick black hole in the hollow between her collarbone and shoulder joint, nearly spurting blood with each breath she took. "You need a doctor."

"Just get it out."

"I'm calling 911—"

"No, no, you can't. He'll kill me."

"Who will?"

"Nate," Leila murmured. "Just get it out."

I was afraid she was going to pass out in my lobby. Clearly the rundown on what had happened would need to wait. "Leila, I can't. You need to see a doctor."

Leila whimpered, her eyes closed, shaking her head. "I'll just leave, sorry . . ."

Catherine touched my shoulder. "I have an idea. Leila, would you let a doctor examine you if it's somewhere safe, and private?"

Leila didn't answer at first, but then she nodded. "If it's safe."

I looked at Catherine. "What?"

"I'll explain later. Let me make a phone call."

Catherine had taken a cab over to Olde Towne, but since she'd barely touched her drink, she got behind the wheel of my rental car.

I rode in the backseat with Leila, doing my best with a shirt to stanch the blood flow. For the second time in a week. Leila's head was in my lap, her eyes narrowed and unfocused. "You were right," she said. "About Nate. The car. He was there."

"He was where?"

"At the print shop. I told Vincent. About the car. Then Derek came. He shot me."

"Derek did?"

She went quiet, moaning slightly as her weight shifted when Catherine turned onto her street. At this hour, it was empty, no signs of life except for a silver car in her driveway, taillights gleaming. As we got closer, I saw that it was a Porsche.

"Whoa," I said.

Catherine pulled in next to the sports car as a tall, ash-blond woman got out of it. She held a large nylon duffel bag at her hip. "Evelyn, thank you," Catherine was saying as I helped Leila out of the vehicle too. "I know it's late."

The woman, Evelyn, gave a terse smile. She was fiftyish and stern-looking. "I didn't think I'd be hearing from you again, Cat."

We helped Leila into the house. There was no natural place to put a bloody person with a gunshot wound in a nice house like this, but Catherine dashed into the bathroom and emerged in a hail of shower-curtain rings with a clear plastic liner, which she spread out on her sofa. Leila sank into the cushions, her eyes closed while Evelyn opened her bag and pulled out a pair of scissors, which she used to cut open Leila's shirt. She peered at the wound, her mouth a flat line.

"Get it out," Leila mumbled.

"Hon, it is out," Evelyn said. "Through and through, a clean shot. You're going to be fine. I'm going to give you a shot of Demerol to take the edge off, okay?"

Leila nodded.

The doctor dug through her bag for a few seconds, then looked up at us, a syringe in hand. "Cat, you need something too?"

Catherine's expression hardened and she shook her head. She took me by the arm and pulled me into the kitchen.

I said, "Who in the hell is this woman?"

Catherine went over to the sink and washed off her hands and arms. Her jeans, formerly white, were now various smeary shades of red and brown. "A neighbor," she said, which did not satisfy my curiosity at all. "A friend, sort of. One of Wystan's friends. She brings the adrenaline needle to the party, usually. For when things inevitably go too far."

"I can't tell if you're joking right now."

"Oh, I'm not." She shook off her hands and dried them on a paper towel. "I'm trying to stay away from those parties. But Wystan, he's probably at one right now. I don't even know where he is, to be honest. But listen, that's neither here nor there. I knew Evelyn could help and wouldn't make a fuss."

She was speaking to the granite-tile floor. From the other room, a gasp of pain and a gagging sound. Catherine closed her eyes, her brow furrowing.

I slipped my arm around her and she leaned into me. "I'm sorry," I said. "This isn't what either of us had in mind for tonight. But thank you, for your quick thinking." I rested my cheek against her soft blond hair. "And I'm sorry. About your husband."

"Now it's my turn to not want to talk about something," she said. We stood like that for a while, not speaking. Then she said, "Tell me about this case. The whole thing."

Catherine always liked hearing about my cases, about the secrets that lurk between people. So we sat at her kitchen table while the doctor worked on Leila in the other room, and I told her about Marin and Arthur, Leila and Nate, Agnes and Sam, Herodias, the house, the case manager. "But why did Nate shoot the woman at the print shop?"

"I don't know."

"Why is Marin dead?"

"I don't know that either."

"Did Nate shoot his own mother?"

"Maybe. This morning, or yesterday morning, I guess," I amended, because it was closing in on 5 A.M now, "he was scary. Unpredictable. Leila seemed very uneasy when I suggested that Nate had shot Pomp's daughter, so I guess she found out that he did and alerted Pomp, who sent his son Derek to, I don't know, do something with Nate. But obviously that went awry." I pulled up the *Dispatch* website on my phone, scanning through the recent articles for any details. "Oh, here we go. 'Columbus police are investigating a shooting in the Short North Tuesday night.' No kidding," I muttered. "'This is a developing story.'"

I looked up as Evelyn walked into the kitchen, snapping off her bloody rubber gloves. "I'm leaving the Demerol," she said. "A hundred milligrams, every three to four hours, sub-cu. You have needles in the house?"

Catherine nodded, her jaw bunching.

"The cuts on her face—some of them are deep. She'll probably want to see somebody about that, if she doesn't want them to scar. But she'll be okay." She tossed her gloves in the trash and stood next to the counter, drumming her nails on it.

Catherine got up from the table, opened her freezer, and reached in for a frost-covered plastic bag. I looked away while she counted bills from a thick roll into a neat stack on the counter.

"And make sure she changes the dressing once a day. She'll be fine."

Then Evelyn took the cash and left.

TWENTY-TWO

I woke to the sound of hard rain on the window and a crick in my neck from sleeping in an armchair. The shower curtain had been removed from the couch across from me, the room more or less put back together. I checked my phone: eleven o'clock. I rubbed my eyes. From elsewhere in the house I heard a television and smelled coffee. I unfolded myself from the chair and went into the kitchen, where Catherine was watching an infomercial about a blender.

"Good morning," she said. She had showered, her hair wet, her face free of makeup, wearing only a black kimono. "Tea?"

"Please." I leaned against the wall. "I didn't peg you as an infomercial type."

She gave me a smile. "I'm so tired. I don't even know what's going on. Go ahead, put on the crime channel."

I picked up the remote and flipped to the midday news.

"One man was shot last night at the corner of High and Prescott," a reporter was saying, "and he remains in stable condition this afternoon at Grant Medical Center. Police are looking for these two individuals for questioning in connection with the incident." The screen flipped to a fairly bad computer sketch of Leila and a decent one of Nate as the reporter rattled off instructions for what to do if you knew anything.

"Leila is in the guest room. I gave her some toast. I don't really know what you're supposed to give someone who just got shot."

"Toast seems good."

Catherine turned on a burner under her teakettle and folded her arms over her chest, not looking at me. "I just keep remembering, like, that actually happened. Last night."

"Yeah. It did." I went over to her and rested a hand on her hip, and she leaned backward against me. "I'm sorry. That I got you involved in this."

She shook her head. "You didn't know. And I'm glad I could help, to be honest. I haven't been feeling particularly useful lately."

"Is that why—?" I started. But I changed my mind.

Then Catherine finished it for me. "Why I'm acting like this? A crisis of self-esteem?" She turned around and pressed her face into my neck. "I'm never not missing you."

That didn't answer the question, but I didn't press it. The teakettle began to hiss and she pulled away.

Cup of mint tea in hand, I went down the hall to the first-floor guest room. Leila was stretched out on the bed under a sheet, very still but awake, her eyes on the doorway.

I said, "So there were witnesses."

"Many witnesses," Leila said. Her voice was hoarse. "Many people out and about last night."

"So you want to tell me what happened?"

She nodded.

I dragged a stool over from the vanity table. "Okay, let's have it. Nate shot Tessa and you told Pomp about it?"

Another nod. "I couldn't stop thinking about what you said."

"About his car."

"Yes. I confronted him. Then I was terrified of what he might do, so I called Vincent. He told me to keep Nate there. A while later,

Derek showed up. I let him in and it went bad right away. Nate and Derek both shooting at each other."

"But you're completely innocent in all of this."

"Innocent," she said, closing her eyes for a second. "No, but I wasn't going to hurt anyone last night. I don't even have a gun. However, I don't think Derek stopped to evaluate the scene before he started shooting. It was complete chaos. I went out the back of the building to get away from them. I don't have my phone, my wallet, anything. But I had to get out of there."

"And Nate?"

"I didn't see where he went."

"Why would Nate shoot Tessa?"

She closed her eyes again. "It's unfortunate, that she was there. Nate came for Arthur. He believes Arthur shot his mother. It had nothing to do with Tessa. But Nate knew about what was going on at the print shop. I don't know why he would bring such attention, except that he's not thinking clearly. Paranoid."

I chewed my lip. If Nate thought Arthur killed Marin, that meant my theory that Nate had done so was useless. But then again, I had to consider the source.

And the fact that schizophrenia did run in families.

"Tell me about Agnes."

She sighed. "Marin and I became friends, before Nate got out of jail. She introduced him to me. He's very charming, when he wants to be. But disturbed. And the relationship between them— odd. Obsessive, in some ways. He was fixated on getting her out of the situation with Arthur. He thought it was beneath her. That she was owed. That they both were. Do you know about Nate's father?"

I nodded.

"It was a wrong that needed to be corrected, what had happened with the money. Nate spent a long time in jail, thinking about that. He knew that his aunt had been the one to dismantle the whole thing. So he wished to punish her. Rob her. But it all went too far. Everyone takes things too far—did you ever notice that?"

"I did."

"Not just rob her, but rub it in her face. He watched her for a while, saw her feeding the alley cats. Then he and I, together, we befriended her. She didn't recognize him. She hadn't seen him since he was a child. So she didn't even know who she was talking to."

"When did all this happen?"

"It was last December. She was a lonely old lady. I thought we were just going to strip the house of all those gorgeous antiques and sell them. Which we started to do, but Nate is impatient. It wasn't enough. He wanted the house, too. He wanted to get the house and sell it for a million dollars, cash."

"Who buys a house with a million dollars in cash?"

"No one, of course, it's impossible. But Nate insisted. I helped him with the paperwork. The deed. He even got her to sign it, telling her it was just to ensure the cats would be taken care of."

I shook my head, disgusted. "Then what?"

"Well, then she found out. I don't know how. I wasn't there when it happened. But Nate came to me, very upset. He said they argued and she fell. It was an accident, though. He didn't mean to kill her."

I took a moment to process that. "He told you he killed her?"

She nodded. "We avoided the house for a while, one month, maybe."

I watched her face for clues that she was lying. But she gave away nothing, and I wasn't sure if she was lying, or if Nate had lied to her about Agnes. "What about the case manager?"

"I don't know anything about that."

"Your boyfriend didn't tell you about the other person he murdered?"

Her face hardened a little. "I am not proud of what happened.

And I don't know what murder you're talking about. I forged some documents. I don't know what all Nate did."

"You need to talk to the police."

She laughed, the first time I'd heard her laugh. Then she winced. "I can't do that. You know I can't. Not now."

"A lot of innocent people have gotten hurt here. Even if you don't care about Agnes Harlow, I know you care about Tessa. I saw it in your face yesterday."

"It doesn't matter now. Vincent will take care of Nate."

"And what about Arthur? The police think he killed Marin too."

"Maybe he did."

"No, Nate's the homicidal maniac in the family, remember." I sipped my tea. "What happened the night Marin died? Were you with him?"

Leila went quiet for a while before she continued. "She called. After she had dinner with Arthur." She turned to look at me. "Ranting and raving about some private investigator tailing her— you. She took it hard. I think she had a soft spot for Arthur, I really do. He is a good guy."

"Everyone keeps saying that, while also screwing him over."

"Maybe that is a case against being good."

"Maybe it is. So she called after dinner."

She nodded. "Nate and I were at my place, and Marin came over to tell us about it, about how she hadn't been to the house for a while because she thought someone had been following her for a few weeks and she was trying to lay low. So she was vindicated, you see. That she'd been right. Almost happy about it. Nate was angry though, wondering how much this investigator—you—knew about the house. They argued about whether or not the house was safe. But when they'd argue, things could get ugly. Not violent, but nasty. Both of them, absolute pricks sometimes. So I told them to take it elsewhere, and they left."

"Okay, what happened next?"

"Nate came over later and said we should stay away from the house for a bit too, just in case. He said nothing to indicate Marin was dead. We heard about it together on the news, and he fell apart. Nate was crazy about her. He wouldn't hurt her."

"But you just said, things could get nasty between them. And he left with her that night."

She didn't say anything in reply.

"Where do you think he went last night?"

"Part of me thinks that he is smart, that he has no choice now. That he'll try to run." She paused for a second, swallowing thickly. "I don't know how much money he has. He's bad with money. Marin kept his share for him. Hopefully she had a good hiding place for it."

I thought about the Bitcoin receipts. "She did," I said. "In her nightstand, along with her weed and her vibrator. What's the other part of you think?"

"That he is a vindictive person, and he will want to hurt me for telling Vincent what he did."

I scooted my chair backward. "The police," I said. "You need to talk to them, now." Although Tom hadn't called me back last night, surely this could get his attention and usher me back into his good graces.

But Leila shook her head. "I can't. Not now. What would I even say? I can't talk about Nate and Marin without talking about Vincent, and even you would not be able to save me from Vincent. Not to mention the fact that I don't have any evidence. Of any of it. If I say *I helped to do all these things,* but can't prove I had help, I am on the hook for it."

I got up and paced the length of the room. Evidence. She was right about that: there was precious little of it in this case. Just rumors and partial paper trails. "Why did you come to me yesterday?

Did you think I could nurse you back to health and then let you disappear into the sunset?"

She sighed. "You think so poorly of me."

I watched her, my hands spread wide in frustration.

"I came to your house because I thought I would be safe. With you. Nate would never expect me to go to you. Not when you know so much already. I was just trying to survive, yesterday."

"And today?"

"And today," she said, "I am aware that I owe you, and Cat, and I would only ask you to give me a few more hours to rest. I'm sorry. I'm very tired. Can we talk later?"

I nodded. "Okay."

I found Catherine in the living room, curled up in the chair where I'd slept. She was still awake, but barely. I crouched down in front of her. "Hey," I said. "*Cat*. When did you start introducing yourself to everyone as Cat?"

She gave me a sleepy smile and leaned forward for a kiss. "I don't know," she said, "do you hate it?"

"A little. You're a *Catherine* to me, through and through."

"Maybe I turned into a different person after we first met," she said, which was kind of true. "And maybe now I'm turning back."

Something hurt, in my chest. I couldn't tell if it was a good hurt or a bad hurt. Knowing our history, probably a little of both. "There are a few things I need to check on," I said, "hopefully something to back up her story. But I don't want to leave you here alone with her. I can call someone to come over and keep you company—"

"Oh, there's no need," Catherine said, sitting up. "Leila and I were having a good conversation while you were asleep. Artist to artist. It's really okay. She can barely stand up. And it's not like she's a stranger or anything."

I studied her delicate features. "She's not an honest person," I said.

"Maybe not honest, but it's okay. Don't you think if she was going to try to run or something, she would've done it while I was in the shower?"

I didn't say anything.

Catherine kissed me again. "Go. I'll be fine."

TWENTY-THREE

I wanted to talk to Alecia Watson, but first I wanted to be dressed in non-bloody clothes. I stopped at home and gave a thorough inspection of the cars parked on the street before I got out, but nothing was out of the ordinary. And inside the building there were no traces of what had happened last night except for a single drop of blood on the edge of a worn Oriental rug on the landing. With the light still out, no one would ever notice.

I told myself to remember to call the landlord. Later, when I wasn't in the middle of this mess.

I was freshly showered and wearing clean clothes when I heard the door to the building creak open. Heavy footsteps that stopped at my apartment, and a loud, forceful knock.

I shook my gun out of its holster and said, "Who is it?"

"Vincent Pomp. I just want to talk."

I felt my jaw bunch up. "I'm in the phone book."

"I'm sure you are."

Neither of us spoke for a while.

"You came to Tessa's service yesterday," he said finally. "Why?"

"I was there when she passed. It seemed like the right thing to do."

"I wish I could believe you. Where is he?"

I parted the curtains and looked out at him. He seemed startled by the gesture. He was alone, his suit jacket rumpled and dotted with rain. I opened the door and stood facing him, my gun at my side. "You're talking about Nate Harlow."

"Where is he?"

"I don't know. But I'm looking for him too."

"Why?"

"I think he's responsible for everything that's happened. But I told you to call first next time. This is my home. You don't just show up here acting entitled to answers."

Pomp narrowed his eyes at me. "You're not afraid of me," he said.

He apparently couldn't see the tremor in my hand or hear it in my voice. "It doesn't really matter if I'm afraid of you or not. I don't know where Nate is, so I can't tell you. I imagine that he's trying to get away from this city by now."

"He killed my daughter. He shot my son last night." He slumped a little against the wall. "Derek has a collapsed lung and might not make it. All he wanted to do was make a little cash."

I knew he was a bad guy, but I almost felt sorry for him. His world was caving in because of Nate, and he didn't even really know the guy. "Not enough cash in the Pomp family business?" I said.

Pomp was quiet for a moment before he answered me. "Derek always has to do things his own way, on his own terms. He ran into some trouble with drugs a while back, and I wouldn't let him near Phoenix after that. He just wanted to show me he could do it—be a responsible businessman. He didn't ask for all this."

I wasn't so sure that the word *responsible* applied here. But I didn't want to let on that I knew what Derek was involved in yet. "All what?"

"The print shop. The police found things inside. Things that tie my son to some criminal activity. It's quite serious. And now, even if he does pull through, he might wind up in prison for the rest of his life. That's what."

"Lucky for you that you never ended up buying the print shop from Arthur," I said, taking a guess.

His nostrils flared. "You know about that?"

"I know Arthur didn't want to sell it," I said, "but he had no clue about what Derek and Leila were up to. Did he?"

Pomp shook his head slowly in a resigned sort of disbelief. "No, he didn't. I made him an exceedingly generous offer, too, because Derek had proved to me that there *was* money in it, even though the print shop had been operating in the red for the last three years. But Arthur wasn't interested—not in one and a half times what the dump was worth on the up-and-up." He shrugged. "They always say that everybody's got a price, but I'm not sure what his is."

"So if you wanted to go into business counterfeiting passports with your son, why not just start over? Why bother buying the print shop from the last honest man in the city?"

He almost smiled. "The last honest man," he said. "Right."

"That's not an answer," I said. "Why not build your own?"

"Efficiency."

I thought about what Leila had said. Archimedes.

Pomp added, "Why reinvent the wheel, when all the pieces and parts were right there."

"But he wouldn't sell."

"I thought I figured out a way around that. I bought the entire office complex."

I studied him, picturing the office I'd followed Leila to yesterday. The recently removed vinyl letters. "How is that going to help?"

"Derek said the print shop was having trouble making rent

some months. So even if Arthur wouldn't sell to me, once he owed me, he could be controlled. You don't have much leverage against a person you already owe."

I raised an eyebrow. "That's pretty clever on your part."

He didn't say anything.

"Because that way, you're pretty insulated from all of it on paper, aren't you?"

He laughed without humor. It turned into a wounded howl. "Fuck being insulated. I want my children. And I want to smash in Nate Harlow's skull."

"You're not the only one. But I still don't know where he is."

Pomp shook his head. "If I find out you're lying to me," he said, but his heart wasn't even in it.

Rattled from my conversation with Pomp, I called Tom as I drove over to Lilley Avenue. Once again, it went to voice mail. This time, I waited for the beep. "Tom. It's me," I said. "I need your help." I gritted my teeth as I had to slam on my brakes to avoid running a red light. "You said to tell you if I needed help, and I do. Please, call me so I can explain."

Everything was going to be fine.

Tom would call back.

Neither Nate nor Vincent Pomp had any possible way of finding Catherine's house.

Before the light turned green, I grabbed my phone off the seat and tapped out a text to her:

Everything okay?

Her response was immediate.

> I told you it would be and it is :) The alarm is on and
> she's asleep. Stop worrying.

Then, a few moments later, the same three dots she'd been sending for months.

Alecia Watson lived in a brick Cape Cod with bright, happy flowers out front. She answered the door with a stack of mail in her
hand, expression hard. She wore hospital scrubs, light blue. She was
clearly the same woman smiling in the photo in her husband's obituary, only with nothing to smile about now. I wondered who had
planted the flowers. "Can I help you?"

"Yeah, hi," I said. "My name is Roxane. I'm a private investigator and I'd like to talk to you about your husband."

She narrowed her eyes slightly behind her purple-framed
glasses. "Do you have some ID on you?"

"Sure, of course." I showed her my PI license, which she in-
spected with more care than anyone ever had.

"Sorry," she said, handing it back to me. "You never know. I've
had some real weird visitors. So you are who you say you are. What
about my husband?"

"I'm sorry for your loss, first of all," I said. She nodded curtly.
"And I've read your blog, so I know that there hasn't been progress
on the investigation."

Alecia drew in a slow breath. "No."

"I came across A.J.'s name in the course of another investigation. Into something that happened to one of his clients, actually."

She flinched slightly when I said her husband's name. But then
she tipped her head to the side and stepped back from the doorway
to let me in. "One of his clients?"

I followed her into the kitchen. "A woman named Agnes Harlow," I said.

Alecia shrugged. She sat down at a small round table and gestured for me to do the same. "He never talked about his clients by name. So this Agnes person—something happened to her?"

"She fell and injured a hip."

"That's terrible." She looked at me. "What does that have to do with a private investigator though?"

"It's kind of a long story. It boils down to the fact that she said something to me about your husband, that makes me wonder if he might have helped her with something. Found something for her."

Her eyebrows pushed together. "He helped his clients with a lot of things. That's what his job was."

"Right," I said. "Bear with me here. A real-estate thing. Does that sound familiar to you?"

"A real-estate thing for his clients? No."

"He never mentioned anything troubling him?"

"Troubling him? What in the world are you getting at?"

I didn't really know how to say it except to say it. "Agnes fell down a flight of steps on or around Easter Sunday," I told her. "I think she was pushed down those steps, because she had discovered that her nephew had transferred ownership of her house into his own name. I talked to her about it, and she mentioned A.J. She said that she told him."

Alecia studied her fingernails for a while. "Told him what?"

"About the house. That something was going on with the house. I don't really know, but that's my theory right now."

She shook her head. "I have no idea about any house."

I showed her photos of Marin, Nate, and Leila, but none of them looked familiar to her.

Alecia seemed a little frustrated. "So are you trying to say A.J.

died because of something to do with this, or what? Because if that's what you're saying to me, I hope it isn't just some wacky theory. A.J. was the kindest, smartest man I have ever met, and he only wanted to help people. It kills me every day to get up and act like everything's all right, knowing the person who took his life gets to continue living theirs. So if you know who that is, you're gonna need to tell me if you want to keep talking."

I tapped Nate's picture on the table. "Him," I said. "Only I'm not sure how to prove it."

She picked up the photo and studied it with the same focus she'd used on my license. "He looks like an Abercrombie model."

"I know. But he's already killed at least one other person."

She put the image facedown. "How do you prove it?"

"Can you tell me about the days before he died? I know this is hard."

"Well, I hadn't seen him in four days. I was working nights, he worked long days what with his classes at OSU, we were never home at the same time anymore. It was only supposed to be for a while. I was moving to the day shift starting May first. But anyway, we knew we were going to have an ugly couple weeks, but we were hanging in. Talking mostly through texts. I joked that I was married to a chatbot." She smiled, but it quickly faded. "I was working that night. Easter. Seven to seven. He'd gone up to Cleveland to see his mama, and he said he might swing by the hospital and bring some leftovers for me and Karen, my good friend who works with me. Since, you know, hospital food. That was going to be around ten. But by ten, the police had already come and told me. I didn't even know I should be worried." Then she bit her lip like she was remembering something. "A real-estate thing, you said."

"Yes. The deed to a house in the Short North."

She said, "He texted me that evening to ask for Karen's husband's number. I figured to make plans to hang out or whatever. I didn't have his number and Karen's shift didn't start till nine. I told him, you can get it tonight. Since he was bringing the food. But then . . ."

I waited.

Alecia took off her glasses and took a long time polishing the lenses on the edge of her shirt. "I don't know if this has anything to do with anything . . . but Karen's husband works for a real-estate attorney."

I met the Kinnamans at Brighton Lake. Sam, Suzy, and I sat around a small table in the lobby while Molly and her daughter worked on a puzzle together in the common room. I placed a printout of the deed to Agnes's house in front of them. "I'm sorry to be the one to tell you this," I said. "I really am. But Agnes was conned into signing over the entire property to your cousin Nate."

Sam blinked at me and said nothing. Suzy snatched up the deed and furiously turned the pages. "She signed this. That's her signature."

"Yes, it is."

"She just signed it?"

"Yes. But she was misled as to what it was."

Her face was growing red. "This—the house—can he *do* that? Just *one piece of paper* and it's suddenly legally binding?"

"Suze, lower your voice, hon," Sam said. "Is it really that easy? A signature and boom?"

"Unfortunately, in a case like this, yeah, it can be—"

"This is why," Suzy said. She shook her head quickly. "This is why I said about the power of attorney. That house is how we're going to pay for her care here, after the ninety days is up. That's what the insurance covers. She doesn't have any money left. She only has that house. Oh my God." She stopped speaking abruptly, the color draining from her cheeks. "That's what she was telling me."

The rest of us stared at her.

"I thought she was talking nonsense. The dungeon of Machaerus, Herodias and Salome. The last time I saw her, at Christmas. She was saying it. They were back, she said. They were back. I thought she meant the—the delusions. And when I got to the hospital, right after. She kept saying they tried to take the house. They threw her into the dungeon. This Herodias thing, John the Baptist, it's something she's said off and on for years. I didn't think. Dad," she said, clutching her father's arm, her eyes overflowing, "what did I do? Did they hurt her? Is that why she fell?"

As gently as I could, I said, "I think Nate caused your mother's fall. Yes."

Suzy turned and buried her face in Sam's shoulder. "I am a horrible daughter."

While Sam rubbed her back, he looked at me. "What can we do? There has to be a way to undo it, right? It's fraud."

I nodded. "It is. I have to tell you, I'm not an expert about this kind of thing. You'll want to talk to an attorney, someone who specializes in real-estate law. And I'll send the police your way, too." I paused to check my phone, hoping for a callback from Tom. But there wasn't one. My stomach hurt. "I don't know what's going to happen. But the important thing is that you know now. You can take steps."

Sam nodded as his daughter wept into his shirt. "I hope you're right about that."

TWENTY-FOUR

Tom still hadn't called me back. A little pissed off, I dialed his number, listened to his voice-mail greeting again, and left another message asking him to call me. This time, the message was rather terse. I called Catherine next, and she didn't answer either. No one wanted to talk to me. As I drove back to Catherine's house, I fumbled with the spaceship-like controls of my rental car, trying to get the windshield wipers to operate at a reasonable speed. Rush-hour traffic had taken hold of the city, and 315 was a parking lot. Every vehicle seemed to be personally standing in my way. I called Catherine again, and when she didn't answer, I imagined Vincent Pomp somehow tracking her down, holding her hostage. *No, stop it.* I forced myself to breathe deeply and listen to the rain. But I didn't want to do either of those things. What I wanted, I told myself, was a trip in a time machine back to the day I took on Arthur Ungless's case. Maybe all of this would still have happened regardless, but it would've been someone else's problem.

I could almost believe that, but not quite.

I crept along in my lane, counting out a chronology on my fingers to pass the time. One, Leila starts making and selling fake IDs. She brings her lover's son into the business to help with production. The fake-ID business is booming, and Derek wants to expand. Passports. Leila thinks it's a bad idea. Vincent Pomp offers to buy the shop from Arthur to get a piece of the forgery business, but Arthur isn't selling. Six—was that six?—Derek finds a new partner in Bobby Veach, who cuts Leila out of her own scheme. Marin, meanwhile, falls in fake or real love with Arthur and they get engaged. She immediately commences stealing cash from him under the guise of wedding planning, because she's the scorpion and he's the frog. Nate gets out of jail and Marin hooks Leila up with him. Nate is full of ideas about how he can get his mother out of the world of small-time cons, and it all has to do with Agnes Harlow, who's the one responsible for their fall from grace in the first place. They transfer the house into Nate's name, but it's harder than expected to sell a million-dollar house for cash. At some point, Agnes and/or A.J. figures it out, A.J. ends up dead, and Agnes is badly injured in a fall down her steps.

I tapped my thumb impatiently on the steering wheel. I was only to Ackerman. Neither Catherine nor Tom was calling me back.

"Then things get even weirder," I said, to keep my mind off the worst-case scenario. "Something happens to spook Marin badly enough that Arthur thinks she's having an affair. He hires me. She buys expensive pens for a week and does nothing suspicious at all while I follow her." I thought about what Leila had told me earlier. Marin had thought someone was following her, and had been avoiding Agnes's house. Either Marin was very, very good at spotting a tail, or I wasn't the only person following her. Maybe that could explain the behavior that tripped Arthur's detector. But who?

Vincent? Derek? The latter was clearly no stranger to criminal activity. Leila had told me that Vincent and Marin had been an item in the past. Maybe Derek was deeply protective of his mother? I frowned—that seemed like a stretch, especially since that particular affair had been over for a while.

What have you done, the man's voice had said in the alley that night.

What *had* Marin done?

After everything I'd learned, I still didn't understand Marin's death.

From the sound of it, she was the most innocent out of everybody.

Which wasn't really saying much.

I finally hit I-70 and went east as fast as rush hour would allow.

Catherine opened the door on the third knock like nothing was wrong. I said, "Jesus, I was worried. You didn't answer your phone."

She pulled me inside, brushing raindrops off my shirt. "Sorry," she said, "I told you, I'm bad at phones. It's probably upstairs. We were watching TV."

I let out a long breath. "Ah, so you're BFFs now."

"*No*," Catherine said, "she's zonked on Demerol and not much for conversation. We were just watching a documentary. About fonts."

"Fascinating."

She slid her hands down to my hips. "Yes." She kissed me. "It was." Another kiss. "I was thinking of ordering pizza for dinner, if that's okay."

I nodded, but then remembered I was supposed to be at my mother's house for dinner tonight. "Fuck," I said.

Catherine raised her eyebrows. "What's wrong?"

I pulled out my phone to text my brother. "Nothing. Family dinner at my mother's house tonight, but I think this situation trumps regular obligations." I saw that I had a message from Andrew already:

Where are you?

I typed

> Something came up, please make a good excuse for me
> and put the phone back in my pocket.

Leila was lying on the couch, paging through a magazine, and she glanced up when I walked into the room. I said, "It's later. Let's discuss going to the police."

She bit her lip. "Nothing has changed from this morning."

"So what's your plan? We already established that letting me nurse you back to health, then riding off into the sunset was an unfairly cynical accusation."

"You're all business today."

I sat down on the edge of the coffee table. "I'm stressed," I said, "because you put me in the middle of a bad situation, and I can't just do nothing. Nate is still out there, and who knows what scheme he's planning next."

Leila shook her head. "He doesn't have any other schemes. He isn't that smart."

"He's smart enough to do this much damage. So I'm not going to take any chances. Don't you want to stop him?"

She closed her eyes for a second. "Of course I do. In the morning."

My phone buzzed in my pocket. I got up and paced the length of the room—she had that effect, of frustrating me to the point of pacing. But I stopped cold when I read the text from my brother Matt, who texted me about once a year.

> You need to get over here. Something's happening.

I felt sick as I walked up the front steps to my mother's house. There were two unmarked police cars parked at the curb, and the front door was closed. Usually in the summer, the door was open to the screen almost constantly, even in the rain. And speaking of which, it was raining even harder now, the sky a bruised greyish blue. Inside the house, I found my brother Matt sitting in the living room, watching *Pawn Stars*. My mother's voice echoed from the dining room.

"Matthew Weary," I said, my hands on my hips in front of the television, "what the fuck? You can't text me to get over here ASAP and then not explain what's going on."

He motioned me to get out of the path of the TV, which I refused to do. "I don't know, it's something about the lawyer's office, Dad's estate—she's really upset. She sent Andrew to go pick something up for dinner. And *Tom's* here now. So you know she doesn't want to talk to me."

I felt myself grinding my teeth together so hard my sinuses ached. Of course Matt would view whatever crisis this was as an attack on his own ranking in the family likability poll. "What? Why?"

"Would you move, please?"

"Christ, I hate you sometimes," I said. I left him to his show and went into the dining room, where my mother was sitting with Tom and an older guy I didn't know, tall and heavyset, with thick black hair threaded with grey, and bushy eyebrows to match. My mother was crying—the gasping, red-faced type of emotion that I hadn't seen since after my father died. I swallowed hard and said, "Mom, hi."

"Roxie," she managed between sobs, reaching out her arm to me. I squeezed between Tom's chair and the wall so I could give her a hug.

"Mom, what happened?"

"It's—I'm—I'm so stupid," she said, before covering her face with both hands and crying so hard she couldn't speak. I rested a hand on her shoulder, my chest tight.

Tom stood up and pushed his chair in. "Roxane, this is Rafael Vega, he's a detective in Frauds," he said.

The older cop held out a hand. I shook it, stunned. "Frauds," I said. I felt my mouth hanging open, a sour taste of bile in the back of my throat. For a moment I couldn't speak.

Frauds could mean a lot of things, I told myself. Just because *my* current case involved fraud didn't mean that this was related.

My mother grabbed for my hand. "I was at the lawyer's office yesterday," she said, her voice gripped with tension. "Signing papers. Afterwards, a young man from the office came by here with something I'd forgotten to sign. I signed it and went about my day. But it was—I told Rita and she—your father, everything he worked for, and I just signed it all away. Like an idiot." She stopped there, consumed by tears again.

Rafael Vega gently touched her trembling shoulder. "Mrs. Weary, it's going to be okay."

I felt a wave of panicky emotion. This sounded all too familiar. "What the hell happened?" I asked Tom.

He nodded toward the kitchen and I followed him there. Rain was pounding against the window over the sink. "Genevieve was telling your neighbor about it, this document she signed, and it raised a red flag to her." He spoke quietly, almost a whisper. "The paper was a quitclaim deed, and the man from the lawyer's office said it was to transfer the house to you and your brothers automatically in the event of her death—but that's not how quitclaim deeds work. Your mother called me in a panic, rightfully so, and I brought in Rafael. He's seen this kind of thing before. Someone uses deceit to coerce a homeowner—usually someone older, older than your mother, actually—into signing over the rights to their property. Effectively selling it without money changing hands— What?"

"Tom, this is about Marin Strasser," I said.

His expression turned exasperated and a little bit concerned, maybe for my sanity. "What are you talking about?"

"She had a son. His name is Nate Harlow, and he's done this before. I tried to call you, like three times." My sinuses burned. I was not going to cry in front of him. "I didn't *try,* I mean, I did call you, and I left you two voice mails about this, and I just—forget it, Tom," I finished, escaping to the steps so I could have my break-down in private. Hot tears gushed down my cheeks as I climbed the stairs two at a time. Nate Harlow had been in my mother's house. Nate Harlow caused her to feel this way. *I* caused her to feel this way. This was my fault. My thoughts spun to the conversation after the funeral, when he'd hissed *you'll see how it feels* to me when he accused me of terrorizing Marin. This was an act of malice, nothing else. Malice toward me, enacted on my mother, who had nothing to do with any of it. At the top of the steps I pushed into the first doorway—my father's office—and slammed the door behind me.

This was only the second time I'd been in here since my father died, and the smell of him hit me in the face. Aftershave and whiskey. I bent at the waist, my forearms on my knees. I couldn't breathe.

The steps creaked as Tom walked up to the second floor of the house. He said my name gently, the way you talk to a crazy person. He tapped faintly on the door to the office. "Can I come in?"

"No," I said. I straightened up, wiped my face, tried to get a grip. "Please?"

"No."

He sighed. "Listen, I didn't see your calls. I dropped my phone on Monday and haven't had a chance to replace it yet."

I sat down on the edge of my father's desk and ran my fingers over the fake wood on the front edge, where the finish was warped from years of a glass of melting ice sitting in the same spot. With the lamp off and the thin, grey light from the window, the room was ashy and dim. "But my mother called you and you answered."

"Yes, at my desk."

"You weren't ignoring me, then."

"Of course not, Roxane, I wouldn't do that—look, can I come in?"

I didn't answer. I was thinking about the fact that my mother called Tom, instead of any of her kids. Instead of me. Not that I would've been any help, especially since this was my fault. He waited a few seconds before pushing the door open. In the dark, I saw his jaw bunch as he looked around the room, which somehow belonged more to my father than it ever did even when he was alive. I said, "I'm pretty sure it's haunted."

Tom sat on the edge of the desk next to me. "Tell me what's going on."

"Are you just humoring me?"

"No, I'm asking you to explain. We have Marin's cell phone, and the number she called most often was saved under *Nate.* Please, tell me."

There were footsteps in the hall. "Hey, Rox?"

Andrew pushed open the office door. "I got Chinese," he said. "Oh, sorry—um, I didn't know you were busy. Hey, Tom."

Without meaning to, I moved a few inches toward the window to put some distance between Tom and me. "We'll be down in a bit," I said.

Tom turned on the lamp that sat on my father's desk so he could take notes. I told him the whole story, from my complete failure to stay out of it on Friday, to the Harlow family, the Kinnamans, Bobby Veach, Vincent Pomp and his son, Leila, right up to the drama of last night. As he wrote I saw that he was left-handed, which I had never noticed before. Absurd that you could know someone intimately without ever seeing them write something down, but there we were. "I'm going to reach out to the Ds on the shooting last night, to see where they are," he said when I was finished. "And I need to talk to Leila, either bring her downtown for a formal interview or, if she needs a hospital, we can do it there. Plus Sanko, and we can loop in the rest of the Frauds team too." He reached into his pocket, came up empty-handed. "Dammit, I don't have a phone. I keep forgetting."

I offered him mine, but he shook his head. "I rely on it so much that of course I can't remember anyone's number. Vega will have it, though. We're going to get this guy, okay? Your mom is going to be fine. Probably we can intercept the paperwork before it ever even gets filed with the county, which would make it basically like it never happened. But even if we can't, there's exactly zero chance of a judge letting his claim on the house stand."

I turned away from him, my eyes welling again.

He reached out a hand, skimming it across my shoulder blades. "Hey, no, no, it's okay. I promise."

"I don't need to be comforted," I said, "I'm pissed off. And you know you can't promise that."

But he kept his hand there for a while and I let him.

TWENTY-FIVE

In the dining room, Vega and my brother had calmed my mother down to the point of being able to push lo mein listlessly around her plate. Tom motioned Vega into the kitchen, where they had a whispered chat. I sat down at the table with Andrew and my mother, shaking my head at the offer of a plate.

"Mom, I'm so sorry this is happening," I started.

She looked up at me. Her eyes were dry now, her features tense and stunned. "I don't want to talk about it any more, dear."

She got up from the table and squeezed past me, and a few beats later the bathroom door slammed.

I dropped my head into my arms. Andrew said, "So, do you have anything you want to tell me?"

I wiped my nose on my forearm and looked up at him. "Such as?"

He lifted one eyebrow. "It looked like you two were having kind of a moment, upstairs."

"What?"

"You and Tom."

"A moment?"

"You were sitting awfully close."

I put my head back on the table. "No. There was no moment."

"Because I'm pretty sure I saw a moment."

"Just stop. Please. I'm about to fall apart, here. This is all my fault."

"What is?"

But I was spared from answering by a hand on my shoulder. "Roxane, hon," Vega said, "mind stepping in here for a minute?"

I joined them in the kitchen and leaned against the counter for support.

"I filled Vega in," Tom said, his voice low. "Sanko is on the way over, and we're putting out an all-points on the Cadillac, and Vincent Pomp's vehicle as well."

I nodded. This conversation should've happened days ago. I could've mitigated some of this by acknowledging I was in over my head sooner. Like, maybe, on Monday when I first realized how many people were involved and how much was at stake. By calling Tom yesterday, I'd tried. Sort of. If my mother was smart enough to try him at his desk in the case of an emergency, why didn't I think of that? Some detective I was. I snatched a paper towel off the roll on the counter and dragged it across my face. I felt, and probably looked, like shit. But both Tom and Vega gave me the professional courtesy of not telling me so.

Vega was saying, "Usually the types who run this scam, they're strictly white-collar. Paper tigers, I call 'em. They can make a mess, but none of it stands up. This guy, though, he's different. Unpredictable."

I covered my face as another round of tears sprang from my eyes. Just an hour or so earlier, Leila had said that Nate wasn't smart enough to have any other scams. Maybe this was just more of the same, but my mother's house was small and unassuming—nothing like Agnes's. He hadn't done this out of greed, but rather, specifically to hurt me. He'd probably followed my mother to the lawyer's office and made up a story—a convincing one—to get to her. To me.

Something else was needling at me, though. He'd been to my mother's house yesterday. Yesterday afternoon, right after he talked to me. Before Leila ratted him out to Vincent Pomp. She'd said that she went to my apartment because it was the last place he'd think she'd go, that I was the last person he'd expect to help her. Why— because she knew about this?

Because she was capable of far more than she let on?

The icy panic that gripped me as I sat in traffic earlier wound its way around my heart again as I dialed Catherine's number, listened to the flat tone as it rang five times before it kicked to an automated voicemail greeting.

"I just left her there."

"What?"

"Who?" Vega said, confused.

"Catherine. With Leila. Oh my God." I called her again. "Just because it was fine earlier doesn't mean it's fine now. I trusted her too much. I thought she was telling me everything but she wasn't— no, she gave me just enough dirt on herself to make it believable, but—Tom, I need to go over there—"

"First we—"

"Please. Trust me on this."

He met my eyes for a long time, and finally said, "Right, of course. I trust you."

We took Tom's car, or the department's car—a tan Impala with a bar of flashing lights behind the grille in front. He turned them on as we sped south on 71 and he used the radio in the car to talk to someone in Patrol, trying to get a unit to check on Catherine ASAP. But because her house was technically in Bexley, a tricky jurisdiction issue arose. It was a hard story to explain in the first place, and around Spring Street, he gave up. We were almost there anyway.

I kept calling Catherine's number, and she kept not answering. Nothing had been wrong earlier, but this was different. She'd had her phone when I left—she'd shown it to me before slipping it into the pocket of her robe. I pressed my forehead against the rain-dotted window and tried to breathe. But my insides hurt as I pictured her, long blond hair sweeping against the black satin that covered her thin shoulders. Catherine was no damsel in distress, but she was physically delicate, small. Leila was too—and she was injured—but she was also duplicitous and dangerous. I had been more worried about Vincent Pomp than I was about her, and that was my mistake. One of many. I unholstered my gun and checked the cylinder.

Tom glanced at me but said nothing.

The house looked just as I'd left it, lights glowing in the lower level and one upstairs bedroom, door closed, driveway empty. Tom parked in the street and turned to me. "Let me—" he started, but I was already out of the car, sprinting up the slippery grass to the front door.

I pounded on it with my fist. "Catherine!" I shouted as I squinted through the sheer curtain behind the pane of glass in the door. I didn't see anything, or hear anything, but she didn't come to the door this time. Tom was right behind me, about to say something. But I was already grabbing a waterlogged daisy in a small, dense pot, which I chucked through the glass in the door so that I could reach in to unlock the deadbolt.

"Okay, stop. Roxane." Tom grabbed my arm and stepped in front of me, his own weapon drawn now too.

The alarm on the wall was silent. It should have been pealing. If it was still armed, that is. Catherine had armed it when I left. Tom started down the hallway, calling, "Police, is anyone here?"

I wanted to throw up. My thoughts were blaring static. I didn't even know what I was afraid had happened.

But something had, because Catherine would've opened the door otherwise.

We went through the lower level, and found nothing. Heard nothing. A pizza box was on the kitchen counter, one slice missing. Two plates beside it, untouched. Two napkins. Catherine's phone. An empty cardboard sleeve once containing twelve cans of grapefruit fizzy water was balanced on the lid of the kitchen trash can. A single can of the fizzy water was on the counter.

I looked at the can, the plates, the pizza. She would've had to disarm the security system to open the door for the delivery guy. Then she set it down, got out plates, a single beverage. Because there was only one can left in the box? I opened the fridge, saw an open space where the box had been, and then I bolted to the garage.

Catherine was on her side on the oil-stained concrete, an ugly gash at her temple. My stomach turned inside out as I dropped to my knees beside her. "Tom," I yelled, "I found her. Garage. She needs help."

She moaned softly as I felt along her jaw for a pulse, which was faint but steady. She turned her face toward my hand. A lump was forming at the edge of her eyebrow, purple and angry, bisected by a wide swath of broken skin that ran past her hairline, and there was blood dripping from her nose. "I'm so sorry," I whispered. "I'm so, so sorry. Just hang in there." I pulled my phone out but my fingers had gone numb, uncooperative. It skittered out of my hands and across the concrete. Tom dashed into the garage and collected the phone off the floor.

"Is she breathing?" he said, his voice low and serious, his face bathed in the glow of my phone as he dialed.

"Yes. Her pulse is like sixty and faint. Her car is gone, too."

He hit the garage-door button on the wall, and the door slowly ratcheted up. He paced outside, speaking urgently into the phone.

I stayed where I was, my hand clutching Catherine's, willing her to clutch back.

At some point, Ed Sanko decided he liked me, or at least didn't hate my guts anymore. He sat next to me in the waiting area of Grant's ER and listened to my story again, not calling me Veronica Mars even once. Not that it really mattered, since I'd obviously let him call me anything he wanted if it meant the universe would take back what was happening.

As if the universe had ever worked that way.

Catherine had been wheeled away for a CAT scan, and for the last thirty minutes, detectives and uniforms had been traipsing in and out of the waiting area as a plan was formulated. There was a warrant in the works for Leila's apartment, for the security-camera data for Catherine's house; there was an APB on the Cadillac, and on Catherine's stolen car as well; there were patrols at the airport. Sanko and I were making a list of places Leila might be. She was hurt—which maybe narrowed her options—though it was hard to say how bad the gunshot wound really was; her weak-voiced list-lessness could've easily been an act.

Sanko was saying, "So can you think of anywhere else she might go, any place she might have mentioned? Family?"

"Vincent Pomp," I said, "she is or was involved with him. And I don't know about family. She speaks with an accent, not sure where she's from."

"What about Nate Harlow?"

"She ratted him out," I said, "I can't imagine she's with him."

Tom, who was pacing back and forth by the elevator, said, "Humor us."

"Nate lived with her, with Leila. His mother is the only other associate I know about, and he's obviously not with her."

"Marin's associates, then."

I shook my head.

"The Victorian Village house, maybe," I said. "It's empty, except for the antiques. But she knows that I know about the house. Unless she'd try to sell something for cash."

"Sell something, at this hour?"

Tom, still pacing, said, "There's a twenty-four-hour pawn shop on the west side."

Sanko shook his head, but I held up a hand. "Pawn shop," I said, nodding. "She might go to Arthur's house. For money. Well, Bitcoin slips, whatever you call them. I found a bunch of them in Marin's stuff, and Leila asked me about it, offhand." Like she was fishing for information, now that I thought about it. I sighed.

"What does that have to do with pawn shops?" Tom said, while Sanko muttered something about Bitcoin.

"Bitcoin ATMs. They're—it's—I can explain Bitcoin to you another time, but it's like digital cash, untraceable. Marin had a pile of Bitcoin serial numbers in her nightstand, I guess her and Nate's share of the loot, and anyone can use those to get cash out of a Bitcoin ATM, which you can find in places like pawn shops." I was holding Catherine's black leather purse, and I squeezed it to my chest. "So that's my best guess, Arthur's place."

Tom and Sanko looked at each other. "Worth a try, I guess," Tom said.

I stood up. "Can I come?"

Both detectives said, in unison, "No."

"But you don't know where it is."

"We can find it," Tom said, "and you should stay here for when she wakes up."

They left, Tom promising to call me from Sanko's phone if anything developed. I knew he was right—Catherine would be scared when she woke up, and I didn't want her to be alone—but I also wanted to watch someone slap handcuffs onto Nate and Leila more than I'd wanted anything in recent memory. I took up Tom's beat by the elevator and paced the yellowing linoleum. Other things I wanted, in no particular order:

A drink
A hug
A time machine

There were none of the above on offer in the Grant ER.

I sat back down and called my brother.

"She's asleep," Andrew said. "I got her to take a Valium."

"Will you stay with her?"

After a pause, he said, "She's asleep."

"Andrew."

"Matt's still here."

"If you leave, Matt will sit on the edge of her bed so that he can be the first thing she sees when she wakes up, and he'll immediately remind her of what a fuckup I am. Please, stay with her. He'll get sick of you and leave eventually."

"You're not a fuckup."

"I appreciate the sentiment, but let's be clear: This *is* my fault."

Andrew sighed. "That guy, Vega, he said things would be okay. And, I mean, when do cops ever say that? So he was probably lying, I guess. But there are things she can do—there are options."

"But Andrew, she was terrified. Because of me, because of this, whatever this mess is. My fault. Don't argue with me about it."

"Fine. It's your fault."

"Thank you."

"Does that make you feel better?"

"Not at all."

We listened to each other breathe for a few seconds. "I'm gonna go," I said finally. "Please stay with her."

"Okay."

"Promise me."

"*Okay*, I promise."

I sat back down, was too restless for sitting, and got up again. Finally, the elevator doors opened and an orderly wheeled Catherine out. She was awake, her green eyes wide and scared.

"You're here," she whispered.

I followed her gurney down the short hallway to the curtained-off corner that constituted her room for the moment. The orderly gave me a dirty look but said, "Dr. Sethy will be in shortly."

I put Catherine's bag on the foot of her bed and leaned down to kiss her cheek. "I am so sorry this happened," I said. "The one time I think maybe you aren't going to hurt me, and then I turn around and hurt you."

She grabbed my hand. "You were right about her. Not honest."

"Not that right," I said, "because I left you with her like it was nothing." I nodded at her head. "What happened?"

"I went out to the garage to get a drink," she said, "and then there was this man there, behind me."

I stared at her. "A man."

She nodded, wincing.

"Young, old, what kind of man?"

"Young. Blond. He hit me, with a gun. He took my car."

"What—how? How did he find your house?" I said, though this was not a question Catherine could answer. "Where was Leila in all of this?"

"She told him not to touch me."

"When?"

"After. After he hit me. Then they got in the car."

"She went with him willingly."

Another nod.

Jesus Christ, was any of Leila's story true? I bit my lip so hard I tasted blood.

Catherine said, "My phone."

"It's right here," I said, "do you want it? I can call someone for you—"

"No, no, she was using it. She was using my phone. She asked if she could use it to check her voice mail, since she didn't have hers. I didn't think . . . she only had it for a minute, maybe two. She didn't even speak to anyone. Just listened." She squeezed her eyes closed. "That was stupid, wasn't it."

"No, it wasn't. You didn't know. Can I look at the phone?"

She nodded again, her eyes still closed.

I took out the phone and clumsily clicked through its old-school menu. If she hadn't talked to anyone, she'd probably texted Nate. But the inbox and the outbox were both completely empty, like she'd cleared them after she used the phone. I said, "Did she actually call her voice mail?"

"She called something. I heard a recording, and she pressed a bunch of buttons."

I clicked to the recent-calls list, which she had not cleared. At 8:40, when I was sitting in my father's office having a breakdown, she had called a single number, toll-free.

I used my own phone to call it.

"*Hi*," a recorded voice told me, "*thanks for calling Greyhound.*"

I went out to the lobby and called Sanko's number. "They're together," I said breathlessly once Tom was on the line, "Leila and Nate—"

"I know, one of Ungless's neighbors saw them. They were here. Not long ago. The Worthington police were just getting here when we arrived, said they got a call about the alarm going off about fifteen minutes back. She bled all over the house. I checked the nightstand. Just a, um, some weed," Tom said, apparently unwilling to say the word *vibrator* to me. "No paper slips. Do you know how much money we're talking?"

"No idea. Marin stole thousands from Arthur. But who knows how much of that is left. Listen, I think they're over at the bus station," I said, and explained about Catherine's phone. I glanced down the hallway, where she was being admitted for observation overnight since she had a concussion.

Visiting hours were long over.

"Stay where you are, Roxane," Tom said, reading my mind. He muffled the phone against something while he spoke to someone else, and then a car door slammed. "Okay, I'm going to get someone from Patrol over there right away, and we'll be there soon. Please, stay where you are."

"But—"

"No. I'll call you back."

He hung up in my ear. I got up and started pacing again. The Greyhound station was a five-minute walk, maybe less. But what was I going to do—stage a citizen's arrest? I kept pacing, telling myself I was doing a good job of not being reckless for a change. Back and forth across the linoleum. The doors slid open and people came in and went out and I stayed where I was.

Until, that is, I heard a voice behind me. A familiar one.

I spun around in time to see Vincent Pomp and his oldest son, Simon, hustling out of the elevator and toward the street doors, talking low. They must have been visiting Derek, I realized. Before too long, we could fill the entire hospital with victims of this mess. I pressed myself against a wall, but neither of them noticed me there. I went after them as far as the door vestibule but they were already getting into the backseat of the black Crown Vic. I watched its taillights head toward Town Street—toward the bus station. I called Sanko's phone again, but no one answered this time.

"I just saw Vincent Pomp and his other son leaving the hospital, with some urgency," I said into his voice mail. "They drove south on Sixth." I bit my lip, trying to decide what else I should say. But there was nothing else, so I hung up as I ran down the steps outside the hospital. The night air was cool and wet, the pavement shiny in pools of light.

Stay where you are.

Pomp could have been heading home, to his office, to a bar. He wasn't necessarily going to the bus station, was he? I folded my arms over my chest and tried to talk myself into staying.

Or maybe he was going to the bus station after all, and not because he needed a ride. He wanted to kill Nate Harlow for what Nate did to Tessa. Would a bunch of bystanders stop that kind of revenge?

I closed my eyes, the image of her body brightening into focus in my mind.

Meanwhile, I was going to do—what—stay where I was?

TWENTY-SIX

I approached the bus station via Town Street, scanning the entrance for signs of any disturbance. Nothing—not yet—but also, there weren't any cops in sight, just a cluster of taxi drivers outside the doors, smoking and chattering in rapid-fire Somali. Pomp's Crown Vic was not among the cars parked at the curb. I doubled back to Fourth to check out the meter spots there, but I still didn't see it, or Catherine's car. I pushed into the station through the side doors and lingered briefly by the package service window—currently closed—while I looked over the people seated on benches in the long space of the terminal. It was about half full, quiet except for a television tuned to the Weather Channel.

No one looked familiar.

I walked the length of the terminal, past the ticketing desk, the vending machines, the bank of pay phones, the empty express-bus waiting area, and the café, where the smell of day-old hot dogs and coffee mingled with old cigarette smoke and diesel. A uniformed employee looked up at me, then back to her phone. I turned around and went back the opposite way, noticing a *NO FIREARMS* sign posted on one wall.

But I still didn't see anyone—not Nate, not Leila, and not Vincent Pomp.

I ducked into the women's restroom and found only an old lady washing out a plastic sandwich container at the sink. I took off my scarf and tied it around my waist to fully camouflage the gun holstered on my hip. As I turned to leave, I caught sight of my own reflection in the dirty, chipped mirror next to the door and hoped that the grim setting was contributing to how rough I looked.

The scarf wasn't helping, and neither was the bruise at my throat.

I weaved my way through the ropes at the ticket counter and waited to be called up, which took nearly a minute despite the fact that no one was in line in front of me. The ticket agent looked like he hated everyone equally, and I was no exception. "Hi there," I said, "I don't need a ticket, I'm just trying to find my friends—we were supposed to meet up. Maybe you've seen them? Good-looking blond guy, cheekbones that could cut glass—"

"Haven't you people heard of cell phones?" he said, cutting me off. I looked at him.

"Your friend, he was here, asking if I'd seen *you*. Dark-haired lady, no luggage, that's you, right?"

I supposed that did sound like me. I nodded with mock relief. "Where did he go? And how long ago was that?"

"Ten, fifteen minutes," he said. "And I don't know where he went. To keep looking, probably."

"What did you tell him? About if you'd seen me."

"Lady, you just walked in here."

"I know, I know." He was losing his patience with me, so I hurried to finish. "But did he buy a ticket?"

"No. Now, if you don't mind," he added, pointing at the small line that had formed between the ropes.

"Right. Thank you."

I went in the direction of the Fourth Street doors, giving the terminal another once-over. Still nothing. I paused at the restrooms again and stuck my head into the men's, but it was empty.

So Nate was looking for Leila, and having enough trouble

finding her that he asked the cranky ticket agent. Dark-haired lady, no luggage. Interesting distinction. Maybe Nate was carrying their luggage. She was injured, after all. But where had she gone? I'd been wrong about her at every turn so far, so it was hard to guess. I placed a hand on the top of my opposite shoulder and imagined the throbbing heat of a gunshot wound, the chemical buzz of Demerol. I could see her going into the restroom, to puke or to splash water on her face. Or maybe outside for some fresh air—the atmosphere inside the bus station wasn't exactly invigorating. I started to push open the door, rearing back into the doorway when I spotted Pomp's driver-slash-bodyguard standing on the sidewalk, meaty arms folded across his meatier chest, eyes on the street. He gave no indication that he'd noticed me, so I stood very still and waited until someone else came out of the station, noisily dragging a suitcase with a bum wheel. I slipped back into the station and made a beeline for the Town Street doors, catching sight of Pomp's elder son milling around by the express-bus area.

Lightning flashed outside—a neon crack of it, followed by an electric whine and sudden murky darkness inside the bus station as the power went out.

A groan went up among the people in the waiting area. "Oh hell no," somebody near me muttered.

Cell phones began to light up, everyone's faces lit from below like people telling ghost stories by a campfire. I joined the back of a group headed toward the Town Street exit and pushed outside. The traffic signal at Town and Third was dead. The streetlights, too. The cloudy, late-twilight sky was the color of wet cement. The rain had slowed to a sprinkle, but far-off thunder still rumbled. The street was filling in now, a stream of people walking south on Third as if an event at the theater had just let out when the power died. There was an air of disbelief on the street. I walked to the corner of

Town and Third and looked up and down the block and took a few steps, and then I froze.

A dark figure leaned out of the bus-only driveway and looked up and down the block, as I had, then ducked back inside the fence, then stepped out, facing in my direction.

But he wasn't looking at me.

He was looking at something behind me.

I stepped backward until I was pressed up against the brick wall of the building and looked to my right, squinting in the near-dark.

Vincent Pomp.

The figure by the driveway was Nate.

They both had their guns drawn, and I was right in between them.

I covered my mouth with my hand. It didn't seem like either of them had seen me. But they certainly had seen each other.

No one spoke.

I was barely breathing.

Then Nate turned slightly and took off running across the street, firing off two shots in the general direction of both Pomp and me as he dodged between cars. The shots both went into the brick wall. Pomp ran after Nate amid the shriek of braking cars and the scatter and gasp of pedestrians. Nate ran down the throat of the underground-garage entrance, Pomp close behind. I nearly collided with the elder Pomp son as I ran the opposite way on Third— toward the oncoming crowd of theatergoers—and our eyes met, but despite the recognition that flashed in his, he kept running after his father.

I hurried across the street too, waving my arms. "Don't go into the garage," I shouted at the southbound traffic. I could see the edge of the Statehouse lawn up ahead. There had to be police there, I thought. "Go towards the Statehouse."

A woman driving a RAV4 with its windows down rolled them

up, like *I* was the danger. Finally, red and blue lights started swirling from up the street and a cruiser squealed to a stop at the entrance to the park. Two uniforms got out and looked at me like they thought I might be the danger too. "There's an active shooter in the garage," I said, pointing south toward the ramp. There wasn't time to explain. "I saw three people at least, all with guns."

They exchanged glances, but then two more shots boomed around the block.

TWENTY-SEVEN

"Everybody down! Everybody down!"

One of the uniforms ducked back into the cruiser and reversed into the street, effectively blocking off the traffic. The other spoke into his mic in urgent tones. More sirens lit up a few blocks away. The people on the street scattered in every direction—into the hotel, between the stopped cars, back toward the theater, over toward the bus station. I ran into the center of the mass of people, urging them back and away from the whole area. A twenty-something woman—dressed for a night out and drunk already—slurred to her friend, "What's going on? Fireworks? We can't get to the car because of fireworks?"

"We can get into the garage through the hotel," the friend said, "don't worry."

My stomach flip-flopped. She was right. The garage connected to the hulking Capitol Square building, which connected to the hotel, the theater, maybe more.

I ran up the block and flagged down a kid in a lime-green valet windbreaker who was on his way back to his post. "I need your help," I told him. "Get hotel security. They need to shut down access to the hotel, including the garage, okay? Nobody in. There are men with guns in the garage."

He stared at me. "Are you a cop?"

I showed him my gun, which was apparently proof enough. Nodding, he grabbed a walkie-talkie from the valet stand and headed inside the hotel. I walked back along the edge of the park. There were still people hanging out, maybe expecting a fireworks display too. "You guys need to clear the area," I announced as I walked, my voice shaky to my own ears, "go out to High Street and head towards the Statehouse, okay?"

Against a chorus of *huh* and *what*, another trio of police cars converged on the area, lights swirling.

I intercepted a family with three small kids as they rounded the corner out of the tunnel that led over to the Statehouse.

"No, the park is closed, go over to the Statehouse. That way." I pointed. "Hurry. Please. Tell anyone you see not to come down here."

I pushed open the back entrance to the building and called Sanko's phone again. This time, Tom finally answered. "The power is out downtown, and Nate and Vincent Pomp are in the garage under the Commons," I said, "and I've heard four shots already—"

"Roxane, where are you?"

It was cool and dark and very quiet inside, insulated from the chaos outside but also somehow scarier, because I was that much closer to whatever was happening down there. "I'm in the Capitol Square building, in the back where the shops are. I'm not in the garage. Tom, there are people everywhere, and the garage is connected to all these buildings—I'm just trying to keep people from going down there. They have no idea. Everything is pitch black."

Through the windows I could barely see cops halfway down the park with flashlights, clearing people away from the entrances to the garage. I unholstered my gun and crept slowly along the wall, bumping into a table almost immediately. I winced at the loud sound; being stealthy lasted about a minute. But I didn't hear anything else, no other signs of life. The businesses were all closed at this hour, their glass doors locked tight. Out on State Street, police lights swirled and horns honked, nobody understanding. My wet shoes squeaked on the tile floor as I made my way farther into the space.

"We're three minutes out, maybe less," Tom was saying, "we're coming from Broad Street. Will you please stay where you are this time? Please?"

"Yes," I said, meaning to do exactly that.

But then I heard someone else's footsteps on the terra-cotta tile.

I dropped into a crouch behind a trash can in the center of the row of shops and pressed my phone to my chest to muffle the light from its screen. I kept my breathing soft and even and didn't move a muscle, not even when I heard those footsteps echoing toward me.

Heavy footsteps.

He bumped into the same table I had and swore at it softly.

The footsteps zigzagged across the hall, and he jiggled some doorknobs.

I heard Tom's voice, tinny and muffled against my shirt.

I ground my teeth together and wished more than anything that I'd just kept moving toward State Street. But I hadn't, and so here I was. I squeezed my eyes shut, willed the footsteps to stop.

About eight feet away from me, they did. Then pale white light lit up the hallway, just for a second. I didn't dare to pop my head out for a look. Instead I listened as hard as I could: heavy breathing, like someone who had just run a great distance.

The flashlight or phone screen or whatever it was flipped off, and the space plunged back into darkness.

And the footsteps kept approaching me.

One, two.

Somehow the quality of the darkness above me changed, and I knew that he was standing right in front of the trash can. He stood very still, impossibly silent. I was afraid to move even the few inches I'd need to move in order to see if he was looking at me, or just standing there oblivious to my presence.

Then, soundlessly, the muzzle of a gun pressed into my temple, hard. "Where is she?" Nate Harlow said.

Every muscle of my body contracted, as if I could shrink from view via sheer isometrics. I didn't say a word.

Nate grabbed my arm and yanked me upright. My phone slipped out of my grasp and skittered away down the tiles screen-up, still connected to Tom. Nate twisted my revolver out of my hand, snapped open the cylinder, and shook it; the six rounds clanged onto the floor and scattered. He squinted in the darkness at the gun. "Piece of shit," he said.

He tossed it down the hallway in the direction he'd come from. "Now. Where. Is. She. Tell me what you did with her."

"With who, Nate?"

His voice was strained and desperate. "With Leila! With Leila. Jesus Christ. Where is she?"

"I don't know."

"Don't lie to me."

"I *don't know.*"

"You just couldn't stay out of it. My business."

"Speak for yourself," I said, "you went to my mother's house—"

Abruptly, he hushed me, clamping a hand over my mouth. The doors from the park opened slowly. Nate pulled me against the glass wall of one of the shops. His fingers dug into my skin. At first there was no sound, just a mounting tension in the air. Whoever had entered bumped into the same table and knocked it over.

The next sound was my gun sliding across the linoleum as someone stumbled over it.

My phone was too far away to reach, its screen still lit up, still connected to the call.

I squeezed my eyes shut, though it didn't make much of a difference whether they were open or not in this darkness.

I heard the cylinder of my gun snap out and in. "Does this mean you're bone dry, Harlow?" Vincent Pomp said.

Without hesitation Nate moved his gun away from my temple and fired two shots in the direction of Pomp's voice. The sound boomed around the corridor, punctuated with the treble of breaking glass as a bullet struck one of the shop windows. The door facing State Street swung open, a cry of "Police!" interrupted with more gunfire.

"Nobody moves," Nate barked, "nobody comes in here. I'll shoot her if anybody else comes in here."

The door at the other end opened too, and Nate dragged me away from the wall to shoot three times down there. I lost my balance and fell, and Nate caught me by the hair. I cried out as he yanked me across the hall and into a slight alcove made by the doorway of a store.

The darkness was disorienting, my brain showing me shapes that weren't actually there in front of me. I touched my scalp, expecting blood but not finding any. The State Street doors were still open, a few uniformed cops visible in the flashing police lights from the street behind them. The other end of the hallway was silent and dark, Vincent Pomp either hiding or dead.

I plunged my hands in my pockets, looking for anything that could function as a weapon: a receipt, two quarters, and my keys. I had a Swiss army knife on the keychain, though it was old and more like a nail file than a knife. Still, maybe it could do some damage. I ran my fingers over it, starting what I could remember of the rosary in my head.

"Hey, Nate?" a familiar voice called from the State Street doors. Tom.

I pressed a hand over my mouth so I wouldn't scream.

Nate said, "I told you, nobody comes in here."

"No, I know, I know," Tom said. "I'm just here in the doorway. Nobody's coming in."

Nate was quiet.

"You can call me Tom."

Silence.

"Right now, Nate, things could go a lot of different ways, right? Nothing's set in stone. You can still change the outcome here."

Nate lifted the gun from my head again and fired at the ceiling, where something shattered and *ping*ed back down to the floor. "Shut up," he snapped. Then he jammed the gun back against my skull.

On the park side of the corridor, a stunned grunt was followed by a slumping sound.

"You son of a bitch," Vincent Pomp yelled, and he shot once toward the doorway Nate and I were in. "Simon. Simon. Where are you—"

"I'm okay," Simon Pomp said weakly. "It's not that bad."

It sounded a little bit bad.

I reached the first decade on my Swiss army rosary as Nate pressed the gun harder into my head.

"You shot my other son, now," Pomp said. "What the fuck did I ever do to you?"

"Fuck you. This is all your fault. Listen, I have demands. Okay? I have demands. You're supposed to listen to my demands, right? Are you listening?"

"Yes, Nate, I'm listening," Tom said.

"First of all, I want everyone to back up, I want a fifty-yard perimeter around this place."

Impossible, especially considering the fact that the street was gridlocked with cars. But Tom said, "Okay, that's easy, I'll work on that."

"Next, I want Leila here, now."

A tense silence followed.

"Where can I find her?"

"You tell me, asshole."

Then Pomp yelled from the other side of the hallway, "Leila is gone, kid. She sold you out. She sold you out yesterday."

Nate fired two shots in that direction. Another silence. I dug hard at the edge of my Swiss army knife, still trying to free its blade.

Tom spoke next. "You miss her, huh? You're close with her."

Nate kept the gun on me as he leaned into the hallway. "Yeah. That's it. I *miss her*. So nobody's leaving until you bring her here."

"That's the thing though," Pomp said, "she's gone. She got on a bus. To Cleveland."

"No. We were going south. Huntington. She had the money. From the antiques."

"She lied, bud. You're never going to see her again."

Some of the pressure from Nate's gun let up, but it didn't seem like a conscious choice. He was getting fidgety, physically anxious. He paced the width of the doorway, the hand with the gun moving loosely around my head.

"It sounds like you just need to talk with her, clear all this up," Tom said, "right?"

I could tell what he was doing: trying to find a common ground with this lunatic, get him to relax, establish empathy, eventually create a rapport. But Nate only seemed more keyed-up, not less. It didn't help that Pomp did not have the same objective as Tom.

"She's *gone*," Pomp said. "Jesus, this is pathetic. Nobody loves you, kid. Not Leila, not your mommy. Did you know she was afraid of you? She told me, she said when you went to jail, she was re-lieved."

"Don't talk about her. She'd still be alive if it wasn't for you."

Nate fired across the hall, shattering another window. Kernels of safety glass showered the corridor and momentarily caught the light from the police cars on State Street. In that split second, I could make out a human shape crouching along the glass wall to my right while Nate paced, agitated as hell, to my left. Pomp? I squinted in the dark until the face came into view: not Pomp, but his bodyguard, Bo.

The darkness had been so complete that I hadn't even realized he was in here. And, more importantly, neither had Nate.

Bo raised a finger to his lips, and I nodded.

"How do you figure?" Pomp called.

"If you would've just taken care of her while I was gone. She wouldn't have wound up with him. He was obsessed. Obsessed with her, and he killed her."

Pomp chuckled. "And here I thought you killed your mommy."

So did I.

"I would never hurt her. Never. All of this was for her. To get what she deserved. She earned that house. My father's house. For putting up with that whole fucked-up family for all those years. It was all going to be hers when he died. But they were so horrible to us. They took what was hers. Ours."

"Mr. Pomp," Tom called, "what do you say about letting Nate and me work this out?"

"Like I care about him getting it worked out. He killed my daughter. My Tessa. She was nineteen years old. Nineteen years old. He shot *both* of my sons. Simon, you doing okay over there?"

"I'm hanging in," the younger Pomp said, his voice weaker this time.

"We're gonna get you some help, okay? As soon as I put a bullet in this asshole's forehead."

Tom said, "We can get help for your son right now. We just need the guns to go down on the ground."

In reply, Pomp fired at the ceiling this time. A chunk of plaster came down with the bullet. I finally got the knife open in my pocket and slowly slid it out and showed it to Bo. He nodded and made a gesture I couldn't follow.

"I just need you all to back up, like I said." Nate stepped out of the doorway, his foot only inches from Bo's hand. "Okay? No more psychology bullshit until that happens."

He stepped back into the doorway, still oblivious to Bo.

But also still waving the gun in my general direction.

Once Nate resumed pacing, I craned my neck so I could make out the shadow of Bo's face again. He pointed at my hand—at the knife. Then pointed at the back of his own knee, pantomiming a stabbing motion. Then a nod at Nate.

I pointed at my chest, wishing telepathy were real. He was asking me to stab Nate in the back of the knee?

Another nod.

It seemed like my other choice was to wait until Bo made a move himself, which might or might not take my personal well-being into consideration.

I couldn't believe I was about to cooperate with a demi-gangster.

But I nodded back.

"I don't see anyone fucking moving!" Nate screamed. "Get the fuck out of here."

He stepped out into the hall and fired at State Street, where the civilians were, the cops. Where Tom was.

Suddenly, a deep hum sounded in the building. As the lights began to flicker on, I took my Swiss army knife and jammed it into Nate's popliteal as hard as I could. He yelled in pain, the knee buckling and sending him sideways to the floor. Bo rolled forward and landed with an elbow on Nate's wrist, which made a sickening crunch and pop of bones.

The gun landed on the tiles.

I pulled myself out of the doorway and grabbed it, released the clip.

It was empty.

The doors on State Street opened and the hallway flooded with cops. I saw Tom among them, his face ashy as he met my eye.

Nate writhed in pain, blood soaking his pant leg and the floor beneath him. My knife stuck out from the tissue behind his knee, dead in the center.

"Jesus," Bo said, "good aim."

I heard someone laughing, and realized it was me.

TWENTY-EIGHT

The entire thing had gone down in twenty-three minutes. It felt like at least a hundred times that long, but American Electric Power reported that the electricity, which had gone out in the general downtown area owing to a blown transformer, was restored after only twenty-three minutes, thanks to the swift response from its team.

"I call bullshit on that," Sanko said, turning off the television in the small kitchenette near the homicide unit. "Twenty-three minutes. If that's true, then how the hell is it after five a.m. already?"

"Time flies," Tom said, "when you're doing paperwork." He tapped a pen on his report and continued to not look at me, which was what he had been doing since we got here. The interrogation rooms were all full—Bo, Vincent Pomp, and Simon, who had been treated and released for the wound where Nate's second-to-last bullet had merely grazed his forearm. I was just a pesky witness, more or less; I didn't rate a proper interrogation room. Nate, meanwhile, was in the hospital. The same hospital as three of his other victims: Arthur, Derek, and Catherine. There was maybe something poetic about that, or maybe there wasn't. And Leila was, like Pomp had said, long gone. By the time the cops were able to touch base with the bus line, her Detroit-bound coach had already stopped in Marion and Leila had already cut and run. The driver remembered the pretty woman with her arm in a sling, but he had no idea where she went. So for now, she'd gotten away with her part in the whole thing.

For now.

It all could've turned out worse, but it sure as hell could've turned out better.

I picked up another stale cruller from the box on the table. *Fresh from us to you!* it told me. I wasn't so sure about that. But I shoved half of it in my mouth anyway.

Sanko rolled his eyes. "You two and the crullers. Disgusting."

"Why does everyone rag on crullers?" I said. I held up the remaining half of mine. "Right?"

Tom's eyes flicked up briefly but didn't meet mine. He just bit into his doughnut and frowned. "Christ, how old are these?" He pitched the rest of it into the trash and went back to his report.

I slumped in my chair and polished off the rest of my cruller. I wanted to ask how much longer it would be before I was allowed to leave, but I was sort of afraid that Tom would say *eternity* and throw me in jail forever based on the degree of fondness he was exhibiting for me at the moment.

Sanko pushed his chair back from the table and picked up the doughnut box. "I'm going in search of better options," he said, tossing the box in the trash on his way out of the room.

"I had no idea cops were so discerning about doughnuts," I said mildly.

Tom stopped writing for a second but still didn't look over at me. "Yes, we have highly refined palates from years of putting up with bullshit from civilians."

"Hey. Look at me."

He still wouldn't.

"Can we stop with this fight? Please?"

Finally he looked up. His warm brown eyes were tired and strained and not all that warm. "You can't ignore every single thing

I say, and then act like you have no idea what I'm pissed about, Roxane. Do you remember last night at your mom's? How I set that aside to help you out, no questions asked? And then you turned around and did the exact same thing again, except it was worse this time, and I just—I've been doing this for, what, seventeen years? And I've been in a lot of situations that weren't great, and felt a lot of different ways when I was in them. I have *never* felt like I did last night." He pushed away from the table and walked to the sink, arms folded over his chest. "Like I was powerless, nothing I could do. Because you put yourself right in the middle of a thing that you knew was bad, on purpose, and there was a chance, a really big fucking chance, honestly, that you weren't getting out of it."

It was the most he'd said to me in the last six months, and he wasn't done yet. He sat back down across from me and said, "I asked you to stay at the hospital. You told me that you would. But then you followed three pretty bad guys to a fucking bus station, looking for two other bad guys? And when that didn't put you into harm's way enough, you went right into ground zero of the whole thing."

"Isn't it to my credit that I didn't go into the parking garage?"

"No, Jesus Christ, are you hearing me at all? It's like you want to punish people for caring about you, and that is so many kinds of fucked up, Roxane. And all of this, every last bit of it was pointless. Because Ungless, who is apparently more important to you than your mom, or Catherine, or me—he's still guilty." He flipped his notebook closed as if that was the end of it. "You can go, we're good."

"Hold on, I don't think you can say we're good after that," I said, leaning onto my forearms on the table, so stunned by what he had just said that I couldn't even respond to the part that mattered. "After all of this craziness, you still think Marin is dead because of a lover's quarrel?"

He looked at me with something like disbelief. "Do you have another theory of what happened to her?"

"Um," I said, because I didn't really, other than the fact that Nate was obviously nuts, "how about the guy who killed two people *that we know of* and tried to kill three others? Four, counting Agnes."

"You heard what he said in the dark."

"Right, and Nate Harlow is completely rational and trustworthy."

He got up from the table again. "We found his prints on shell casings from the scene."

"Nate's? Great. He's your guy. What's the problem?"

"Arthur Ungless's fingerprints. Casings. From Hunter Avenue."

"No."

"No, what? You're telling me what we did or didn't find now?"

"That's impossible."

"How so?"

"He—no. He wouldn't."

"His fingerprints were at the scene. That's concrete. Direct evidence. Not only that, but he remains the only one with a coherent motive here anyway."

I shook my head but didn't say anything right away. If all of this—what had happened to Catherine, to my mother, to my car, to me—came to pass because I couldn't believe that hapless old Arthur could ever hurt anyone, I was done. I'd enroll in dental hygienist college after all.

Tom added, "If you have any other ideas, I'm all ears."

When I came out of the police station, I looked around at the street for a second, not at all sure where my vehicle was. Then I remembered I had the ketchup-scented rental car, and that it was at my mother's house on the north side. I decided to walk over to the hospital—maybe it would clear my head. The sky was that kind of orangey pink that looks pretty like a sunset but really means trouble, at least according to the sailors. The air was dry for the moment, though, and faintly cool. Rush-hour traffic was starting up downtown, the drivers sleepy-eyed and oblivious to the fact that a few hours earlier, the scene of their daily commutes had been a hostage situation.

I walked east on Long Street, past the YMCA and a series of boarded-up storefronts and the exposed pit of earth where they were building more overpriced condos that no one would buy, or another parking garage that we didn't need. I tried walking fast, but my body wasn't cooperating. I wasn't angry at Tom like I had been the other day—I was just bewildered.

Because he was probably right.

There was no benefit in caring about me.

No one had benefited from even *knowing* me lately, including Arthur, who maybe didn't deserve my help anyway. I still couldn't picture him shooting his pretty fiancée, not even after discovering the extent of her deceit. But I couldn't ignore the fingerprints. I probably shouldn't have ignored the gun in the first place. The gun he owned and claimed not to know the whereabouts of.

Maybe it really had been stolen. By a random thief who then used it to murder Arthur's fiancée twenty years later.

I sighed. Hoof prints, horses. If Tom was just telling me about this case, I'd easily say that Arthur was guilty. A no-brainer. But I'd met him, and I thought that meant something. That my instincts told me he was a good guy who'd never hurt Marin.

But my instincts had also told me that Leila was trustworthy enough to leave alone with Catherine.

So maybe my instincts weren't worth shit.

Catherine was asleep when I got to her room. I stood in the

doorway for a while, watching her breathe out and in, out and in. Her head was tipped to one side and I could see the patch of skin where her hair had been shaved, the wound thick with spiky black stitches. A heinous bruise had bloomed behind her ear, across her temple, around her eye. I wanted to throw up and for a second I thought I would. But I swallowed a few times and my stomach calmed to a regular old sinking sense of dread.

I sat down in a chair against the wall of Catherine's small room and looked at the whiteboard mounted next to the door. *Discharge date: TBD. Today's plans: Neuro-oto consult. MRI.*

"Jesus," I muttered.

I leaned against my hand, closed my eyes for just a second, and fell into a flat, dreamless sleep immediately.

I woke up when a nurse bustled into the room and checked Catherine's vitals. "Your blood pressure is staying up, hon, which is great news. Can you tell me where you are?"

"The hospital," Catherine mumbled, her voice hoarse.

"And do you know who the president of the United States is?"

"Unfortunately."

The nurse laughed. "Okay, sister, back in a couple hours, okay?" She shot me a smile as she left the room.

Catherine murmured to me, "Don't go anywhere."

I started to unfold myself from the chair and go to her side, but she dropped off to sleep again.

I leaned my head back against the wall. I thought I stayed awake, but when I heard Catherine's voice again, the light in the room was different.

"Are you just going to sit over there like a weirdo?" she said.

"No. Hi. Good morning. Sorry." I got up and moved to the edge of her bed. "I didn't mean to fall asleep."

"I'm sure the chair is incredibly comfortable."

"I'm thinking of replacing my mattress with one. Catherine,

I'm so sorry. I'm sorry that this happened, and I'm sorry I left you here last night—"

"Hey, stop. No." She put her hand over mine on top of the thin blanket she lay under. "We aren't doing that. I don't want to talk about how very sorry you are."

I nodded. That was fair enough. "How are you feeling?"

"You can probably guess."

That was fair enough, too. "Do you need anything? What can I do? When do you get to go home?"

"They don't know yet." She gave a soft little sigh. "Please. Stop with the questions. Just sit with me."

I nodded and kept quiet and held on to her hand.

Finally she said, "It's not just the concussion."

"What is it?"

"It's called a temporal fracture? That's the part of the skull over here." She pointed at the deeply bruised area around her ear. "Um, so I guess my brain is now exposed to bacteria from my ear canal, which is cool."

"Catherine—"

"Stop, stop," Catherine said. She squeezed my hand. "Just listen. I'm supposed to stay calm, and so you have to also. Calm. Okay?"

I looked away and nodded, a white-hot anger poking my heart.

"I have to be on antibiotics, because of the, it's called a CSF leak? A cerebrospinal fluid leak. And I'm having some trouble hearing right, from this ear. And vertigo like whoa. Which sounds bad, I know, but it might not be."

I squeezed my eyes shut. None of this was fair, not least that I should've been comforting her, not the other way around. But I didn't trust myself to speak yet.

"There's an ear doctor who will come by at some point today and I'll know more. Sometimes they have to do surgery, for this. Sometimes not. It can heal on its own too, without the surgery. If there aren't complications, I could be out of here by tomorrow. The head, the brain, it's apparently good at fixing itself. It's smart, literally."

I cleared my throat. "Especially yours."

"Hopefully."

I turned back to her and brought her hand to my mouth. "Whatever you need," I said, "just name it. Even if what you want is for me to get the fuck away from you."

She closed her eyes for a second and I was afraid she was going to say yes. But instead she whispered, "I never even got my orgasm, so no."

I laughed a little bit. "Okay."

"I want you to tell me my hair looks great."

"It does, it really does. This is a good look for you. Very edgy."

"I want you to say that it doesn't matter if I look like this for months. They said it could be months before the bruises go away."

"Catherine," I said, "what matters is that you're alive. It doesn't matter what it looks like. But if you're worried about not being your usual flawless self, we can get you a masquerade sort of mask. With feathers and everything. Cat ears, even."

She gave me a small smile. "We."

"If you want this to be a *we* situation, then yeah. We."

Neither of us spoke for a bit, the silence punctuated by the beeping heart monitor she was attached to. "Do you think that maybe all along, the problem with us, it's been that we do this?"

"We do what?"

"We say, *Should we give it another try?* We make a big deal about it. *Yes, we are officially giving it another try.* And that puts all this pressure on it, scares it away."

I did not think the problem with us could be summed up so simply. But I said, "Maybe." I watched her for a while, trying to make sense of everything. "So what do we—I mean, you and I, separately and independently, do now?"

"I am going to stay right here," she said, "because I don't have a choice. And you, hopefully, are going to go home and sleep. On a bed, not a chair. And when you wake up, go to my house and bring me a sketchbook and a real pillow because this thing is bullshit."

I nodded, recalling the broken window, the potting soil all over her foyer. I needed to deal with both of those too. "Pillow, sketchbook. You got it. But I don't need to sleep. I'm fine."

"Lies."

"Really."

"No, I gave you the terms. I need you in one piece."

I opened my mouth to comment on that but changed my mind. Maybe she was right. Maybe that was the problem with us. That every expression of a feeling or a connection was called out, highlighted, unpacked. Maybe just saying it was enough. *I need you.* "Okay."

"I mean it."

"Okay. Sleep, sketchbook, pillow."

"And flowers."

"And flowers," I said.

I picked up her hand and kissed her knuckles. "Anything else?"

"You."

"And me." I stood up, realizing just then how tired I was; it tugged at my consciousness like an anchor. "See you soon."

When I got to the doorway, she said, "Did you find them? Leila and the guy?"

"Him, we got," I said.

I didn't continue and she didn't ask.

———

The thing I should've done was go home, like she asked me to. But as I pressed the down button for the elevator, I realized that Arthur's room was only one floor up. He was the last person I wanted to see at the moment, but the only person who could tell me what I needed to know. I pushed the other button as well and both elevators—down and up—arrived at the same time, like an angel and a devil on my shoulders.

Arthur was playing cards with a young woman, strawberry-blond like him. The daughter, I assumed. "Hello," I said.

They both looked up.

"Roxane!" Arthur said. His color was better, and he was partially sitting up in his adjustable bed. "This is my daughter, Charlotte. We just started another round of gin rummy, do you play? We can deal you in."

"I can only stay a minute." I folded my arms over my chest in an attempt to restrain myself from grabbing him by the shoulders and shaking him. Gin rummy, while Catherine was one floor down with a fractured skull. "Listen, Arthur, glad to see you're doing better, but I need to talk to you. About the fingerprints on shell casings the cops found in the alley where Marin was shot."

Charlotte frowned at me but didn't say anything. Arthur's eyebrows went up. "The what?"

"The thing I told you the cops found, when you insisted there was nothing to find. Your fingerprints. Are on the shell casings. How do you explain that?"

"No, this isn't—no." Arthur placed his cards facedown on the bedside table. "They're lying. Or they made a mistake. I wasn't there. I swear to you, I wasn't there. I left the restaurant and went home. That's all I did. You think I would lie to you? After all this?"

I just stared at him. I didn't know what to believe anymore.

"You don't—they don't still think that I did something to her, do they? I would never—no. You know I didn't, right? Please, I need you on my side."

I swallowed thickly and avoided looking at him. It was suddenly very important that I get out of this hospital. "It'll all be in my report," I said. "I need to go."

TWENTY-NINE

I took an Uber back to my mother's street with the intention of getting right into my rental and going home, but I spotted her on the porch step with a paper cup of coffee and a cigarette.

And company.

Rafael Vega sat beside her on the step, coffee in hand as well. I noted with relief that he was wearing a different rumpled dress shirt today, meaning he hadn't slept here, which might have bothered me for reasons I couldn't entirely explain. I thought about ducking behind my rental car's fender and waiting for however long it took for him to not be on the porch anymore. But my mother spotted me and smiled, giving me a little wave.

"Detective Vega lives just over off of Maize Road," my mother said. "Isn't that funny, what a small world it is."

I stood on the sidewalk in front of the porch. The world was a lot of things. At the moment, small did not feel like one of them. Or funny. But my mother didn't look at it the same way I did, and that was probably a good thing. I nodded and said, "Indeed."

"We just got back from the courthouse," my mother said. "We rode together, since he's so close by."

"How did it go?"

"The document was still in the queue to be processed," Vega said. "So we just took it right out of there and ripped it up. I know the guy's in custody, with some very serious charges. But we don't even have to file the quiet title motion or anything." He turned to my mother and patted her hand.

"You know an awful lot about the litigation side of this."

"My wife used to work for the county recorder."

My gaze flicked to his ring finger, on the hand that had recently patted my mother's. The gesture did not go unnoticed.

He added, "She passed away a couple years back."

Then I just felt like a jerk. In an effort to make up for it, I said, "Well, I'm glad you're here." My voice didn't exactly sound convincing. "And Mom, I know 'I'm sorry' doesn't cut it, but truly, I am—"

"Nothing you could've done, Roxane," Vega said a little quickly, shooting me a small wink. "Nobody gets to blame themselves here. Not you, not Genevieve, nobody. Some people are just born bad, ya know? The important thing to remember is that a lot of the time when this happens, nobody even finds out about it for months, and it takes twice that long to unravel the whole mess at the courthouse. This was a scare, but it isn't going to amount to more than that."

My mother smiled. "I'm lucky to have such good people around me," she said. "Rafael, I'm just going to run in and check on the pie. Roxie, you want to stay for lunch?"

"No, I need to get my car and take off."

"Okay, well, give me a hug then. . . ."

I hugged her with one arm, my eyes squeezed shut against a sudden, piercing sadness. So no one had told her about the mess I'd made, how this *was*, actually, my fault. Maybe Tom was right. Maybe I did punish people for caring about me—not intentionally, but maybe I did it all the same. And why? Because I didn't care enough about them? No. That couldn't be further from the truth. But maybe I didn't care enough about me. The fact that I didn't have to face the music right now with my mother somehow made me feel worse.

Meanwhile, she thought she was *lucky*. Not for the first time, I thought about how she deserved better than she'd gotten: a dead husband who could be a real asshole sometimes when he was alive, three borderline fuckup kids who drank too much and end up hurting the people they were supposed to care about.

I couldn't do anything about most of that, but I could do something about me.

After she went into the house, I didn't quite know what to say. But I was still there with Vega, so I figured I had to say something. "Pie?"

"She's making something called nacho pie for lunch." He stiffly pulled himself to his feet. "She already assured me it's not racist, it's just what she had in the fridge for lunch today."

I laughed, and it took me by surprise. "She's not a great cook, but she means well. But you're probably not staying for the cuisine, are you?"

He raised a bushy eyebrow. "Meaning?"

I shook my head. If my mom wanted to make nacho pie for a friend of Tom's, what was it to me? Instead I said, "I guess I owe you, for keeping my part in all this quiet."

"If you want to tell her someday, go for it. But maybe after all of this settles down, yeah?"

"Yeah."

"I know it's a long story. The time isn't always right for long stories. And if the time is never right, that's okay too. The secret's safe with me."

We looked at each other for a while. If my instincts about anything were to be believed, I'd say he had kind, trustworthy eyes. I said, "You probably think I'm an awful person."

He chuckled. "No ma'am. I know we just met, but I also know

that Tom thinks the world of you. I never knew your dad but Tom and I go way back. He's as good as they come."

"Yeah," I said. I took a few steps toward my car, eager to get out of here. "Hey, after the dust settles with all this, there's another family who could use your help figuring out the quiet title or whatever. Another one of Nate Harlow's victims."

"Anytime, Roxie."

When I got home, my ancient landlord was on the sidewalk in front of the building with a stepladder, trapped in conversation with Bluebell or whatever her name was. "And on top of the power outage, there was blood all over the landing yesterday," she was saying. "Blood. Actual blood. That is not normal. Are you trying to say it's normal?"

"Lady, what's *normal*? All I'm saying," Glenn said, "is that I don't see any blood."

"Well, I can't live here. It's been one thing after another with this place."

"Then move when your lease is up. In March."

"I can't wait till March!"

As I squeezed past them and up the steps, Bluebell touched my arm. "You saw the blood, right? Roz—Rose . . . anne?"

I looked at her. She was wearing a beaded headband across her forehead and a Slayer T-shirt, though I was willing to bet she didn't know a single Slayer song. If she hadn't already demonstrated herself to be a terrible neighbor, I might've offered an explanation— such as it was—for the blood. But she had, so I didn't. I said, "I have no idea what you're talking about."

I went into the apartment and closed the door behind me and sighed, so overwhelmed with relief at being in my own space that I had to steady myself for a second with a palm against the wall.

Shelby stuck her head out of the guest room. "You're back," she said.

"I am. Sorry to disappoint. How was camping?"

She wrinkled her nose. "Not disappointed, obvz. Camping was okay. The cabin was cool, but the weather sucked. So we came back yesterday, just in time for the power outage."

"Shit. Did you manage okay in the dark?"

"Why, because you have zero candles or flashlights anywhere in the house?"

I laughed. "Yes. That is exactly why."

Shelby shrugged. "It wasn't out for that long. I just went out onto the porch. People started playing music and stuff. It was kind of cool. Where were you?"

"Working," I said.

"Well, next time the power goes out, you'll be all set. I went to the dollar store in Whitehall this morning and got you three flashlights. And batteries."

I took a few steps down the hallway and leaned against the wall. "You," I said, "are too responsible for your own good. Your dad doesn't know what he's talking about. You have your head on better than most grown-ass adults I know."

Then it hit me. "Hey, come out here for a second," I said, heading back down the hall.

Outside, Bluebell was still whining about the epic unfairness of not being able to break her lease, while Glenn had possibly died standing up. I said, "How serious are you about moving out?"

Bluebell put her hands on her hips. "Oh, I'm moving. Tomorrow. The blood was the last straw."

"Tomorrow? Dammit, I don't have time to find a new tenant again. I already went on the internets once this week," Glenn said, at the same time as Shelby whispered, "Blood?"

"Maybe you could find someone to take over your lease," I said.

"Like who?"

"This is Shelby," I said. "She is literally the most responsible person I know."

Shelby was clearly still wondering about the blood. "What's going on?"

"Shelby, you're looking for an apartment. B—I'm sorry, I have no idea what your name is either—you don't want to break your lease. Glenn, you don't want to have to go on the internets to find a new tenant. Discuss amongst yourselves. I am going inside and sleeping."

I left them there on the sidewalk and went back into the apartment and lay down on my bed with my clothes still on. I was the keyed-up kind of tired now, my thoughts an incoherent jangle about Catherine and Tom and Marin and my mother and, somewhere in there, me and the spectacular mess I made. I stared up at the stars on the ceiling for a while, then got up and went into the office and parted the miniblinds to check on the progress outside. Glenn was smiling at Shelby, nodding. Shelby looked over her shoulder at my window, saw me standing there, and gave a thumbs-up. I smiled back.

I turned away from the window and went to the kitchen to make a cup of tea. While the water buzzed to a boil, I considered the bottle of whiskey on my counter. I couldn't pinpoint any specific, poor choices that were made under the influence of alcohol during this case. But having a drink as my first meal of the day did not seem like a step in any right direction. I put the bottle away and stirred a teaspoon of sugar into my mug instead.

THIRTY

There was a small army of men—boys—loading Bridie's eccentric furniture into the back of a cargo van when I left the house on Friday morning. She was drifting from one end of the yard to the other in some sort of kaftan, chatting on her cell about which shade of white she wanted her new walls painted. "Is this good-bye, then?" I said as I walked by.

"Hang on," she said into the phone. Then she looked at me. "Yes, sadly, but I feel really good about leaving the place in your daughter's hands."

She held out an arm for a hug, but I gave her a hearty handshake instead and looked flatly at her. "It won't be the same here without you."

I drove up to Brighton Lake. The sky was clear and bright, the air warm but not hot. A perfect summer day that did not suit my mood, but when had the weather ever paid anyone the favor of matching a mood? A proper night's sleep had restored my ability to think, but that wasn't necessarily a good thing.

Because what I kept thinking about was mostly how everyone came out of this worse off. How if I'd been following Marin that night, she might still be alive—and the chain of events that led to Tessa Pomp's death might have been averted. Or at least postponed until I was out of Arthur's employ altogether, meaning that Catherine and my mother wouldn't have gotten involved at all. At the end of the day, that was what mattered. I could take the heat, but it wasn't fair for other people in my life to have to put up with it as well.

And honestly, maybe I couldn't take the heat as well as I thought I could.

I was meeting Suzy and Rafael Vega at Brighton Lake but I got there a few minutes early so I could go in and see Agnes. She was holding the same bible, running her fingers over the edges of its cover. She looked up when I entered the room, and she pointed at me. "You again. Strange stranger, but good listener."

I smiled. "I'll take that compliment."

"Will you read this to me?" She thrust the book at me. "The words are loose. Again."

"Sure, Agnes. What would you like to hear?"

She looked up at the ceiling and smiled faintly. "Psalms. Just pick."

I flipped the bible open and looked for something suitable. The text ran together in front of my eyes. I read out loud, "'Surely, I wait for the Lord; who bends down to me and hears my cry, draws me up from the pit of destruction, out of the muddy clay, sets my feet upon rock, steadies my steps, and puts a new song in my mouth, a hymn to our God . . .'"

When I was finished, I sat there quietly until Agnes turned over on her side and faced away from me. "Thank you, dear."

"My pleasure," I said.

A few minutes later, Suzy bustled into the room. "Sorry I'm late," she said. "Sorry, sorry, sorry. Did I miss the detective?"

I stood up and took a step into the hall. "No, but he should be here any minute."

She nodded and ran a hand through her short blond hair. "Thank you, by the way."

"Don't mention it."

"And listen, I know I wasn't the nicest to you, when you first came around. I apologize for that. I had—have, really—a lot of complicated, messed-up feelings about my mother."

"Understandable."

"I won't let it go four months without seeing her again, is what I'm trying to say. This has been a wake-up call. So thank you for that too."

"Of course," I said. "Did Sam come with you?"

She shook her head. "He's at home, helping with the garage sale."

"It's finally Molly's big moment, huh?"

"Yes, high hopes."

"Well, I hope it's a smashing success. And tell your father I said hello, okay?"

"Will do." She chuckled. "He's so funny. This morning, we were eating breakfast and I was reading the paper. Marin's obituary ran today, did you know that?"

"No."

"Well, it says a bunch of crap like Marin loved interior design and traveling with her fiancé. Like she's this totally normal person."

I sighed. Good old Arthur, still not getting it. "Yeah."

"So I read it out loud, and my dad said, we ought to go and wear matching sunglasses." She laughed, but I didn't. "Oh, come on, it's a little bit funny, isn't it? I know I told you that story."

I nodded. "Your dad was there that day? At Bill's funeral?"

"Yeah, of course. Bill was all Mom had left. Even though they'd been divorced for a long time by that point, Dad came for moral support."

I stared at her, thinking. "For some reason I thought your dad didn't know Marin."

The reason was because he told me.

"No, he did. Mom and Dad were divorced by the time she came

around, but Bill was still my uncle. So we'd still see them at holidays and all that. Sometimes with Mom, sometimes without. Dad and Marin got into a fight once, a big fight. Nate smeared chocolate pudding on this sofa that she'd just gotten, like three of us saw it happen. But Nate said it was Mom, and Marin flipped her shit about it. Yelling at Mom, over something she didn't do, over a damn couch. Bill didn't want to get into it, you could just tell. Dad put her in her place good about that, he said something like *just because you say something, doesn't mean it's true.*"

"Ha," I said, but my voice sounded weird.

There was no way. Right? Maybe he misspoke when he told me he didn't know Marin or her son. Had never met them. Maybe he was trying to protect his family; after all, I was a random stranger who just showed up and started asking questions.

But I hadn't told him that Marin was dead, and he hadn't asked.

I assumed that Suzy had filled him in.

Maybe she did. But maybe he already knew.

Why would he lie to me?

He wouldn't. No.

This couldn't happen.

Or could it? Marin's death was still a weak spot. Tom didn't think her killer was Nate, and I didn't think it was Arthur. Sam was a sweet old guy, and he hadn't known about any of this till Wednesday.

Unless he'd been lying about that too.

Molly Kinnaman's garage sale was in full swing when I arrived at her house: four old ladies perusing the knickknack table and a crowd of young mothers pawing through the mountains of baby clothes, all to the soundtrack of Sam's piano playing.

Molly, with her daughter on one hip, grinned at me. "The sale is finally open! So if you need any bowling equipment or costume jewelry, please, stock up."

"I'll take a look," I heard myself say, my palms going sweaty. "Do you think I can chat with Sam a minute?"

Molly nodded and sent me into the house through the garage. My heart was hammering in my chest, not nerves exactly, but something worse. I went through the kitchen and around the corner to the living room, where he was sitting at a piano, a folio of sheet music in front of him. "Hi," I said, and he turned and looked at me, and from the expression on his face and the way I felt, we both knew that I knew.

"You lied to me," I whispered.

He turned back to the piano, his shoulders slumping.

"You said you didn't know Marin. Never met her. That's what you said."

He dropped his head into his hands, elbows hitting the piano keys in a dissonant chord. "I know."

I forced myself to cross the room and sat on the arm of the couch next to him. "Sam, *why*? What happened? Just—why?"

Sam straightened up and pushed his glasses to the top of his head and rubbed his face. Then he turned to look at me, his hand grabbing for mine. "I was just trying to talk to her, okay? Talk. Just talk. Then all of a sudden there's a gun in her hand."

"Start from the beginning, Sam."

He told me that when he got back to town after Agnes's accident, he went over to the house to get some of her books. "I still had a key. But I got there and this woman was out front, carrying off a box of Agnes's good silver. Blond woman, good-looking, dressed all fancy. I didn't recognize her at first. The last time I saw her was fifteen years ago, and she looked different. Obviously she'd had work done, you know. Facelift and whatnot. I asked her what the hell she thought she was doing," he said.

"You just confronted her?"

"Hell yes I confronted her—she didn't belong there."

"What did she say?"

"Oh, it was rich. She acted like she didn't know who I was. She claimed she was an antiques dealer, that Agnes hired her months ago to sell some of her antiques."

I nodded and motioned for him to go on.

"So she put her box into this shiny SUV and drove away. If I'd had a car I would have followed her, but I didn't. So I went up to the house and tried my key, but the locks were changed. Agnes is a mess, new locks on her house? Something wasn't right. Not right at all. So I watched, and I waited. I watched that house for days from a bench next to the tennis courts right there, and I wrote everything down in a notebook. All the comings and goings. I didn't see Marin again. But after a while somebody called the police on me. An officer showed up, wanted to know how come I was sitting there all day every day."

"What did you say?"

He sighed. "Looking back, I guess I seemed a little nuts. I tried to explain about Agnes and Marin and all that, and they got real caught up on the fact that we got divorced years ago but I still had her key."

I could see that. "Okay, so what happened then?"

"Well, that didn't go anywhere, needless to say. He told me to find somewhere else to sit, I said I could sit wherever I want because this is America, he said I could literally sit on any other bench *in* America, just not that one. I didn't want it to turn into a thing, you know. And it got me thinking, maybe I was wrong. Like maybe it wasn't her after all. Sometimes my memory, you know. I'm seventy-three years old. Sometimes my memory just isn't the best."

Sam backed off for a few weeks, but then Agnes said something that gave him pause.

"The hospital freaked her out. It wasn't good for her, and she was really struggling. But after she was healed up enough not to need the hospital, they moved her to the care home. That was better for her. She calmed down some. And she said the thing about the house, Herodias and Salome stealing the house. See, you ask Agnes what her name is, she'll tell you. Agnes Harlow. She knows who she is. But she also knows that in a past life, which is also unfolding simultaneously, she's John the Baptist. Herodias was what she'd always called Marin."

"So you knew."

"Just like you knew." He rubbed his eyes. "And I've heard about this kind of thing before. Sick people, getting taken advantage of. It happened in California to my daughter's neighbor. He went into a hospice facility and these random young punks *sold* his house, right out from under him. I went over to the library and I asked them, is there a way in the computer that you can show me if a certain house has been sold. This cute little librarian gal pulled a database right up for me."

I was shaking my head. If he'd only told me this on Sunday. "And you saw what I saw. That Nate Harlow's name was all over the house."

"I wasn't even thinking about him. I was thinking about Marin. But yeah, there it was. I started sitting on the bench again, in front of the house. Nothing happening, mostly. Then this one night, there she is. I saw her park the car and walk into the alley. That was where. I didn't know why I was there, not really. I wasn't even going to speak to her, but she saw me, and she just pulled a gun out of her bag and—and she pointed it. At me." He took off his glasses and polished them, slowly. "And it just happened so fast, she pulled out this gun, and we were yelling and I was trying to—I didn't want her to point it at me and we struggled over it, so quick, it was over so quick, Roxane, the gun just went off and there was this bloodstain blooming on the front of her dress, like when you put a drop of food coloring into vinegar, like for dyeing eggs at Easter, you know? It just billowed out and she was on the ground, looking up at me and I was standing there holding a gun. I just turned and ran. I didn't know what else to do." He put the glasses back on but they fogged up immediately as he began to weep. "I was so angry, and so scared. I came home, right home, and I hid that gun where no one would ever look for it."

"Do you still have it?"

He nodded, sighing. Then he struggled to his feet and lifted the lid of the piano. He reached in and pulled out a bundle of newspaper with a trail of duct tape hanging from one side. I took it from him and gently unfolded it, careful not to touch.

"I'm so sorry," he whispered, tears streaming down his craggy face. "When you showed up, I thought—at first I thought you knew. But then I realized you didn't, and I thought maybe there was a chance. That no one would need to know. But that isn't right. Whatever she did, it's not my place. To play executioner."

The gun was a silver thirty-eight semiauto, just like Arthur's.

No, not *like* his—*his*.

Marin had his gun all along, maybe because Sam Kinnaman was borderline stalking her.

She *had* been shot with Arthur's gun. His fingerprints were on the casings because he'd probably loaded this gun years ago.

But he wasn't the one who pulled the trigger last week.

THIRTY-ONE

By Saturday I'd been ignoring texts for the last two days—most of them from Andrew, who wanted to know what the hell was going on with me, and Pam, who wanted to touch base about a few last-minute party things. That was her expression: *touch base.* I had no intention of touching anything. I had added exactly zero songs to the party playlist I was supposed to be making, and I suspected I wouldn't be very good company anyway. So maybe I wouldn't go. I lay on my couch, listening to Shelby and Joshua moving a dresser across the floor in the apartment above me. I thought I might just lie there all day like that. But when Tom himself texted me to ask if I had time to grab a drink at the Tavern today, I stared at the words on the screen of my phone until my vision blurred. What would it mean if I said no? Would I ever *have time* again, or would he?

An hour later, I found him sitting at the end of the bar with a bottle of Newcastle Brown in front of him. He looked tired and sad, which was probably how I looked too. It was certainly how I felt. I perched on the barstool next to him and said, "Happy birthday."

He gave me half a smile. "Thanks."

"May you live to be one hundred, with one more to repent."

"What's that?"

"An Irish something or other. I don't actually know."

"Well, thanks," he said again. "Is that what you're supposed to say, when someone recites an Irish something or other at you?"

"I have no idea. I usually just punch them in the face."

Tom laughed. "That would not surprise me, actually."

Neither Tom nor I said anything for a while. The bartender brought me a Crown on the rocks without me having to order it—such are the benefits of having a local bar.

Finally, I asked, "So what's the story—what you really wanted for your birthday was a tense conversation with me?"

"No." He sipped his beer and met my eye in the mirror over the liquor bottles behind the bar. "I just want to talk. No tension. Just friends, talking."

"So talk." I sipped my drink. "Or was I supposed to do the talking?"

He sighed. "First off, I had a visitor yesterday."

That didn't sound very friendly. I waited.

"Samuel J. Kinnaman." Tom spun his beer bottle slowly on the bar top. "He told me that you suggested he come talk to me."

I let out a breath. "Yeah."

"Next time, maybe a heads-up about that would be appropriate."

"Yeah."

We sat in silence again, until Tom said, "If he hadn't come forward, would you have ever told me?"

"I knew he would," I said, which wasn't exactly true.

"No, you didn't."

That was more true. I'd left Sam's house with a promise to check in with him on Monday, to see where things stood. I didn't know what I'd intended to do on Monday—not then, and not now. "I was just trying to figure out a way to, I don't know, get Arthur off the hook without throwing Sam to the wolves." I looked up at the pressed-tin ceiling. "It's not like I never would have told you."

"Right."

"I would have."

"When? Take Arthur out of it."

"I can't do that. He's the reason why any of this . . . you know." I drank some of my whiskey. "Maybe I wouldn't have. I don't know. Is that what you wanted to hear?"

"You'd be okay with nobody answering for Marin's murder."

"I don't think it's that simple," I said, and he nodded.

"I know it isn't."

We sat in silence for another while. The bartender passed by and served us another round.

"For what it's worth," Tom said finally, "I think the prosecutor's office is open to a plea. Manslaughter, maybe involuntary, maybe a suspended sentence. He's seventy-three years old, and he's not the one who added a gun to the encounter. He doesn't belong in prison."

"No, he doesn't." I studied the ice in my glass and said, "I'm sorry I didn't tell you right away. I was sorting through it. I thought it didn't matter much either way, because Marin is dead regardless."

He nodded again. "And I probably wasn't all that approachable, after the other day."

"No."

"I was harsh with you."

"Kind of, yeah."

He swiveled on his barstool to face me. "Look at me. I want to tell you something."

I remained facing forward.

He continued anyway. "I think we underestimated," he said, "how hard it would be. To, you know. Just be friends."

"What, without sex to defuse the inevitable tension?"

"Well, yeah." He cleared his throat. "Don't you?"

"Hey, I wasn't the one who wanted to stop—" I said, then shook my head. "Sorry. Okay. Yeah, I do."

"And I hate it that things are awkward between us, because you're the only person who gets it sometimes."

I finally looked at him.

"And listen, I'm aware that you were right, here. About Marin. And Arthur. If not for what you put together, I'm not sure we ever would've figured it out. And that kind of weakens my argument that you should have stayed out of it. But maybe we could've worked together differently or something. Had a conversation, instead of just going to the nuclear option."

He was right. He often was. "Last week, the day after Arthur was shot. I *was* rattled. But it really pissed me off that you tried to say that's all it was," I said.

"I know. I'm sorry."

"But I didn't want to admit it."

"I know that too."

"Looking back, I should've. It would have been easier than the way all of this went down."

"I hope you don't think that's what I'm saying. That this is your fault."

I shrugged. "Some of it is. My mother, sobbing her eyes out. Catherine, in the hospital with a fractured skull."

His eyebrows shot up. "Shit."

I nodded. "She'll probably get to go home tomorrow or Monday, but yeah. It's brutal, looking at her. The bruises. She had some hearing loss right after but it's getting better."

"So you and her," he said, "a thing again?"

I felt myself smile. "I don't know. I've been keeping her company and sneaking her in dirty chai. Does that constitute a *thing*?"

"Aw, who the hell knows," Tom said.

We sat together in another long silence. After a bit he said, "I don't want it to be weird between us."

"No."

"Can we work at it?"

My instinct was to ask what that meant. But it occurred to me that my instincts weren't serving me that well lately where relationships were concerned. So I just nodded.

"Instead of shutting down and walking away, let's just talk through it. The truth is just easier. I know how you feel about talking. But I also know how you feel about the truth. And, you know, sometimes, you're all I have."

He didn't say *of him*. But I heard the two words anyway, whether he meant them or not. I didn't especially mind, not as much as I used to. I blinked a few times. "You talk enough for the both of us, to be honest," I said.

He laughed and raised his beer bottle. "To the truth, even when it's uncomfortable."

I clinked my glass against his bottle. "To the truth."

My phone vibrated in my pocket—another text from Pam.

> Would you mind picking up my order at Pistacia Vera? I'm
> so behind on everything!!

I smiled.

So much for the ice-cream cake and my efforts to make the surprise party less terrible.

"I should probably get going soon," Tom said, as if he could read my mind. "Pam and I are going to Milestone for dinner and it's this awkwardly early reservation, like five thirty. Makes me wonder if she's planning something else, later."

Talk about an uncomfortable truth. I said, casually, "Like what?"

He looked at me, eyes narrowing. "You know something."

"No."

"What about the truth, even when it's uncomfortable?"

"*If* I knew something, you wouldn't really want me to tell you."

He laughed. "Hell yes I would. What do you know?"

I debated for a second. "In the interests of our renewed friendship and the newfound openness between us," I said, "and not because I am incapable of keeping a secret, because I most definitely am, I must tell you that fifty of Pam's closest friends will be waiting in her house when you get back from dinner, with party hats and fussy little snack foods."

He looked up at the ceiling. "Well, shit."

"Surprise!"

"Party hats?"

"I tried to tell her that you would hate it. I really did. She actually wanted to lure you over to her place under the guise of distress, like an intruder in the house."

"Jesus."

"I told her that was a terrible idea. I don't think I had much sway on the rest of her terrible ideas. She sent out invitation cards with sparkly crap on the front."

For no clear reason, we both started laughing then, that kind of sudden, loud, breathless laughter that strikes without warning and leaves you feeling shaky but acutely alive. I put a hand over my sternum, trying to get control of myself. My rib cage hurt. "She invited my brothers, too. I mean, Tom, has she met you?"

He wiped his eyes, his face ruddy from laughing. "I told her I didn't want to do anything. I didn't even want to do dinner, after the way this week has gone."

"Did you tell her that?"

"I did. But she insisted."

"She doesn't understand you at all!" I said, lightly.

"I know. She's great," he said, "I know she is, but sometimes it doesn't make any sense. Her and I together. Right?"

"Aw, I wouldn't go that far," I said. "Opposites attract, and all that. You clearly care about each other. Plus my mom definitely wants you to propose to her."

"Oh, Jesus." He pinched the bridge of his nose, struggling to maintain composure too. "Sparkly crap. Why was that so funny?" He sighed. "Thanks for telling me. I can just see myself saying *thank God you didn't try to throw me a party, because I hate that shit* over the dessert course or something."

I finished my drink and crunched an ice cube between molars. "Maybe it'll be fun."

"Maybe."

Our eyes met in the mirror behind the bar again. Tom said, grinning, "Remember my birthday last year?"

A little of bit heat rose to my face. "Yeah."

"That was a good night," he said.

It meant something to me, that he thought so too. "Yeah."

We sat there for a little while longer as he finished his beer, and then he reached for his wallet but I shook my head. "I don't think so. Nobody buys the drinks on their birthday."

"Wow, sparkly crap and free beer?"

"It's your lucky day, truly. Now go home, be chill, do *not* tell her I ruined the surprise."

"Our little secret." He winked at me in the mirror. "Promise. Hey, Roxane?"

"Yeah?"

For a second it looked like he was going to say something profound. But he changed his mind and just shrugged. "See you later?"

I nodded. "You bet."

He slid off his seat and I watched him walk out of the bar and into the warm afternoon, his tall form turning to shadow in the flare of light from the open door and the city street beyond.

ACKNOWLEDGMENTS

It's quite a thrill, to be writing the acknowledgments for my second book. I first want to thank everyone who read *The Last Place You Look* and sent me nice emails or social-media messages, wrote reviews, requested it from the library, talked about it, recommended it—you helped get the word out, and that means everything to me.

The Last Place You Look was ushered into the world last year with the help of many fantastic individuals, without whom I'd be so, so lost.

First, thanks to my agent, Jill Marsal, for her continued support. I'm thrilled to have her in my corner, and I value her expertise beyond words.

Huge thanks to my editor, Daniela Rapp, for believing in Roxane (and for introducing me to picklebacks). The whole team at Minotaur has done so much for me—shout-outs to Lauren Jablonski, Sarah Schoof, Allison Ziegler, Joe Brosnan, and everyone else who touched the book behind the scenes.

I also want to thank Faber & Faber for introducing me to U.K. readers and showing me the best time ever at Harrogate, especially my editor, Angus Cargill, and Lauren Nicoll.

Big thanks to Dana Kaye and Julia Borcherts of Kaye Publicity for their excellent work on my behalf.

Thanks to Karen Brissette for rallying the Goodreads troops and generally being awesome.

Thanks to indie bookstores like The Book Loft, Gramercy Books, Mystery Lovers, Centuries & Sleuths, and Trident for welcoming me in and taking good care of me.

I'm tremendously grateful to some fellow crime writers who've been generous and patient in helping a newbie out, from blurbs to blogs to shared train rides, and so on, including: Lori Rader-Day, Christopher Coake, Rob Hart, Chris Holm, James Renner, Michael Kardos, Sophie Hannah, Val McDermid, Martina Cole, Hank Phillippi Ryan, Alafair Burke, Erica Wright, and Andrew Welsh-Huggins.

Thanks to my Pitch Wars family, especially Kellye Garrett and the class of '15. Also to my 17 Scribes family, for almost always having answers. And to my actual family, especially my parents, for being the best salespeople anyone could hope for.

I want to thank Ernie Chiara, for being a good friend, a good reader, a good writer, and also for making me try oysters since I've now written about them in both books. They did taste like "the sea," as described.

Finally, thanks to Joanna Schroeder for all the things, including but not limited to: watching bad movies with me, watching good movies with me, petting cats, taking trips and awkward selfies, being good company, your sense of humor and kindness, and believing in me even when I don't.